Unspun

A Collection of Tattered Fairy Tales

Unspun

A Collection of Tattered Fairy Tales

Anika Arrington   Sarah Chow   Katherine Cowley
Scott Cowley   Chris Cutler   Sarah Blake Johnson
Ruth Nickle   Kaki Olsen   Robin Prehn
Jeanna Mason Stay   PJ Switzer

Edited by Sarah Blake Johnson

Cover and Interior Art by Ruth Nickle

Additional Editing by Jeanna Mason Stay, Sarah Chow, Katherine Cowley, Brian Kenison, Marianne Von Bracht, and Anika Arrington

After Ever After Publishing
Ruth Nickle and Katherine Cowley, Editors-in-chief
1st Edition: April 2018
Published in the United States of America

CONTENTS

Heart of a Thief   3
by Chris Cutler
The man who sold Jack the magic beans must find his own way to the sky.

Rumpelstiltskin's Daughter   27
by Ruth Nickle
A girl raised as a princess tries to discover her true heritage.

Tsar Vislav, Tsarina Vislav, and the Firebird   41
by Sarah Chow
Neighboring kingdoms demand the return of their stolen treasures.

Tatterhood and the Prince's Hand   57
by Katherine Cowley
An ugly, magic-wielding princess is not certain she wants to find her missing husband.

The Little Mermaid   137
by PJ Switzer
The mermaid embraces the possibilities of being sea foam.

Ásthildur and the Yule Cat   141
by Sarah Blake Johnson
The Yule Cat searches for a child to eat on Christmas Eve.

Perfectly Real   147
by Robin Prehn
After sleeping on a pea, a princess finds herself in a gilded cage.

The Pied Piper's Revenge 161
by Scott Cowley
Kidnapping young children may not have been the pied piper's brightest idea.

Ethical Will 179
by Kaki Olsen
Generations later, the Nutcracker still maintains a connection with our world, but so does the Mouse King.

Breadcrumbs 233
by Jeanna Mason Stay
Gretel confronts her past by returning to the gingerbread house in the woods.

Spring's Revenge 249
by Anika Arrington
As Snow White's son prepares to take the throne, he discovers there is more to his mother's story than an evil queen and true love's kiss.

The Original Tales 275

About the Authors 281

"Sometimes what you think is an end is only a beginning."
Agatha Christie

HEART OF A THIEF

Chris Cutler

The crowd was overflowing with thieves. They might think themselves hidden, but from his seat on the inn's roof, Gerund could see them all. One good eye was more than enough to spot their greedy grasping. They stood at stalls around the edge of the crowd, selling roasted nuts and chilled melon and watered beer. Charging three times what their wares were worth, robbing buyers of even more than they would have at a festival market. Taking because people let them.

Other thieves lurked nearby, hungry fingered, ready to snatch any wares left unattended or within reach. Taking because they wanted to.

Still more thieves mingled through the crowd, picking pockets, jostling and smiling and lifting. Taking because they could.

But the master thieves congregated in the center, claiming pride of place. Climbing greedily over the giant's corpse, arranging riches pulled from his pockets, arguing over the enormous brass belt buckle. There was a competition of sorts underway to see which faction of thieves could convey the most self-importance: the swaggering men in bright soldiers' helms, the mincing women in white scholars' caps, or the drifting figures in peaked magicians' hats. Gerund rather thought the scholars were winning.

In their center was the chief thief, the man everyone was celebrating. Jack. The youth still stood in his ridiculous triumphant pose on the giant's chest. Axe over one shoulder, goose at his feet, golden egg held so that it glinted in the sun with every gesture.

Gerund scowled and spat over the side of the roof. This was a complication. Jack should have been on the run with that goose, leading the giant away. The people, drawn to this threadbare village by Jack's recent fortune, should have been cowering or fleeing. That would have given Gerund the opening he needed to climb the beanstalk and rescue Meena. Instead, a thousand people were standing in his way, robbing him of that chance.

Chance to do what, though? Jack had *cut down* the blasted beanstalk. There was no leafy ladder to climb, no way up. The crowd couldn't be in his way if he had nowhere to go. And it wasn't as if he could grow another one. That had been the last of the beans.

Gerund shaded his good eye—the left one—and scanned the scene again. Jack had the goose and the axe. His other prizes, stolen earlier in the month, would be guarded somewhere nearby. The harp would be no help to Gerund, but the coins might be of use. The magicians had scavenged a dozen items from the giant's body. Those were bound to be magical, and some might be useful, but Gerund had no way of knowing which. He wouldn't test himself against the magicians' wards for an unknown tool. The soldiers had claimed a small pile of baubles and jewels for the treasury. Not what he needed. The scholars had gathered some oversized items for the university: a large nail file, a spade, a belt, a . . .

Gerund shook his head. None of those possessions would help him. Then again, the corpse itself meant that he was no longer racing against the giant's return. He had time to make a new plan. That meant he had time to rest his old bones. With a sigh, Gerund made his careful descent down the ladder into the inn's yard, then climbed slowly up the inside stairs to his pallet on the upper floor.

The words might as well have been magic. A simple incantation of "I've come to settle my bill" conjured such an enthusiastic smile onto the innkeeper's face that Gerund knew he was about to be robbed.

"Master Gerund! Moving on so soon?" Silas was the tallest, lankiest brownie Gerund had ever seen, which meant that with Gerund's geriatric stoop they saw nearly eye to eye.

"I'm afraid it's getting a bit too exciting for me around here, Silas."

"Well, I suppose that could be so," Silas said. He lifted a plate of sausages onto the sideboard and wiped his hands on his apron. "That business with the giant is for our grandchildren to sort out, one might say."

Gerund grunted. A grunt could mean anything.

"How did you mean to pay?" Silas asked. "I don't suppose you've come into coin after the festivities? Hedge wizard like yourself could be mighty popular at a time like this, even with those university folk hanging about with their flashy spells. Fireballs may be good for pleasing a crowd, but your skills are *useful*. Affordable, too."

Gerund scowled. Silas knew he'd studied briefly at the university before everything went wrong. He couldn't tell if Silas was trying to mock him or commiserate.

"Find myself suddenly rich like young Jack?" he finally said, deciding not to take offense. "I can't say I have. Services would suit better, if you'll accept them."

"Of course, of course." Silas waved him toward the cellar door and followed down the steps. Halfway down, Gerund stopped. A new cask of wine sat in the center of the floor, and the table beside it was covered with cheese wheels. At least twenty cheeses, each wider than a plate.

"Surely you're joking. I only stayed a month!"

From behind, Silas laughed. "Just as you say, good man. Lead with the high bid and all that. I rather expected to haggle over the number of cheeses."

Gerund spluttered. "That's ridiculous. The wine alone is worth twice what you charged me the first time I came through."

"Mmm, perhaps. But last summer you ate your own food. And with the growing crowds since Jack started showing off that harp a month ago, I'm sure you can understand that there's been a shortage of rooms. Had to raise my prices with demand."

"If that's the case, my services should be worth more, too." Gerund waved at the table. "You clearly need this spread to keep up with the meals you're selling. With the giant's death yesterday, the crowds will just keep growing. I'll bet you're nearly out of ripened cheese."

Silas nodded. "A fair point, to be sure. But I've also been stabling your cow, as requested. I could have been renting that space to a fine horse for more than I charge my lodgers. Seems to me you could have grazed her on the common with the rest, for a lot less trouble all around. But I don't cast out paying guests." He didn't bother to emphasize *paying*.

Gerund didn't say anything. He'd needed that cow out of sight.

"Half the cheeses," Silas proposed, "and a year on the wine."

Gerund shook his head, but took another step down into the cellar. It was inevitable, no matter how much he haggled. Taking advantage, that's what Silas was doing! The thief. Even if he'd had coins, there was no way Gerund could afford these higher prices.

Gerund capitulated after two quick counteroffers and sat tiredly on the bottom step while Silas whistled his way up out of the cellar. All twenty-seven cheeses for six weeks, and eight months on the wine. He shuddered.

Well, there was no point in waiting.

He waited anyway. Why should the innkeeper get what he wanted right away?

The wood step was hard beneath him. His left hip ached the longer he sat. But it was the crick in his neck that finally convinced him to end his pointless petulance. He pushed himself up and, creaking a bit, moved to lay his left hand on one of the cheese wheels. He took a breath.

Spots of white mold began to appear on each cheese, slowly at first, then spreading as fast as broken dreams to cover them completely. The wheels shrank a bit as moisture left them, the cheeses ripening two weeks in the space of a song.

Gerund lifted his hand away and inspected the wheels. One had bubbled and cracked, a hollow forming inside; this he set aside to discard. Three of the wheels had an odd orange mold mixed with the usual white. He cut away the orange bits and rubbed those wheels down with brine from the tub on the corner of the table. Oh, yes, Silas had been prepared for him. He placed his hand on top of the pile again, watching as the cheeses continued to cure. When they were six weeks old, he stopped.

He cradled his hand as he returned to the steps, then sat flexing it for some minutes. He pulled out his belt knife and set to trimming his nails, which had grown unmanageably long. It was easy enough to push things forward through time, but some piece of you had to stay in contact, had to travel with it. Early on he'd made the mistake of channeling everything through his right thumb. In hardly more than a month the nail had blackened and fallen off completely, and the knuckle had seized up to the point he couldn't grip anything. He flexed it now, to test the range of movement. Slow care had brought some of its strength back, but the bones still felt brittle. He knew better now, knew how to spread the damage of years across himself, and how to preserve

the parts of himself that needed to stay young. Teeth were especially important, and his remaining eye.

Yes, time magic was considered first-term drudgery. Gerund
thought of the university-trained magicians who had come to
loot the giant's corpse. That life had been stolen from him, along
with everything else. But the magic he had could still do remarkable things. Important things.

And profitable things, of course. He took off his boots and
socks, then stood and walked to the wine cask. Eight months.
This was going to be unpleasant.

His cow's rope was disgustingly mildewed. As Gerund watched,
the senile beast drooled an oozing stream of cud onto the coil
under her head. Was that still the same rope that Jack had tied
around her neck? Silas hadn't cared for her properly after all, the
cheat! Just stuck her in the stable and forgotten about her. It was
a wonder she was still alive! Gerund should have come to check
earlier that their bargain was being met. Had he seen this neglect
he would never have agreed to age the wine. If it were possible to
undo his work, remove the weight of time he had settled on the
food in that cellar, he would have done so. But time cannot be
turned back. He had learned that lesson well.

Gerund regarded the rope for a moment. No. He wouldn't
touch the thing. He pulled a knife from his pack and found a
section behind the cow's neck that was dry enough to hold so he
could saw through the fibers. He left the ruined rope where it fell
and collected a new one from the tack hanging across from the
horse in the next stall over.

Holding the new, much cleaner rope, Gerund led his cow
past the rear of the inn. He grimaced at a mild stench; then he
grinned. It only took a few moments to find the cat's body in the
tall grass nearby. It was an old village stray with mange across its
back, and kind Providence had struck it down in the night so that

Gerund could exact some measure of justice. He carried it to one corner of the inn where a burrowing creature had made its home. Kneeling as quickly as he dared (not very quickly, with his knees in the state they were), he shoved the cat as far back into the hole as he could reach. Then he pushed it through time. Just a day. Just enough for the rot and the stink to take full hold and for the juices to seep into the ground so that the smell would linger after the cat was discovered and disposed of.

He wiped his hand in the grass and led his cow out of the yard, away from one corpse and toward another.

The walk was longer than it would have been the night before. With substantial effort, the villagers and visitors had dragged the giant's body several hundred yards closer to the forest. It wasn't wise to leave eighty feet of carrion lying beside the road, even ignoring the imminent swift decay under the summer sun. Already there had been signs of foxes, wild dogs, and a bear, and it would only get worse.

In contrast, the downed beanstalk wasn't as destructive as he had expected for something so large. Rather than toppling like a felled tree, it had mostly collapsed onto itself, spilling over several crushed fields in a huge pile with only a few stray vines looping away. As Gerund made his way around it, he shuffled past a lone farmer staring blankly at his ruined grain. A bit farther on, two scholars were examining a partially open bud. That killed his last hopes for a simple solution. Of the few buds he had seen, only this one had begun to open into a blossom. He'd already known there wouldn't be bean pods, but he had still hoped the plant might be induced to grow at least one. It would have been tricky to entice beans from a plant that knew it was dying, but he could have done it if it had been just a little closer to seed. He was very practiced at pushing things through time. But if none of the flowers had even opened, it was hopeless.

So. The giant.

The dregs of a crowd clung around the body. Faces here and there looked rested and alert, but most of these people had clear-

ly stood vigil through the night. It couldn't have been on the giant's account. They had to have been guarding their stake, their
take. Which meant he needed to be careful of what they saw him
touch. Best to start with the body itself, see if they had missed
anything.

As Gerund had expected, Jack and his mother were nowhere
to be seen. The "hero" was doubtless sleeping off his celebra-
tions, and Jack's mother wouldn't have let him too far out of her
sight. No one else was likely to recognize his cow, so Gerund let
her loose to graze while he approached the body alone.

The corpse had not been moved until after it stiffened, and
death rigor held it in an unnatural pose. The giant had landed on
Jack's house and barn, then lain arched over the ruin. Here, with a
small hillock under his right leg and a gray boulder stabbing into
his shoulder blades, the giant appeared to be straining for the sky,
pushing himself away from the ground that had killed him. His
face was turned to the side and glassy eyes stared. There were no
cartwheel-sized pennies to hold them closed—or if there were,
someone had claimed a better use for them—so those eyes stared
at Gerund. No, past him. Toward the ruins of Jack's house. Ger-
und stepped farther to the side, and the eyes did not follow him.

Gerund walked a slow circuit, one hand on the body for balance. Most in the crowd were civil, or at least distracted by something else, and moved aside for him to pass. Other than a bit of
residue in the giant's left pocket, the only magic he sensed came
from the magicians and scholars around him. Everything useful
had already been removed.

Well, everything useful to Gerund. A team was working to
cut through the seams of the giant's overshirt and load the huge
panels of cloth onto carts to haul away. With the giant's back
arched like that, they were able to salvage nearly all of it. It had
been green once, but most of the color was hidden by blue and
brown soil.

Gerund moved a short distance away and stared at the back of the giant's head. The tan hair was still thick around the sides but gave way to a round bald patch near the top.

"Ha!" Gerund couldn't hold back a laugh. "Balding at *your* age, Tomas? Did you comb the rest over the top to hide it, I wonder?" There wouldn't have been much reason for him to try; few would have been in a position to notice.

But Meena would have. That thought brought a scowl with it, and Gerund closed his left eye, letting the world blur into a churn of color. He listened to the mutter of arguments, the shout of instructions, the . . .

Blue.

He looked again at the body, both eyes open. The worn green overshirt was fragmented, the pieces trundling away to the village. One cart carried a panel from the shirt's back, thick with brown dirt and old manure from the fields it had dragged through when the body was moved. Another cart held the shoulder and collar, caked in brown. A third held one of the sleeves. It too had a coating of brown, but not only brown. On the cuff, the soil was a deep blue.

Gerund lurched to his feet and stumped up a small rise until he was high enough to see. The trouser knees were blue. Before his fall, Tomas had been gardening.

His half-run drew too many eyes, so Gerund pretended to stumble. Then his knee twinged and the stumble became real. Several pairs of hands steadied him.

"Careful, grandfather."

"Steady, uncle."

One of the friendly strangers fingered Gerund's nearly empty purse. She didn't bother to take it.

Gerund grumbled and massaged his knee, then made his way more carefully to the dirt-crusted boots. Someone had already started to harvest the worn leather, and little mounds of blue were scattered all around Tomas's feet where soil had been dislodged and discarded. Trying not to attract attention, he felt and sifted through each pile. He found nothing.

But of course, the body had been moved. Collecting his cow, Gerund walked back along the track made by the dragged body, watching for clumps of blue soil. Around noon he reached the base of the beanstalk, carrying a small handful of oversized seeds. Grass and carrots wouldn't get him far, but they were a start.

Best not to linger here. Jack would be awake by now, telling his tale and counting his riches. His mother might come to the ruins of her home. She would recognize the cow, and Gerund didn't want to risk the questions that would follow. He had been hidden behind the hedge during her tirade about Jack's "foolish bargain," and later, while he crouched outside the window and pushed the beanstalk through time, he had heard her sobs about ruin and starvation. She would demand answers.

As he walked to the road, Gerund passed the row of prizes taken from Tomas's body. The jewels and glittery bits were gone, of course, but the more mundane items remained, guarded only by a smith's sleeping apprentice. The belt. The nail file. And the trowel, handle thick as a draft horse, blade pitted with rust. There was blue soil clinging to the blade.

In the clumps on the back he found two cucumber seeds and, Providence be thanked, a seed the size of his spread hands. A sunflower.

The plan didn't seem terrible, but it was. Walk two days to find a secluded spot. Plant the sunflower seed and age it to maturity. Climb the stem and walk two days back to find Meena in Tomas's home. He got as far as sprouting the seed before realizing the glaring flaw: cows can't climb.

Even then it might have worked. Instead of climbing a grown plant, he could let the growing flower carry them into the sky. He just needed to keep the cow balanced on the top of the sunflower as it grew. A smarter beast might have cooperated, might have known how to walk in place to keep its footing. Gerund's cow was not such a beast.

He forced the cow to stand over the plant, the leaves pressing against her chest, and pushed the plant to grow. Lowing, she tried to walk away. Gerund hauled on the rope to keep her in place, so she bent at the knees, sliding off the leaves. She sat on the ground protesting loudly, so he struck her between the eyes. That neither calmed her nor convinced her to obey. He spent hours maneuvering her into place again and again, but she fought against the rope and the plant and especially him.

Eventually Gerund gave up on getting the cow's cooperation. It would be far easier to leave her and climb up on his own, but of course he couldn't do that. He had *bought* her from Jack. Bought her with beans and magic, with a change in the lad's fortune. He would not relinquish a possession so easily. So he spent another two days walking back to the village, where he purchased a pair of ice spikes from the smith. That night he found an outbuilding where the villagers had stored the rope used to haul Tomas's body across the fields. There were coils and coils of it, and Gerund loaded as much on the cow's back as she could carry. If it could drag a giant, it would be strong enough to lift an obstinate cow.

Walking back to the sunflower, his cow moved much more slowly than she had before. Gerund hauled on her lead, but she wouldn't walk any faster. Gerund cursed at her. Had Jack known how poor an animal he was selling? Did Jack feel guilty for cheating his buyer? She couldn't even carry a simple load of rope.

At midmorning of the third day they finally reached the sunflower sprout. Gerund stomped up to it and pushed. The flower flew through weeks of growth, reaching into the sky and unfurling pair after pair of enormous leaves until the top vanished from view into low-lying clouds. Good.

Gerund had already fashioned a harness for his cow and tied it to the longest of the ropes. Now he fastened the ice spikes to his boots, shouldered his pack, and, pulling the rope behind him, started to climb. He climbed past the first leaf and looped the rope around the base of the leaf above it to form a pulley. After pausing to catch his breath, Gerund climbed back down and tied the end of the rope tight to the lower leaf. The leaf was heavier than his cow, so cutting it off of the flower's stem would turn it into a counterweight, pulling the cow up toward him. Before doing so, however, Gerund used another rope to anchor himself to the stem. He eyed the distance to the ground and triple knotted the anchor. No sense risking a fall from up here. When he was sure it would hold, he took out his belt knife.

He didn't have the strength to chop through the leaf on his own, and the knife was far too small for that anyway. But by focusing carefully, he could age just a segment of the leaf rather than the entire plant. His weak thumb meant he had to grip the knife in his left hand, so while he cut at the leaf he used his right to push those cuts through time. In moments the many small cuts shriveled and grew fuzzy with mold. He kept pushing until the wounds progressed into frank rot and the weight of the leaf tore through its weakened stem. Swinging free on the rope, it began a slow descent to the ground, lifting the cow into the air. She protested loudly, but Gerund could only smile. It was working!

The cow and leaf collided gently as they passed in the air, but they were moving too slowly to worry Gerund. She wouldn't be injured. The real danger was that he would exhaust himself. Going up and down like this, he would have to climb the whole distance how many times? He had been prepared to climb into the sky once, not repeatedly by stages.

When the leaf reached the ground, his cow dangled in front of him, spinning slowly. Gerund attached the second longest rope to her harness and climbed up to loop it around the next higher leaf. The one he'd used as a pulley before would become the new counterweight.

When everything was in place, he detached the first rope, anchored himself to the stem, and started to cut. The rope had rubbed against the leaf and bruised it during the first ascent, so he had a head start this time. While he slashed and rotted the leaf, Gerund tried to calculate the total distance he would have to climb. Numbers had never been his strength. The pulley rope was how long again? If the distance between leaves . . . Gerund froze, realizing his mistake. The rope wasn't long enough! Under his fingers, the counterweight tore free and dropped away. For a horrified moment he watched it go, then he fumbled at the knots anchoring him in place. The pulley was higher than before, and the counterweight had farther to fall. This time the leaf wouldn't just lift his cow higher, it would pull her all the way up to the pulley and over it.

The first of the three knots came loose under his fingers, and he started on the second. There wasn't enough time! His cow's ascent had felt slow before, but now, racing against his frantic fingers, it was far, far too fast. He was sure he could untie the anchor rope before she reached the top, but if he didn't get free before she reached him then he wouldn't have time to do anything but watch her tumble to her death. Where was his knife? There! He snatched it up and sawed at the tough fibers.

Gerund startled when the rising cow bumped his foot, and in that moment of inattention the knife tumbled from his grip. He grabbed for it, but the rope around his waist held him back. He succeeded only in nicking his palm and knocking the knife into a rapid spin so that it glinted in the sun again and again as it fell.

He was stuck, couldn't get free in time. He cursed. Well, if the anchor rope wouldn't let him budge, then he would use that immobility. He could still save his cow. If he could just link the cow's harness to the anchor, the counterweight would find itself pulling against the entire flower stem, not just a skinny cow. His cow's head was pushing against his knee now, and by leaning out as far as the anchor would let him, Gerund could just barely touch the loop of rope over her shoulders. He strained, slapped, and finally managed to get two fingers hooked around it. All of this was too much for the cow. Already close to panic from dangling in the air, she thrashed, battering Gerund's leg and arm with her head. He lost his grip.

"Fool beast," he yelled. "I'm trying to save you!" He tried again for the ropes, but she writhed. He couldn't even grab the harness, much less secure it to anything, with a hundred stone of distraught cow fighting him. If he tried, she would just injure him on her way to death. The smart thing to do would be to keep his distance and let gravity claim her.

He couldn't. However worthless the dry milch cow seemed, he had paid too much for her. This cow was *his*, and Gerund would not let wilting leaves and empty sky steal her away.

Her face was now level with his, and he hugged it to him with both arms, his hands on the back of her head. She fought him, but he held on and focused, pushing gently and carefully. It was a delicate and tricky bit of magic to make a mind feel the passage of time, to exhaust it into unconsciousness. He had seen it go wrong before. But the cow was at her limit already and required only a brief touch before falling limp.

With the cow insensate, Gerund scrabbled at the harness and caught hold. With one hand he pulled off his belt and looped it first through the harness, then through his anchor rope, and cinched it tight. It took the strain and held, arresting the cow's ascent. Gerund breathed a sigh of relief and, after securing his cow with redundant ropes and knots, he sat back to rest. It had been a near disaster, but nothing had been taken from him this time. As he waited for his heartbeat to slow, he planned out how to raise his cow safely from leaf to leaf. It would take more climbing to tie and untie multiple ropes, but it would work.

First, though, he needed to climb down and retrieve his knife.

The cow slowly grew accustomed to the blue soil of the land above the clouds. She had balked at first, nearly as upset about the strange land as she'd been about the ascent up the giant sunflower. But over the long, slow days of walking she had calmed and settled into a bearable, drooling silence, leaving Gerund with nothing but anxious thoughts.

They had both needed two full days to recover from the ascent before walking anywhere. Gerund hadn't minded too much, since sleeping under the sunflower's enormous yellow blossom had felt luxurious, despite the lumpy ground. But then he had gotten turned around in the strange geography, and days passed with no sign of Tomas's cottage. He kept them away from roads to avoid meeting people, but eventually admitted that he was lost. He approached a bridge and asked its troll for directions. The troll told him they had come entirely the wrong way, so he and his cow had to retrace their steps, hours and days vanishing beneath their feet.

Each mile was a torture of anticipation. Was he too late? Would Meena be gone? She might have left the very day Tomas fell, eager to escape her prison. If she was gone, how would he find her? Would she return to the university? She would at least tell her friends at the university where she had gone, wouldn't she?

More than two weeks after the beanstalk was felled, he finally found it. Tomas's home was an immense building, but clearly not a palace. Just a cottage like any farmer's. Drab. Meena could not have been happy here. There was some sort of ornamentation crisscrossing the walls, though the pattern was odd. Maybe she had tried to decorate, but the giant had stopped her.

Still avoiding roads, Gerund and his cow approached the back of the house across a field of something immense and green and leafy. He caught sight of an enormous white mass in the middle of the nearest one. Cauliflower, then. The rows were not quite in line with the house, so most of it was obscured from view. Through gaps between plants he searched the chimney for smoke, the windows for light, the doorway for motion. There was nothing.

They came out of the field at the edge of the kitchen garden, and he realized that what had seemed ornamental patterns in the stone and plaster were in fact staircases sized for regular feet. They crisscrossed the entire building, granting access to dozens of human-sized doors and windows.

Of course he wouldn't have seen movement in the large windows—those were for Tomas. Towing the cow behind him, he stepped onto a wide path cutting through the garden. Staring at the closest of the small doors, he stepped forward.

"Can I help you?" asked a woman's voice from his blind side.

Gerund clutched his chest and spun to the right. There was Meena, trowel in hand, kneeling in the blue dirt.

"I'm sorry to startle you, sir. I thought you saw me." She took off her gardening gloves and stood. He tried to watch her face, read her reaction, but he couldn't look away from the scar on her throat. It was pink and ragged silver, partly covered by a loose shawl.

His mouth moved soundlessly for a moment, and he wet his lips. "Meena," he finally said. It was scarcely more than a breath.

"I'm sorry, do I know . . . ?" Her throat moved in a sudden gasp. "Ing? *Ing!* Beast's beard, what happened to you?"

Gerund smiled to hear his old nickname, and chuckled. Somehow he had forgotten how different he would look to her.

"I am a bit older than I was the last time you saw me." He smiled his perfect teeth at her. "I am well enough. The important bits are still young."

Meena's eyes were wide. "Well enough? It's barely been five years. I knew you were dabbling in time magic, Ing, but what could you possibly have needed to spend so much for?" She shook her head. "Never mind that. You've clearly been traveling for some time. Come and sit down!"

Meena led him to a long stone bench nearby. It was sized perfectly for Meena's tall frame, so Gerund had to hop a bit to sit on it. When he was settled comfortably, she hesitated a moment, then sat beside him. On his left, where he could see her clearly without twisting.

"Ing, what are you doing here?" she asked. "Are you in some kind of trouble?" He forced his gaze up to her face. Small brown eyes set above lovely brown cheeks. Twin tracks of blue ran down those cheeks, soil clinging where tears had dried.

"Not at all, Meena. I came for you."

"You heard about Tomas, then. But all this way!" She glanced at the cow. "How could you possibly . . . ?"

She stopped, eyes closed, and pressed a hand to her chest. After a moment she faced him with a warm smile and said, "Truly, Gerund, I am touched. It means a great deal to me that you would drop everything to come and comfort me." She laid one hand over his. "Thank you."

"It took so long to get here, I was worried you would be gone."

Meena nodded. "We had a memorial service here last week, but when everyone left I almost couldn't face the empty house. I thought about staying with my mother for a time, but . . . " She shrugged. "This is home."

Gerund kept his expression neutral. "You are happy here?"

"Well, less sad, at least. I won't say it isn't hard. Sometimes the good memories are the most painful, you know? But I keep thinking that if I weren't here to stumble over them, maybe they would all just fade away. There are so many things that feel fuzzy already. I have to"—her voice broke—"I have to think that embracing the loss is better than walling it off."

"Still as strong as ever," Gerund said. "That's my Meena." Then, choosing his words carefully, he added, "Your pardon for speaking ill of the dead, but he treated you well? I've wondered."

She gave a little laugh. "I guess you would have. No secret that you two didn't get on, is it? I like to think he'd be glad you came now, but honestly? It's good you didn't try to visit when he was here."

"But you . . . "

"Yes, yes." She waved dismissively. "I won't deny he had a temper. Just as impetuous and fiery as he was at university. You should have heard him rant when that thief Jack first showed up. 'I'll grind his bones to powder!' and so on. But yes, I was well."

Gerund saw how she cradled her arm when she said it and didn't entirely believe her. That must have showed in his expression, because she laughed.

"What, you thought I needed to be rescued from the big bad giant?"

At his silence her laugh died. More softly, she said, "You did think so, didn't you, Ing?"

"No."

"Oh, Ing. Is that why you came?" Meena clasped her hands in her lap. "I didn't think it through, did I? To get here now, traveling alone, you must have set out long before news of Tomas could reach you. You didn't know he was dead, but you were planning to come anyway."

Gerund closed his eyes. "He was bad for you, Meena. You never belonged with him. Yes, I came for you, to take you away. My plan was to do it while he was alive, but now that he's gone I won't leave you trapped by his memory."

"Ing, stop. I'm not trapped."

"All right. I expected that you would want to leave, but if you really do love this home, we could stay."

A pause. "We?"

"Well, Tomas is gone, so . . . "

She stood, face incredulous. "What!?"

"Meena, you're my love. You always have been. I thought . . . "

"Oh?" she interrupted. "You thought that I would suddenly be eager to replace Tomas with someone else? Is that it? Or is this about the supposed treasure he kept in the attic? Well, Jack has everything now, so there's no point in nosing about here."

"That isn't the treasure I care about. Tomas took *you* from me!"

"Ing, what in the blue sky are you talking about?"

He slid off the bench to stand in front of her. "We were close, Meena. I treasured every moment with you. And then Tomas gave you that goose after I got kicked out of the university. He lured you away with those golden eggs and brought you up here. He didn't even let you finish your final year! But now? Now you're free of that giant and his gifts."

Meena gaped at him. "That is what you think? Ing, nobody took me. I *chose* Tomas. I made my own path, and up here we made a home. That's not a position you can just step into. Nobody could, even someone I thought could someday fill his shoes."

Gerund turned in a circle to take in the cottage and garden and cauliflower field. "This life with you is what Tomas stole from me. Will *you* deny it to me as well? Even now? Meena, I paid my eye to save you!"

Meena's hand flew to her throat, to the memory of a knife. "Don't. Just don't. You saved my life once, and I am grateful, but you cannot use that gift to claim the years that have followed." She turned away. "You should leave. I'm sorry that I can't give you what you wanted."

Gerund threw up his hands. "So, it was all a waste then? I spend my beans, my effort, my *time*. I send Jack. And it's all for nothing?"

She spun around, and Gerund's wrist was suddenly clamped in a grip like iron. And it wasn't just her own impressive strength—he could sense threads of magic hovering under her skin. Her voice hissed into his face. "Jack. You *sent* him? Do you mean to tell me that that I am mourning my husband because you thought you owned me? That Tomas is dead and it's your fault, Ing? *Yours?*"

"No! I didn't want him dead. I just wanted Jack to take the goose so you could see clearly again. Without the gift that stole your heart away, I could . . . "

"Stop! If you say one more word about what was taken from you, I swear I will break this old body of yours in half. Look at your own ledger and find the entry where you stole my husband from me. Where you stole a *lifetime* from me. And you *dare* to say that I owe you something? For what? For holding back time for a moment while healers raced against my death? Yes, you lost an eye, but that is not my debt to pay."

She released his aching wrist and shoved him in the chest. "Go, Gerund. We will not see each other again."

"But . . . "

"Take your cow and go. If your thieving heart leads you back here to steal a single minute from me again, I will show you exactly how much I learned at university. All the time in the world will not be enough to hold your misery."

Gerund blinked several times and knew there was nothing he could say to make her see. She was distraught, obviously not thinking clearly. She would understand when she had a chance to calm down. She just needed to rest, to wake up someplace Tomas hadn't touched.

He grasped her hand and pushed her toward unconsciousness.

"No," Meena said. Her hands sparked with yellow flame.

Panicked, Gerund pushed harder, willing her to sleep.

"No!" she said again. She clamped her fingers shut on his and somehow redirected his push. A dozen shoots of grass popped out of the blue soil at her feet. His hand was blistering with the heat of her grip, and he tried to twist away, but she held tight.

"I may not have graduated," she said, "but that also means I never swore to follow their code. Giants aren't the only ones who can grind bones to powder."

Gerund's fingernails blackened and cracked. The smell of burning hair and skin choked him. She was too strong. Though she redirected it into the ground, he kept pushing time at her because those extra days brought at least a little healing to his tortured hand.

"You fixated on that goose," she was saying, "and never saw the truth. The eggs were a promise of golden tomorrows. Tomas gave me a home in the clouds, he gave me the sky itself. He gave me so much more than just a goose."

He could not push Meena through time, so instead he pushed at the flames around her hands. They flared instantly, becoming a blinding ball of fire. Meena shrieked and released him, and they both fell to the ground as the flames vanished to nothing.

Gerund couldn't see anything but bright spots. He lay on the blue earth, holding his scorched fingers in the air where they wouldn't touch anything. This was his chance! He could make her sleep! Meena would also be blind and dazed, so she wouldn't expect it, wouldn't be prepared to block him. He flailed with his unburnt hand and found his cow's rope. He pulled on it to lever himself in the right direction, then let go and reached toward where Meena had fallen. His fingers grazed her knee, and he started to push.

Something massive crushed his wrist, and Gerund screamed. What had Meena done to him? The weight shifted slightly before lifting away. With short, shallow breaths, Gerund fought to feel anything beyond the pain of fragile, splintered bones. There was a heavy thud nearby, like a step. Something warm and wet dripped onto his arm. Drool. It was his cow. The ungrateful beast had stepped on him!

He tried to lift his arm out of the dirt, but the first movement sent shards of sharp pain shooting through him. He bit off another scream and focused on his breathing. Slowly he became aware of Meena speaking. He turned his good eye toward her but could see little through the tears and the lingering afterimage of the fire.

" . . . crushed, but the skin is not broken," she was saying. "Here, I'll just try . . . " His broken wrist went blessedly numb, followed by his burned hand. He took a deep breath and fought a sudden need to vomit.

"I've only chilled them," Meena said. "Do not try to move or everything will be worse."

Gerund nodded. He didn't think she was talking solely of his injuries.

"I will find someone who can tend to you," she told him. "As I said, we will not see each other again. Goodbye, Ing."

She took the cow's rope and walked toward the house she called home.

"I paid for that cow," he protested.

Meena did not answer, and Gerund could only grind his perfect teeth and watch yet another thief steal away what was his.

RUMPELSTILTSKIN'S DAUGHTER

Ruth Nickle

I t was an impulse too strong to control. The sight of the emerald dangling around the queen's neck sparked a memory so strong, so clear, that Tessa had little choice but to approach the queen and rip it from her throat. The moment of shock from everyone surrounding her was enough to give her a head start. She tore down the corridor, tears of panic and rage and pain streaming from her eyes.

Light from the emerald seeped through her fingers, burning them. Still she clung to the stone. She could see a hazy image of it above her in her cradle. Again when she was four, her father held it out for her to see but cautioned her not to touch.

"*The magic is much too strong for you yet, my dear. But soon enough I will teach you. And then, child, there will be no one greater than you.*" Tessa's father sat next to the fire and held up a chain, the green gemstone dangling from it.

Light reflected off the smooth cuts of the jewel, scattering little green stars throughout the room. They danced off the walls and ceiling, and Tessa squealed in delight as she watched it spin and shimmer in the warm glow of the fire.

"*Would you like to see a trick?*" He grinned. Holding the jewel in one hand and then taking a pebble from the ground, he closed his hands around both and spoke a few words in gibberish. Wiggling his brows, he opened the hand that held the stone.

Tessa leaned in to take a look. The rock was now gold. She put her hand to her mouth and giggled her surprise.

"*Can it do anything else, you ask?*" he said. "*One day you shall find out exactly how much power such a little jewel can hold. But for now, I'm afraid it is time for bed.*" His grin broadened, and he stood to place the jewel gently back in its silver box. He turned, scooping her up and spinning her around. And then when they were too dizzy to stand, the little man sat with his daughter on his lap and spoke the sweet little lie that would forever be etched in her heart.

"*Oh, my sweet girl.*" He put his forehead to hers. "*No one will ever hurt you. I promise you, love, that you will have the life that I never did. You will grow and be loved, and you will have a good life. I promise you that I will do whatever it takes to make it so because nobody, not a single other soul, matters to me as much as you do.*"

When he broke their connection, she was quiet and still.

He cocked his head slightly, studying her. "*What is it, my child? What has made you so sad?*"

Her little eyes filled with tears. "*Oh, Papa! I'm just so . . . so . . . lonely after you leave!*" She nuzzled her head into his neck, wrapping her arms around him.

"Oh, dear, that is a problem," he said, stroking her hair. "What shall we do, then? Hmm?"

She was quiet for longer still as he rocked her gently from side to side.

"I want a brother, Papa . . . " she finally whispered.

"A brother!" He smiled. "What do you know of brothers?" he asked, but she didn't answer. He pulled her in closer and sighed. "All right then, my sweet little one. If that is what it takes to make you happy, a brother you shall have."

What had she done? Oh, heaven and stars, what had she done? Fear clutched every inch of Tessa. It clawed and pulled at her until she felt she couldn't breathe. Demons of her past ran alongside the queen's guards as they chased her down the corridor of her own personal nightmare.

She could hear Papa's voice as if he were there, clear and heart-wrenching. "I've got you, I've got you, I've got you . . . "

"Hush now child, 'twas naught but a nightmare." Papa lifted Tessa into his embrace. Her small hands clung to his shoulders as she hiccupped for breath between sobs. "Besides, there can be no tears when I have brought such good news!"

The joy in his voice, his warmth, his safety soon calmed the frightened girl, and she leaned back to look at her father. He wiped a tear from her big blue eyes and tucked a strand of raven hair behind her ear before giving her forehead a kiss.

"Ah, sweet mint and sunshine." He had always told her how much he loved the scent of her hair. "I have come to tell you that I have finally done it, my dear. I have finally found you a brother. But wait!" he said, putting a finger up to halt her excitement. "We have still a little while to wait as the boy is not yet born."

How had the queen gotten the necklace? And why had Tessa
not seen it until just now? All this time the key to her past was
right there, hanging from the queen's neck. "But how?" the question spun in her mind.

Tessa remembered the morning her father had taken the necklace from its box and left. The kiss he had given before he set out
had lingered on her forehead for years. Slowly, oh so very slowly,
it had disappeared as the days and months, the years had gone by.
Now it was nothing more than a whisper of a memory. Her heart
beat heavy in her ears. Tears clouded her vision. The fear of the
chase and the pain of the memory threatened to break her. Yet
still she ran.

*"Papa!" Tessa cried out. Rain poured down, dulling sight and sounds.
"Papa!" she screamed again. But at just four years old, her voice was no
match for the wind.*

*He should have been home. He had promised he'd be home. As she
inched along the trail that led away from her house and into the forest, the
gray sky turned black. Thunder clapped, striking a tree that seemed much
too close to her. She ran.*

*Something, the root of a tree, a branch, a hand, grabbed at her foot, and
she sprawled to the ground. She picked herself up and scurried under a tree
that offered large branches to hide under. Tucking her knees under her chin,
she clamped her eyes shut until at long last she fell asleep.*

*"What's this now?" A woman's voice tsked. Arms lifted her into a soft
embrace.*

*The woman carried her to the castle, quickly and quietly finding a room
and a bed for Tessa. Night had never been so dark. So dead. Back at her
cottage the night was filled with the sound of owls and bats and life, noises
that reminded her that she was not alone, that she was safe. The only sound*

she heard now in the new, strange castle was a howling that wove through the halls.

"The wind, only the wind," Papa would've said. He would've then held her in his arms as he rocked back and forth, and he would have sung a sweet lullaby until she was finally able to drift off to sleep.

But he wasn't there, and it definitely was not the wind.

The sound, a weeping sort of anguished cry, came closer and closer to where she cowered behind her blanket. The air surrounding her grew colder as the noise climbed louder and louder until she could have sworn that whatever made the noise was at the foot of the bed. And then the howling stopped. Every inch of her trembled as she slowly peeked over the blanket.

A ghost stood there, its shape too faded to tell whom it had once been. Her teeth chattered as she asked, "Who are you?"

The monster held out what she could only assume was an arm and then gave one last shriek. The poisonous noise pierced her soul. She threw her hands up to cover her ears, squeezing her eyes shut tight.

Tessa's feet pounded the hard stone, and she blessed her days spent playing with the prince, weaving through corridors and secret passageways. It was the only reason she was still alive. But even he couldn't save her now.

The sound of armor clashing, of curses and shouting, sent pins throughout her body, making her heart as well as her legs move faster. She had to find the room, and fast.

She barely had time to tiptoe into the room when the prince came bursting out of the trapdoor on the floor.

"Caught you!" She pointed at him and laughed. "I thought you said you were good at this game," she said as she arched an eyebrow.

It was then that she noticed his pale face and a flash of pure fear in his eyes before he was able to mask the look. He met her gaze and grinned. "Yeah, well, maybe I was trying to go easy on you."

"Because that sounds like something you would do . . . " She crossed her arms and gave him a look that said she clearly didn't believe him. "What is it anyway? You know it's not fair to hide where I can't possibly find you."

He shrugged, "I'm the prince. There has to be a place for me to hide if raiders invade, hasn't there? But you must listen to me, Tessa," he said, walking to where she stood, "you have to promise me that you'll never go down there."

With her curiosity thoroughly piqued, she looked over his shoulder. He moved to block her view. "I'm serious! Promise me, Tessa." He kept his eyes on hers, unwavering.

"Fine, but can I at least know why?"

He chewed on his lower lip as if he were debating. Tessa sighed. He seemed to have forgotten, again, that she was in fact a whole three years older than him. But while she was small for her age, he was exceptionally tall for his.

"I . . . I don't want to talk about it. Just promise, okay?"

"All right," she said before giving another sigh.

"Shake on it?"

She groaned. "Fine," she said and spit into her hand as he did the same. When their hands met, he pulled her into a choke hold, rubbing her black hair with his knuckles.

"Come on, little crow. It's time to find us a feast!"

Tessa took a sharp turn and made her way to the staircase of the keep. Up the stairs she ran, winding up, up, up until she reached the door at the top. It was old and rusted, and she knew it would protest when she opened it, so she rammed it with her shoulder, making it burst open. After she entered the small room she turned back to the door and slammed it shut. Finding the wooden beam used to bolt it lying off to the side of the doorway, she picked it up. The wood nearly fell from her shaking hands as she attempted to secure the door. After she managed to slide the piece of timber into the metal brackets on the wall, she hurried to the tall, narrow window that looked out to the courtyard below and squeezed through. With her heart in her throat and her eyes keeping watch to make sure no one noticed her on the ledge, she made her way to the abandoned room only two windows away.

As she crept through the window of the prince's old nursery, she prayed it was still empty and gave the smallest sigh of relief when it was. Not daring to set the necklace down, not even for one second, she placed it over her head. The weight of the gem was a comfort amid the chaos. Her eyes scanned the bare floor, searching for the trapdoor. It was there somewhere, wasn't it? Fresh panic surged through her at the thought that she had gone to the wrong room and then released when she saw the edge of the door hidden among the wooden floorboards. She dropped to the floor and clawed at the edge. Finally her nails caught hold and she pulled the heavy door open.

Her feet found the ladder, and she swung the door shut behind her. Climbing down, she huddled in the corner, her only light the green glow from the jewel. It shined off the wall and the hay. And then she saw it, the reason why the prince had made her swear to stay away years ago. There, among the dirt, mixed in with the hay, a skull stared up at her.

Fog seeped from the cracks in the floorboards above, twisting through the hay and revealing even more bones. The air around her started to chill. Light bloomed from the emerald around her neck as wisps of fog wrapped around the bones on the floor, lifting them into the air to form the shape of a small man.

"Ah . . . " The image breathed. "If only I could smell the sweet mint and sunshine one last time."

Tessa's heart froze and she fell to her knees as she recognized her father. Tears of disbelief streamed down her cheeks.

The light from the emerald grew brighter and brighter until it was nearly blinding. The image of the man began to dim.

"Father? Father, no! Please! I need you! Please don't leave me," Tessa cried out.

"My sweet child, finally I have peace. You have reclaimed what was once mine and is now yours." He bent down and kissed her forehead, but instead of the warmth she had been expecting, there was nothing.

"And now, my little one, my spirit must leave. But remember, as long as you have the jewel, a piece of me will always be with you." She wanted to scream at him to stay, wanted to wrap her arms around the bones and demand answers. But there was no use. Her father was fading, leaving her yet again. The room filled with light and cold until the air seemed to burst.

She covered her face with her arm until it was dark once more. Curling into herself, she sobbed. Why were his bones buried there, deep within the castle and under the castle floorboards? A weight so heavy she felt she would never again be able to stand settled into her bones. The trapdoor above her rattled. It creaked open and light spilled in.

The faces of two guards looked down at her.

They took her by the arms and dragged her out of her hiding place. She raged as one of the guards reached for the necklace, straining her muscles against their iron grasp, biting and kicking and screaming. They couldn't take it away. Not the one piece she had left of her father.

Tessa had hoped that her father would appear at the castle, that he would run to her, embrace her, and then take her away from this place. Each day she would go to the woman who had found her and ask if she had heard any word. All the woman ever replied was that she couldn't possibly know where to look or who to ask for without a name.

Each night Tessa would stay awake, searching her mind for some shred of a memory. Something that would give her a clue as to what her father's name could have possibly been. She had only ever called him Papa. All she remembered was that he had told her a name was something special. Something sacred. And so she would drift off to sleep, tears clinging to her lashes while the name slipped through her thoughts.

One night, however, she remembered something. An R. The next morning, Tessa worked up the courage to ask everyone for different names that began with the letter. She asked those who had barely given her a second glance and even those who never looked upon her at all, the maids, the cook, even the stable hands. Most ignored her, some shooed her away, and the rest gave names that didn't spark her memory. Names like Reagan and Ryan.

By the sixth day, she finally gathered the courage to ask those who hated her most. The children in her class. They were the ones she had once hoped to call friends but who instead laughed at her pale skin and dark hair. They were those who mocked her size and couldn't understand why she, an orphaned pet of the prince's nursemaid, was allowed to attend the school.

With trembling knees and a wavering resolve, she walked toward the group of children during a break in the lesson. She stood at the end of the long wooden table, still too afraid to speak, when a boy took note of her.

"What do you want, Crow?" The boy looked at her as if she were a fly on his meat. She tried to swallow but her mouth felt dry.

"I . . . I was wondering if—"

"Speak up, Crow!" the boy said, throwing his apple core at her while another boy cawed.

She wanted to go hide, but she needed to know. She had to try to figure out who her father was.

"Can you think of any names that begin with the letter R?" she managed to ask.

"Ruben," someone said. Another chimed in with "Robin and Ranaldo." "Rhinoceros!" a boy exclaimed, to a chorus of laughter.

The teasing made her shrink deep down into herself. She ran from the room then. Stopping in the hallway to balance herself against the wall, she closed her eyes to the tears she could not hide.

"What's wrong, Princess?" The prince's voice came from behind her. At fifteen, his voice was getting deeper.

She turned to see him standing a few feet away, a ray of sunshine in her bleak world. Her chin wobbled, and he closed the distance between them.

"My father . . . He is never coming to get me." She covered her face to hide her tears.

With a rare gentleness, he lowered her hands then lifted her chin until their eyes met. "But you have me, Princess. And you know what? We're better than any family." He guided her into his embrace and kissed the top of her head as she cried on his shoulder.

Tessa ran a hand across her cheek to wipe away the last of the guards' spit. The vile insults and names they spewed upon her as they dragged her down to the dungeon could not compare to the damage done to her broken heart. The pain had been great at first. It had left her huddled in tears. But now? Now she sat on the cold, hard ground of the prison cell and felt nothing. Her father was gone, dead, and now the emerald was gone as well.

Her hope had extinguished.

While she sat alone in the cell, everything started to come together. The stories of the queen being able to spin straw into gold. The hushed whispers of a little man who had helped her do it. Those were the tales that were forbidden. The tales she only ever heard snippets of. But now it all made sense. The queen had used Tessa's father. She had made him her slave, and then once she had figured out the source of his power, she had killed him for it.

"Little Crow?" The prince's voice broke through the darkness, making Tessa's head jerk up in response. He came closer until the light from the window lit half his face, shining in one of his blue eyes. His hands clasped the bars between them. She looked away.

"My mother is fading. It's as if that jewel she wore was somehow poisoning her while feeding her at the same time. Her skin is . . . " he paused. "It's gray and wrinkled. Her hair is falling out. If father was still alive, well . . . I'm not sure what he would do, but Tessa, do you . . . " He paused as if he couldn't believe what he was about to ask. "Do you know if her necklace can heal her?"

"*Her* necklace?" she spat the words, finally looking up at him. "You mean the one she stole from my father?"

At least the prince had the decency to look surprised by her accusation. Then with a sigh, he shrank as if the weight of a thousand worlds hung from his shoulders. "Please, Tessa. *Please.* You, more than anyone else, know that I know how cruel she can be." His jaw clenched as if remembering her sharp tongue and wicked strikes. "But, Tessa, she is my *mother.*"

The look in his eyes nearly undid her: The hurt of a little boy.

"I cannot be sure. The jewel was my father's, not mine. I'm . . . I'm sorry I cannot help you more."

Unable to stop herself, she stood and made her way over to stand in front of the prince. She touched his hand that clenched one of the bars between them. "I didn't mean to do it. I . . . I just couldn't help myself." More than anything, she wanted the prince to open the cell door and embrace her, wanted to feel his warmth, his safety.

He swallowed hard. "There is something else." He looked down as if he couldn't bring himself to meet her eyes. "If I could stop it, oh stars, if I could stop it, I would. *Believe* me I would." His voice cracked on the last word while the only tear she had ever seen him shed rolled down his cheek. He coughed as if it were the only way he could get the rest of his words out. "Oh, Princess," he said, finally looking up, his eyes rimmed in red. "You are to be hanged."

Cold dread slipped down Tessa's back, but she remained still, expressionless. What could she say? What could she do? Quiet tears, the empty useless things, streamed down her face. And in spite of herself, she wanted to live.

Happiness had always seemed like such a foreign thing to Tessa. Something she saw in others but couldn't quite grasp. And yet as she sat hugging her knees in the middle of the meadow where the sun melted like warm

honey around her and the grass whispered its hellos, she could feel its once familiar embrace.

The meadow was her place of peace where time moved slower. As she watched the dandelion blossoms float languidly through the air, she heard someone walking up behind her. She didn't need to turn around to know it was the prince. He was the only other one who knew where this place was. Years ago, when she and the prince were playing, they had found it deep within the woods. Ever since that day, she went there whenever the kingdom became too much for her. It wasn't too far away, but far enough as to not hear all the noise and feel all the chaos.

The prince sat down beside her. He settled in the grass and put an arm around her. She leaned into him and there they sat for the longest moment without a word spoken between them. This, she thought, was what true happiness was. If she could have this impossible daydream for the rest of her life, she would be content.

But he was the prince and she was nothing more than an orphan. She would have to be satisfied with the sun and the wind and her daydreams.

Gray clouds were smudged across the sky, blocking the sun and the warmth. The wind was too harsh, too cold. The coarse rope was itchy around Tessa's neck while the trembling of her legs made the stool she stood on wobble against the wooden platform.

A bell tolled in the distance.

"The queen!" The voice rang out above the crowd. "The queen is dead!"

The stool was kicked out from under Tessa. The rope cut into her neck. One last breath; her lungs and throat turned to thunder. She kicked her feet, but it only made the pressure and the pain worse. Her vision began to blur, fading in and out.

The bell tolled once more.

"Wait!" The prince's voice sounded. "Stop! By order of your new king, I command you to release her!"

The world turned black. The burning stopped.

TSAR VISLAV, TSARINA VISLAV, AND THE FIREBIRD

Sarah Chow

Tsar Vislav nervously rubbed one of the golden apples in the basket on the bureau. He'd been in the midst of his nightly routine when Tsarina Vislav returned from her retreat, and his chances of getting peacefully to bed were dwindling fast.

"I take my first month away from home—*ever*—and what do I come home to?" she shouted. "House in an uproar. One son married, two sons dead, new horse stabled in *my* horse's spot, and a shrieking bird in the bedroom!" She jabbed a finger at the luminescent firebird perched in a golden cage beside the dresser.

The tsar gripped the apple. "This was not how I intended things to go, my sweet pear. Please do try to understand."

"Understand?" the tsarina shouted. "When I left we were dealing with nothing more than a simple thief taking your precious golden apples from the orchard. I come back to complete madness!"

"My sweet cherry," the tsar said. "As soon as you left, I sent our oldest son into the orchard at night to watch for the thief, but he slept and saw nothing. So the next night I sent our second son to watch for the thief, but he too slept all night and saw nothing. On the third night I sent our third son, Prince Ivan. He managed to stay awake all night and discover that it was actually this firebird coming to eat the apples. So the boys went off after the firebird."

"You mean to say, you sent them," the tsarina muttered.

The tsar pretended he had not heard this remark. "Prince Ivan returned with not only the firebird, who belonged to Tsar Feliks, but also with a horse with a golden mane, who belonged to Tsar Afron, and with the lovely Helen the Beautiful, daughter of Tsar Hedeon. Prince Ivan's brothers were jealous of his success and attacked him, so naturally he killed them both, and he has now wed Helen the Beautiful and left on his honeymoon."

The tsarina's voice dropped suddenly, soft and menacing. "And did no one even *think* to invite me to my own son's wedding?"

"I tried to delay the wedding until your return. Truly, I did. But Prince Ivan simply would not wait."

The tsar rubbed his temples. "Honestly, I don't understand why you're so angry, my sweet peach. Prince Ivan won all these marvelous treasures through his cleverness and daring. Most tsarinas would be proud."

The tsarina huffed. "A thousand blessings on our youngest son, but 'clever' and 'daring' are not words even our most flattering servants would use to describe him."

The tsar glanced around for support, but the only sound was a squawk from the firebird, so the tsar simply said, "He's a remarkable young man." It sounded unconvincing, even to his own ear.

The tsarina raised an eyebrow. "The kidnapped princess I can understand. Dramatic, but that seems to be the trend with young men these days. The horse I can understand. A bit ostentatious, but a good mode of transportation. The murdered brothers I can understand. Brutal, but there's certainly precedent for that among royal families. But a FIREBIRD? Seriously? You mark my words, that bird will be the ruin of us all."

At that the tsar protested in earnest, "Are you questioning the quest? We simply had to catch him. He was stealing my golden apples!"

The tsarina was unmoved. "So you brought it back here. And now what does it eat?"

The tsar shifted a little so he was standing in front of the golden apples on the bureau.

"I thought so," she said. "Well, if you love your precious apples so much, you can just sleep out in the orchard with them tonight."

And that was that.

The tsar did not have a comfortable night in the apple orchard. His retinue brought out the second-best velvet blanket and the second-softest royal pillow from the royal linen closet. Even so, there was something entirely unnatural about sleeping out of doors. One of the lesser pages held an umbrella over the tsar's head to keep off potential rain. He tossed and turned, longing for the polished cedar walls of his bedroom.

Before long, an entire orchestra of crickets struck up their music from the branches of the nearest tree. "How on earth," the tsar muttered to himself, "did my first two sons manage to sleep through such a racket?"

A few hours later a dewdrop slid off the page's umbrella and struck the tsar's neck. "It would take a feat of will to sleep through this! Perhaps I should have commended my other sons who slept out here all night rather than Prince Ivan who stayed awake and saw the firebird."

At breakfast, the tsarina sat at the farthest end of the table, her hair still rolled in curlers.

"I didn't sleep a wink," she complained, jabbing the toast with her butter knife. "That gleaming bird was so bright I could see it with a pillow over my face."

The tsar thought it unwise to compare their sleeping arrangements, but he could not resist defending the firebird. "You must admit the firebird is beautiful, my sweet blackberry."

"The firebird is absurd," the tsarina said. "Its cage, on the other hand, is beautiful. If you could just get the bird out of it long enough to admire the gold workmanship and the jewels. Maybe if you kept a pigeon in it . . . "

The tsar dropped the argument. "Would you join me, my sweet grape, for a ride this afternoon? I would love to see you ride the horse with the golden mane."

"You mean the horse that was stabled in my horse's stall when I returned last night?"

"Prince Ivan thought you would like the horse," the tsar said. "He was Tsar Afron's finest beast. He's stabled in your stall because he is a gift for you." Prince Ivan had not actually said this, but under the circumstances, Tsar Vislav thought Prince Ivan would not mind if Tsarina Vislav rode the horse. At least sometimes. "My sweet currant, his bridle is encrusted in rubies and his mane is purest gold."

"I don't care what color its mane is, I was quite satisfied with my horse."

⚬⚬⚬

At one o'clock the Tsarina Vislav met Tsar Vislav in the stables, now without curlers on her head.

The tsar grinned his most winning smile. "You look lovely, my sweet plum."

The tsarina rolled her eyes.

Tsar Vislav half expected her to refuse to ride the horse with the golden mane, but she mounted and set off before he could get astride his own black stallion.

After an hour, Tsarina Vislav stopped trying to outpace the tsar and slowed to ride beside him. She was still staring straight ahead, though, so he kept his eyes on the magnificent bridle, all braided with gems, that she held in her hands.

At last Tsar Vislav broke the silence. "How was your retreat?"

Tsarina Vislav sighed wistfully. "Glorious. The food was absolutely divine. I finished a mountain of quilts, two wall hangings, and even some horse blankets. With those peasant clothes you got me, no one even suspected I was a tsarina. I blended right in with all the ladies there. And I connected instantly with these three other women, Katya and Uliana and Bella. I finally have some friends who really understand me."

"That's splendid!" the tsar said.

"It was splendid, till I got home to this mess," she said.

After a moment she went on. "Look, there's something very odd about the whole thing. I simply cannot picture Prince Ivan accomplishing any of the things you've said, yet here are all the prizes to prove it. Not least that glowing bird."

Tsar Vislav chose to ignore this last jab. "Actually, it's been bothering me, too," he said. "It was a bit hectic when Prince Ivan returned, but now that he's left, I've started to wonder about his account. He should be home from his honeymoon in another day or two. We can question him then."

At dinner, Tsarina Vislav still sat at the opposite end of the dining table, but she was not wielding the butter knife as a weapon, so Tsar Vislav took it as a sign that her mood was softening. When the dinner plates were cleared, he approached the other end of the table and sat a few chairs away from the tsarina.

"I made some inquiries this afternoon," he said. "It seems the other tsars did not simply gift the firebird and the horse with the golden mane and Princess Helen the Beautiful to Prince Ivan as he reported. There appears to have been some theft involved."

"Mmmm," said the tsarina, more thoughtfully than triumphantly. "And do you think they will have something to say about the loss of their treasures?"

"Perhaps," said the tsar.

"I'm glad you've inquired," she said.

"May I sleep inside tonight, my sweet quince?"

"Certainly not."

That night the cricket residents of the orchard were mercifully quiet, and the tsar slept tolerably well until a quarter past two, when one of the golden apples fell from the tree, broke a hole straight through the page's umbrella, and struck the tsar's elbow.

"Shriveled apricots!" the tsar shouted.

The page leapt to pick up the apple, grunting as he lifted it with both hands. "Sorry, Your Majesty! I should have caught it." The page quivered.

The tsar growled but waved away his hovering attendants. "Golden apples are much heavier than the ordinary variety."

At breakfast the following morning, Tsarina Vislav sat beside the tsar. He gestured toward several large bundles of quilts, still piled near the entranceway to the dining hall. "You did get a great deal of work done at your retreat," he said.

The tsarina nodded. "I had no distractions there." She reached for a muffin and said, "Prince Ivan claimed the firebird, the horse, and the princess were gifts. Last night you said they were stolen. But in either case, do you really believe Prince Ivan managed to acquire all of those things himself?"

The tsar stirred his applesauce. "Unlikely."

"So who helped him?"

Tsar Vislav shrugged. "There's no way of knowing until Prince Ivan returns."

A few moments later the tsarina said softly, "I'm still sorry I missed the wedding."

The tsar put his arm around her shoulders. "I'm sorry they would not wait."

"What do you think of our daughter-in-law?" she asked.

The tsar paused. "Helen the Beautiful is . . . a good fit for Prince Ivan."

The tsarina smiled. "Not too quick, then?"

"She certainly won't intimidate him." The tsar chuckled. "And she *is* very beautiful, though of course nothing to you, my sweet persimmon."

The tsarina swatted him, but she was smiling.

"I wonder if they named her 'Helen the Beautiful' when she was born, or after she grew up," he mused.

Tsarina Vislav giggled.

A blast of trumpets from the front gate announced the return of Prince Ivan, so the tsar and tsarina left their breakfast and hurried out to greet their newlywed son.

"Mother," Prince Ivan shouted when he saw the tsarina. "You must meet my bride."

He leapt up the path, and Helen the Beautiful bounced along behind him, all golden hair and puffy skirts. "I'm erratic to meet you at last," she said to the tsarina, curtsying a full three times by the end of this unusual sentence.

Tsarina Vislav gave the girl her most formal smile. "I suppose I am too," she said.

"If only you could have been at the wedding," Helen the Beautiful said. "It was absolutely spurious."

"I see," said Tsarina Vislav.

Tsar Vislav clapped Prince Ivan on the back. "Welcome home, my boy! You must both come in and join us for breakfast."

Prince Ivan grinned. "Sure thing!"

The tsar led them all into the dining room, keeping himself between the tsarina and Helen the Beautiful.

"Prince Ivan," said the tsarina after fresh orange juice had been poured. "Your father tells me you gained your bride, a horse, and a"—she gritted her teeth—"shining firebird through your wits and valor."

"Awww, shucks," said Prince Ivan. "Yes, I did."

"He's so inelegant." Helen the Beautiful sighed.

The tsarina was undeterred. "All by yourself?"

Prince Ivan took a swig of orange juice. "Mostly."

"I'm curious about the 'mostly,'" the tsarina said. "Did you have any help?"

"Well, a little," Prince Ivan admitted. "I did most of the work."

"And who was it that helped you?" The tsar smiled encouragingly.

"The Gray Wolf," Prince Ivan said.

The tsar dropped his glass, and orange juice splashed all across the table. "A wolf? You got help from a wolf?"

"Sure," said Prince Ivan. "He said I could trust him."

Helen the Beautiful nodded happily.

"The Gray Wolf ate my horse," Prince Ivan explained, "and then he felt bad, so he offered to help me with my quest. And then he stuck around for all the other favors I needed after that."

The tsarina looked horrified. "How many times have I told you to not trust wolves? Especially ones that talk?"

Prince Ivan looked from one parent to the other, his face drawn up in confusion. "Never."

"Well, I may not have said those words explicitly," the tsarina conceded, "but I thought the gist was implied. Just to make it clear, I'm telling you now: don't ever trust a wolf."

The tsar nodded. "Especially one that talks."

Just then a deep howl echoed through the dining hall. The tsar seized the tsarina's hand, and they dashed outside, Prince Ivan and Helen the Beautiful close on their heels. On the hill across from the guard tower stood a great gray wolf, his thick fur ruffling in the wind.

"Hullo, Gray Wolf," Prince Ivan called to the wolf.

"He's so furry!" squealed Helen the Beautiful.

The tsarina challenged the wolf. "What do you mean by entering our tsardom?"

"I come to gnaw your bones," the wolf rumbled. "Your clever prince has upset every tsar from here to the sea, and when the war is finished, I will have enough flesh for myself and all my brothers to feast for seven lifetimes." The wolf slowly licked his fangs with a long red tongue, as if to emphasize his words, and then sat back on his haunches and gestured with his head toward the great road. "See? Here they come already."

On the road, an army was approaching with the firebird-emblazoned banner of Tsar Feliks, followed by a second army under Tsar Afron's golden-maned horse banner, followed by a third army led by Tsar Hedeon and a banner woven with Helen the Beautiful's image.

"Not sure if I would follow the tactics of a military commander flying Helen the Beautiful's face," Tsar Vislav whispered to his wife.

She smirked a little and jabbed him in the ribs. "Shush. She might hear you."

Helen the Beautiful had not heard them. "That's my father coming! I can't wait to introvert you all!"

"Lovely idea. Let's all sit down for tea together," the tsarina said.

"Actually, tea sounds wonderful," the tsar said. "Prince Ivan, why don't you two go advise the kitchen to prepare some fruit tarts?"

"Oooo, yummy!" Helen the Beautiful said. She and Prince Ivan hurried back into the palace.

The tsarina sighed with relief. "They're gone. Now, should we do something about the invading armies?"

Tsar Vislav took her hand and together they went out the front gate to meet the other tsars. Behind them, Tsar Vislav's soldiers gathered on the castle's walls.

Tsar Feliks, Tsar Afron, and Tsar Hedeon arranged their armies side by side outside the castle. They themselves rode forward with their retinues, swords drawn.

"You have done me a grievous wrong!" shouted Tsar Feliks.

"And me," yelled Tsar Afron.

"And me," called Tsar Hedeon.

Tsar Vislav drew his own sword. "Any wrongs you have suffered were of your own making," he said. "If you have lost your treasures, it is only because you were not clever or daring enough to retain them."

The tsars surged forward in anger.

"Katya?" The tsarina's clear voice rang out with surprise. "Uliana? Bella?" She was staring past the angry tsars at Tsarina Feliks, Tsarina Afron, and Tsarina Hedeon, who each rode in the companies behind their husbands. "What are you doing here?"

"Catherine?" Tsarina Feliks asked. She slid off her horse and rushed forward to give Tsarina Vislav a warm hug. "Catherine! I had no idea you were the Tsarina Vislav! I am in fact the Tsarina Feliks."

"And Uliana was only a name I assumed for the retreat. I am really the Tsarina Afron."

"And I am not really called Bella. I am the Tsarina Hedeon. I came home from our quilting retreat to find this madness."

"You can only imagine what I've been facing," Tsarina Vislav said. "I went from peacefully stitching by the lake to trying to sleep with a flaming *bird* in my bedroom."

All four women laughed. The tsars watched their wives uncertainly, swords still drawn.

"Let's go inside," Tsar Vislav suggested, "and settle all this over some tea and fruit tarts, shall we?"

So the four tsars and tsarinas trooped into the dining hall. The tea was already laid out, but to Tsar Vislav's relief, Prince Ivan and Helen the Beautiful were not in the room. The tsarinas chattered while the tsars crunched slowly through apricot tarts. When at last there was a lull in the tsarinas' conversation, Tsar Vislav spoke up. "Now what can we do for you, good neighbors?"

"I want my firebird back," demanded Tsar Feliks.

"Yes, please take your firebird," said Tsarina Vislav. "Have some golden apples, too. The firebird adores them. We can send you with a bushel." She smiled sweetly at Tsar Vislav.

"Of course," said Tsar Vislav, "we can't return the firebird without his lovely cage. It's an amazing piece of workmanship. Tsarina Vislav was quite bedazzled by it." He returned Tsarina Vislav's smile.

"That's hardly suffi—" Tsar Feliks began.

Tsarina Feliks cut in. "Thank you, that will quite settle our concerns," she said in a final tone, giving her husband a stern look.

"I want my horse with the golden mane back," said Tsar Afron.

"Oh, we really don't need your horse. Please take him back," Tsarina Vislav said. "Along with his beautiful bridle that Tsar Vislav so admires," she added, shooting a look at Tsar Vislav.

Tsar Vislav smiled back. "And you can have these newly finished horse blankets that Tsarina Vislav quilted at the retreat."

"What a generous gift," exclaimed Tsarina Afron before her husband could speak. "I happen to know that Catherine's—I mean Tsarina Vislav's—handiwork is quite impressive." She nodded a head toward the pile of quilts Tsarina Vislav had brought back from the retreat. They were still stacked by the dining hall's entranceway.

"And I want my daughter back," said Tsar Hedeon.

"And you shall have her," said Tsar Vislav, "as well as a son-in-law, for they are wed."

Tsarina Vislav smiled warmly at Tsar Vislav and nodded vigorously. "I'm sure Prince Ivan and Helen the Beautiful will be *much* happier living in your castle rather than here. We can send them home with you today, along with our warmest wishes."

"Oh yes, Helen will indeed be happier that way," said Tsarina Hedeon. "A daughter likes to be near her mother. And between us, thank you for saving us the cost of a royal wedding."

A moment later Prince Ivan and Helen the Beautiful burst into the dining hall, and Tsarina Hedeon gathered them both in a warm hug. After a moment, she forced Tsar Hedeon to join the hug as well.

Tsar Vislav's servants entered with the brilliant firebird in its bejeweled cage and a crate of golden apples. At the sight of his former owners, the firebird squawked loudly. "And good riddance!" Tsarina Vislav whispered at the bird in a voice only Tsar Vislav could hear.

"So, we are settled then," said Tsar Vislav. "Let us bring in some wine and toast everyone's return journey."

As he spoke a howl echoed through the dining hall, much louder than before, and the wolf stood in the doorway.

"Gray Wolf!" Prince Ivan called in delight, waving madly.

"There will be war," the wolf growled, "if I must start it myself!" He leapt at Tsarina Vislav, who was seated nearest the door.

Without even a thought, Tsar Vislav seized the firebird's cage and threw it as hard as he could toward the wolf. The cage struck the leaping wolf, the door flew open, and the firebird burst into flames.

The wolf yelped and fell to the floor, rolling to beat out the flames, but the fire spread to Tsarina Vislav's pile of quilts, and the flames crackled higher and higher.

The tsar pulled the tsarina from the smoky hall, with their guests and servants close behind. Together, they all stood in the orchard and watched the palace burn to the ground.

As the flames died down, Tsar Vislav turned to Tsar Feliks. "I'm so deeply sorry for the loss of your firebird."

"Not at all," said Tsar Feliks. A loud squawk emitted from the smoldering rubble, and the firebird flapped clumsily out of the ruined palace. "He's a firebird. That's what they do."

"That's why we keep it outside," Tsarina Feliks confided.

At long last, all of the tsars left with their armies: Tsar Feliks with his firebird, a somewhat melted cage, and a freshly picked bushel of apples; Tsar Afron with his horse, bridle, and the promise of new horse blankets next year; and Tsar Hedeon with his daughter and new son-in-law. The tsarinas lingered a little before bidding farewell, leaving each other with a promise that they would keep their identities secret so they could all attend next year's quilting retreat in anonymity.

After they had all left, Tsarina Vislav turned to the tsar. "I told you that bird would ruin us."

"I told you he would come in handy," he said.

"No, you didn't," she said. She was smiling. "I'd invite you to sleep up in the bedroom tonight, but it seems we haven't got one."

"Then I will invite you to join me under the apple tree. I have the second-best blanket set up already," he said.

"All right." Tsarina Vislav kissed him.

"Well, maybe not right under the apple tree," she said. "Imagine if one of the apples fell! They are quite heavy."

TATTERHOOD AND THE PRINCE'S HAND

Katherine Cowley

CHAPTER 1

An excerpt from "True Accounts of Nobility, Particularly Queens, Kings, Princes, and Princesses, in Regards to their Interactions with Fairies and Other Magical Creatures"

Once upon a time a king and a queen were cursed to never have children. After many years, the queen found a beggar woman who could break the spell. The beggar brought two pots of water and had the queen wash in them both, then placed the pots under her bed. She instructed the queen to look under the bed in the morning, because a flower would be growing in each pot. She should eat only the beautiful flower and leave the ugly one alone. But in the morning, the queen could not help herself, and she ate both flowers.

Soon, the queen was blessed with twin girls. The second baby, the younger of the twins, was extremely fair and delightful to look upon. Her parents named her Ingridr because of her great beauty. The first baby, the elder twin and heir to the kingdom, was the ugliest child anyone in the land had ever seen. She possessed ugly gray skin and a bit of magic. She spent all her days riding around on a goat, carrying a large wooden spoon, and wearing a tattered hood. Soon everyone called her Tatterhood, and even her parents forgot her real name.

Now once every seven years, in the heart of winter, a band of trolls came and gallivanted throughout the castle, wreaking havoc. The queen, the king, and their daughters hid in the queen's chambers with all the doors and windows barred. This particular year, the princesses had reached seventeen years of age. As Tatterhood heard the racket outside the rooms, she could not sit still. "I will drive them out," she declared. Her parents insisted that nothing could be done about the trolls and begged Tatterhood to stay inside, but she would not listen. She took her wooden spoon and her goat—for, of course, her goat never left her side—and went to the door. "Keep the door shut. Do not open it a bit, for any reason, until the trolls are gone." And out she went and added to the great noise in the halls.

Now her younger sister, Ingridr, fretted and fretted about Tatterhood. Finally she could stand it no longer and opened the door just a smidgen to check on her beloved sister. A troll reached inside and pulled Ingridr out. This troll cut off Ingridr's beautiful head and a troll's head, and then attached Ingridr's head to the troll's body and the troll's head to Ingridr's body. Then all of the trolls left, including the one wearing Ingridr's head.

Tatterhood berated her parents for letting Ingridr open the door, then decided to rescue her sister's head. She sat on her goat and led her troll-headed sister into the forest. After a week, they boarded a ship and sailed through the icy seas all the way to the trolls' castle. When they arrived, she whacked the trolls with her wooden spoon until they gave back Ingridr's head. Tatterhood used a bit of magic to put the head back on Ingridr's body and sailed away with her on the ship before the trolls could change their minds.

Throughout their journey, Ingridr stayed below deck, recovering from her ordeal with the trolls. Whenever she got the chance, Tatterhood rode her goat back and forth along the deck, waving her wooden spoon. She was thus engaged as they passed near another kingdom.

"Is it only you on that ship?" asked the sailors of that kingdom.

"Only me and my sister," replied Tatterhood.

"Can we see her?" they asked.

Tatterhood went below deck, spoke to her sister, and returned. "She won't come out unless the king himself comes to see her."

Well, the king of that land was a widower. He heard of the princess in the ship and decided he must see her. When Ingridr met the king, she fell very much in love, and he fell in love with her. The king asked for her hand in marriage, but Ingridr insisted that as she was the younger sister, she would not wed until Tatterhood did.

The king had two sons. The first was already married, but the second was not, and the king thought it a perfect match. The prince did not want to marry Tatterhood, but finally his father convinced him, for the good of the kingdom and the sake of the king's own happiness.

An extravagant double wedding was planned. The king and Ingridr sat in a grand carriage, leading the wedding procession through the city. Tatterhood and the prince followed after, she on her goat and he on his horse. By the prince's expression, it looked as if he were riding to his own funeral, rather than to his wedding.

As they rode, Tatterhood said, "Do you know why my goat is named Storm?"

"No."

"So I can say that I always ride off on a storm."

He didn't laugh, or even smile.

"Why don't you talk to me?"

The prince turned to her, then looked quickly away. "What should I talk about?" he asked.

Tatterhood thought for a moment, then said, "Ask me, why do you ride that ugly goat?"

"Why do you ride that ugly goat?" the prince asked.

"But I am riding a beautiful horse," she said, and it was so.

The prince glanced at the horse, but when Tatterhood tried to engage him in conversation, he still would not.

After a few minutes, she said, "Ask me, why do you hold that ugly spoon?"

"Why do you hold that ugly spoon?" the prince asked.

"But I am holding a beautiful silver fan," said Tatterhood, and it was so. But still the prince would not talk to her.

"Ask me, why do you wear that tattered hood?" she said.

"Why do you wear that tattered hood?" the prince asked.

"But I am wearing a silver crown," said Tatterhood, and it was so. But still, the prince would not talk to her.

Tatterhood sighed. After a few minutes, she said, "Ask me, why are you so ugly and gray?"

"Why are you so ugly and gray?" the prince asked.

"But I am ten times more beautiful than my sister."

At that, Tatterhood transformed and was truly more beautiful than Ingridr.

The prince fell instantly in love with Tatterhood, and they spoke all the way to their wedding feast. After their marriage they returned to Tatterhood's kingdom, where they lived happily ever after.

End of excerpt

CHAPTER 2

At first, winning a prince's hand in marriage had seemed a grand sort of prize to Tatterhood—after all, she had single-handedly defeated an entire band of trolls *and* saved her sister. Surely she deserved some sort of reward, and Ingridr convinced her a husband would bring her great happiness. But now, six months wed, Tatterhood wondered if she had made a wise decision. Yes, her parents had been thrilled when she returned with a husband who was also a prince, but Prince Trygve was still better at pleasing her parents than her.

Tatterhood rode her nanny goat, Storm, through the fields toward the practice grounds, where she thought she'd find Trygve. She had realized, that morning, that she was expecting a child— she should've noticed several weeks ago—and she wanted to tell him.

Trygve was engaged in a swordfight with one of her soldiers. He swung his double-edged sword with great finesse, expertly blocking the soldier's blows and delivering his own.

Trygve was strong and intelligent—a real warrior. And he was a good man, kind to the people. These were all good traits for a husband who would someday rule by her side. The maids said he was a handsome man, but Tatterhood did not care much about that.

Her people liked him, and Tatterhood liked him for that. But he was always more comfortable with everyone else than with her (except for when she changed her appearance). The previous night they had argued about the new coverlet for their bed. Tatterhood insisted the color didn't matter while Trygve protested that it did matter and the craftsman had not delivered what he had promised and should redo the work. They had said unkind things to each other, and though they both apologized, they had not spoken much to each other since. So now Tatterhood wanted to tell him about their baby—needed to tell him—but she did not know how exactly to start the conversation.

Trygve won his fight. A smile covered his face as he patted the soldier on the back.

"Who will challenge Trygve next?" asked the sword master.

Maybe if they fought in the training arena, it would make it easier to talk to each other. Tatterhood jumped off her goat and raised her wooden spoon. "I will!"

The people cheered, but Trygve's smile disappeared.

"What is your weapon?"

Tatterhood raised her wooden spoon. It was a full arm in length—perfect for fighting against a sword. The bowl of the spoon was about the size of her head and worked well as a mace. The handle was not completely smooth; the front side was flat, to make it easier to hold. The end of the handle curved out, like the end of an axe handle, so that during a fight the spoon could not slide out of her grip.

"Tatterhood! Tatterhood! Tatterhood!" the people chanted.

"Let the match begin!" declared the sword master.

Tatterhood sprang into the attack, using both arms to swing her spoon toward her husband's knee. He blocked and then moved to the offensive, swinging his sword first toward her chest, then toward her abdomen. His strokes came in rapid succession, but his motions had lost some of their normal fluidity.

"What's wrong?" asked Tatterhood as she used the spoon handle to deflect one of Trygve's jabs.

"Nothing," the prince muttered. "You just look very gray today."

Tatterhood wondered again if he was embarrassed by her appearance. Most people got used to it after a few weeks, yet it still seemed to bother Trygve.

She scowled and spread her hands about a foot apart on the middle of the spoon's handle. She pushed her right hand forward, propelling the spoon head toward his arm (if it weren't a training fight, she would've gone for his neck). He barely managed to block. She yanked her right arm back at the same time as she pushed her left hand forward, which pulled the spoon head back and sent the back of the handle toward his other arm. Once again, he barely blocked. He tried to attack, but she planted her feet firmly on the ground and pushed the spoon handle against his sword with all her strength. He stumbled backward.

She did not want to cause him any true damage—he was her husband—but she wasn't going to play easy on him. That was not her way.

She swung toward his knee again. He blocked, and she yanked the spoon back and drove it straight forward, hitting him in the ribs with the spoon head. The hit wasn't hard enough to break any bones, but he would surely bruise.

"This is not a fair fight," gasped the prince. "Your spoon is magic."

"It's not a magic spoon," insisted Tatterhood. "Not exactly." It's not like she had placed a spell on it—there were a handful of ways she could consciously use magic, but for the most part, it did what it wanted. She could not yoke it to her will. (If she had better, more constant control, she could've become a witch, but it was too late for that now.) Yet on occasion, when she used things that resonated with her essence, they channeled a bit of the magic inside her. She couldn't force it to happen, but at times she might fight better or travel faster or jump higher; once she'd even managed to sing a half-decent song while on her goat and holding her spoon, which was clearly magic helping things along.

"It's made of wood," said the prince. "If it were a normal spoon it would be damaged by my sword." His sword had rags wrapped around it to make it less lethal, but even so, he was prob-ably correct.

"Very well," said Tatterhood. "I will fight you with a sword."

She raised her hand to pause the fight and thought very hard of the sword in her bedroom. She willed her wooden spoon and her sword to switch places, and suddenly, her sword was in her hand instead of the spoon. Like Trygve's, it was a stout, two-edged blade, though hers weighed less.

The sword master wrapped rags around the blade.

Tatterhood adjusted her grip on the sword. The metal handle felt cold, lifeless, while her spoon felt as alive as a tree.

Trygve swung his sword, so she parried him.

When it became clear that she would not be an ordinary prin-cess, Tatterhood's parents had encouraged her to take up sword fighting. In this endeavor, she gained proficiency but not exper-tise.

Perhaps the problem was the sword itself. It had a decorative hilt, fit for a princess, and a beautiful shine. It had been forged by the best sword maker in the land, and the sword master declared it perfect for either a parade or a fight. But it did not speak to Tatterhood's essence, and so she much preferred her spoon.

Tatterhood was not as fast as her husband—at least not when she held a sword—and Trygve was very good at this. Though she tried her best, she barely blocked his attacks. She kept shifting her sword's height, but she could not get in a good attack. Yet even if she weren't as proficient at the sword, at least there was a light in Trygve's eyes that she did not see most days, and she liked the way their bodies and their swords moved together. They should fight like this again.

Trygve swung and she moved to block, but it was a feint and now his sword was at her throat. The sword master declared the victor.

Tatterhood bit her lip. She had not wanted the fight to end so quickly, and she did not like to lose. She told herself she would have beaten him if she'd kept her wooden spoon. The soldiers patted the prince on the back.

"Walk with me back to the castle?" Trygve asked.

Tatterhood agreed and asked a servant to take her goat. The servant grimaced but nodded and proceeded to chase the goat. Storm was large, shaggy, and brown. And rather ferocious. She jumped onto a waist-high, wooden fence, bit off the servant's hat, and ran into a field. This did not worry Tatterhood—Storm always came back.

Trygve took Tatterhood's hand. He held it, raised, in the formal manner used to escort a noble woman. Their fingers did not intertwine as the villagers' fingers did when they held each other's hands, but surely it still counted as holding her hand, and in a public, outdoor setting. He must be pleased with her.

They walked through the field. Tatterhood was about to tell him she was expecting a child when a messenger approached. The lass curtsied and declared, "Letters for Princess Tatterhood and Prince Trygve!" Trygve's letter was from his father, King Varg, and Tatterhood's from Ingridr.

They read their letters as they walked. Ingridr was doing well and enjoying the sunny summer weather. She mentioned that King Varg was troubled. "There are reports of the return of a magical creature, but he won't tell me any more details."

Tatterhood looked at Trygve. His face was pale, and his eyes darted back and forth across his own letter.

"Anything wrong?" she asked when he finished reading.

"Of course not," he snapped.

She did not press him or force an answer. She had already discovered that, in marriage, such tactics should be used only in times of great expediency.

They arrived at the castle, Trygve maintaining his stony silence.

"Bring me my horse," he instructed a servant.

The servant returned with Sunset, the prince's prize horse. She was a deep-black beauty with a silver mane. He rode her every day and would touch no other creature. He mounted her and rode to the fields without a word of farewell. Tatterhood entered the castle alone.

Trygve spent several hours with Sunset. When he returned, he was back to his normal self. Whatever troubled him must not be too great if it could be cured by a simple horse ride.

That night she had yet to tell him of their baby. Perhaps she needed to create the right moment. She changed out of her tattered clothes into softer, newer material.

Tatterhood turned to her husband. "Will you lie with me?"

He shrugged, as if to say he did not care either way. Sometimes it seemed he lay with her out of a sense of his duty as a husband, but she did not want that from him tonight. She wanted to please him, wanted to tell him about their baby when she was sure he'd be happy to hear the news.

She considered herself in the mirror, and, as always, found herself satisfied with her own appearance. Tatterhood liked her crooked, lumpy nose; liked the piercing of her eyes and her fierce, bushy eyebrows; liked that her left ear was higher than her right. Above all, she liked her gray skin. It allowed her to blend in with shadows.

She shifted her focus to her husband. There were several ways she could use magic. When she used items that expressed the essence of her soul, magic enhanced her actions. She could switch one object for another if she knew both objects well and knew their location. She could sometimes find a missing object if she had a strong connection to it.

She could also change her appearance for a time, though this was a bit trickier. She sent a wisp of magic toward Trygve, let it prod him, touch his desires. She turned the wisp on herself. She instantly transformed—skin smoother and clearer than her sister's, dainty eyebrows, proportional features. Her hair was still curly but had a reddish tint to it, which surprised her. Normally it turned pale blond.

Tatterhood sat next to her husband on the bed, feeling less like herself.

"It always amazes me when you do that," said Trygve.

Now it was Tatterhood's turn to shrug.

"I wonder what the people would think if you transformed before them," he said.

"I've done it before." As a child, she'd transformed by accident during a festival. Once she recognized the ability and its implications she did it repeatedly until she mastered the skill. But then the novelty wore off for both her and her people. She thought of them cheering for her in the training grounds. "I'm not sure it's necessary to do again." She had told Trygve that she could only change her appearance occasionally because it used too much magic. That wasn't strictly true—magic wasn't like a vial of oil that could be used up—but she liked being herself. She already changed herself two or three times a week, and didn't want him to press her to do it even more often.

"Of course it's not necessary," said Trygve. "But when you change, you look as beautiful on the outside as you are on the inside."

Tatterhood chuckled. "I don't think I'm like this on the inside." And then she opened up to him, in a way that surprised her. "On the inside I'm muddy, always ready for a fight. I'm rough edges and frightening cliffs. I'm disheveled, and not always sure what I should do."

Trygve put his arm around her. His hand wore the ring she had made for him as a late wedding present. "That sounds beautiful to me."

Beauty didn't matter to Tatterhood, but she liked his warmth so she leaned into him and kissed his neck. He kissed her on the lips, and soon they engaged in the same activity that led her to be with child. After, they held each other on the bed, and she knew this was the right moment to tell him the news.

But before she could, Trygve combed his fingers through her hair. "I like the red. Why did you add that?"

"I don't choose what I'll look like."

"You don't?"

"Well, I *can* choose, if I have something particular in mind. Sometimes I make myself look like a troll. And when I was young, I always made my face look like a frog to frighten Ingridr. Most of the time, though, I make myself appear like what someone else desires to see in me. You always want me beautiful, and so I become beautiful. Today you must like red hair."

Trygve sat up and wrapped his arms around his knees. "How very strange."

"It's not strange at all," said Tatterhood. "You probably saw someone with red hair and—" The realization hit her like the punch of a two-headed troll to the face. "The new serving girl has red hair. You think she's beautiful." At least only Tatterhood's hair had changed to match Mette's, and not her entire face.

"I, I—" stuttered Trygve. His face was flushed. "It's not like that, Tatterhood. Yes, she has nice hair. But I've never looked at her in that way—I don't desire her."

"Then why is my hair red?" she said, tugging at it.

"Your hair isn't red anymore." He pulled on his nightclothes.

She turned to the mirror. Her hair was back to its normal grayish brown. She'd lost control of the magic, lost the will to make herself what she was not. She curled up in the bed, pulling the blankets around her. She wanted to take her wooden spoon and hit Trygve with it, but she also wanted to hit herself. This was all her fault—all her fault for marrying a prince who did not want her, all her fault for changing her appearance for their wedding.

She had wanted to show him that appearance was transient and unimportant. She had wanted him to talk before their wedding. But she should've stayed ugly and gray, and waited for him to like her as she was, if such a thing was even possible.

"I'm sorry, Tatterhood."

She could not bring herself to turn and look at him, could not accept such a simple apology. She waited, listened as he fell asleep beside her. Then she let three tears—only three—fall down her face and onto her pillow. She was not the crying sort, and so she blamed the tears on her pregnancy.

She had still not managed to tell him about their baby. She wondered if their child would look ugly like her or handsome like Trygve, and if their child would care either way.

CHAPTER 3

When Tatterhood woke in the morning, she found herself alone.

During their first few months of marriage, every morning they held each other before rising for the day. It seemed the natural thing to do during the almost endless nights of winter, when the sun awoke for only a few hours in the middle of the day. Now, in summer, the sun slept for only a few hours, creating almost endless illumination. The light often caused Trygve to wake hours before Tatterhood, and she would find him reading a book in a chair. She wished she could hold him this morning, because if they had fought the night before, it always softened their feelings toward each other.

"Trygve?" she called.

Silence.

A sense of unease enveloped her, a fear she could not shake. She walked through their rooms, slowly at first, then more rapidly, peeking her head in every nook and corner. The prince was gone.

Her head ached and her jaw felt tight and sore. She must have clenched it as she slept.

She looked on her table, where he always left her notes if he went to do something or meet with someone. There was nothing.

Her heart sank. Trygve never wrote her the sorts of romantic letters featured in ballads, but he always jotted down a few words to let her know if something demanded his attention. She gripped the edge of the table. Maybe he didn't want her to know where he had gone.

"He's left me," she said aloud, and there was no one in her rooms to disagree with her.

Tatterhood dressed hastily in a ragged dress. Rather than brushing her hair, she pulled her hood on top of it. She grabbed her wooden spoon, rushed out of the room, and addressed her attendant, who sat in the hall, doing embroidery and waiting to be called upon.

"Lady Tove, have you seen Trygve today?"

The woman curtsied. "No, Princess. I assumed he was with you."

The soldier posted in the hall spoke up. "I took the shift before dawn. He must have left before then."

She wanted to scream that the prince had not just left their rooms, but left her, for good. Yet she should not do such a thing unless she was absolutely certain. She stuck a finger through a small hole in her sleeve, pulling at it until the fabric ripped, creating a much larger hole. She fiddled with the frayed threads. She wished she could ask Ingridr for advice, but her sister was kingdoms away.

As she walked to breakfast, she stopped every single servant in her path to ask if they had seen Trygve. No one had.

One of the servant's daughters, Anna, came running down the hall. She jumped into Tatterhood's arms and gave her a sticky kiss on the cheek.

"Where's Trygve?" the little girl asked.

Surprised to hear her own question turned back on her, it took Tatterhood a moment to mumble, "I don't know." Someday, would her own child ask the same question, and would she be forced to give the same response?

"I want him to play with me," said Anna.

"I can play with you," said Tatterhood, wanting anything to distract her from her worries.

The girl shook her head and ran back down the hall toward her mother, Elin. "It's more fun with both of you."

"You shouldn't say things like that," Elin rebuked her daughter. She turned toward Tatterhood. "I'm sorry, Princess. Is there anything I can do for you?"

"Have you seen Trygve?" she asked, already knowing the answer.

"No," said Elin, and she got a faraway look in her eyes.

Tatterhood wanted to know the woman's thoughts but did not dare to ask. Elin's husband had left her last summer. And she wasn't the only one in the castle to experience such a thing. Years before, the stable master's wife had left him for another. These sorts of things happened. But they did not—they *should not*— happen to Tatterhood.

She tightened her grip on her wooden spoon, trying to channel her emotions away from grief, toward anger.

She stomped into the private, family dining room, nodded to her parents, and set her wooden spoon on the table, none too gently.

The queen cleared her throat. "What do I always say about spoons at the breakfast table?"

"There are dozens of spoons on this table."

"But none made of wood, and none that large."

Tatterhood pinched her lips together. She moved the spoon onto the floor, beneath her feet.

"Much better," said her mother.

The serving girls came in carrying fruit. The red-haired girl— Mette—spooned bilberries onto Tatterhood's plate. Tatterhood tried not to look at her.

"Where's Trygve?" asked her father.

"I don't believe he's coming to breakfast," Tatterhood said between gritted teeth.

Mette walked out of the room with a bounce.

Tatterhood grabbed a handful of the blue bilberries and shoved them in her mouth, daring her mother to correct her for not using utensils. She knew she was behaving much younger than her age, but she did it anyway.

"You didn't argue about the coverlet again, did you?"

"No, Mother."

"I took care of the problem. I ordered another in the color Trygve requested, and, to make you happy, since you hate to see someone not compensated for their work, I purchased the coverlet with the wrong colors. I am sure I will find a place for it."

Her mother was rather stingy when it came to new furnishings. She had finally replaced the castle curtains a few weeks before, and had made all sorts of complaints about the cost. The fact that she was willing to buy an extra coverlet to make both of them happy meant she must be worried about the state of their marriage.

"Thank you, Mother." Of course, with Trygve gone, the color didn't matter.

Mette brought in the cheeses. The sunlight shining through the windows glinted off her long red braid. Tatterhood gripped her silver fork and knife, picturing Trygve talking to Mette, putting his hand on her shoulder, perhaps escorting her to her room . . .

Mette smiled at her as she returned to the kitchen.

Tatterhood tried a bite of cheese but did not like the taste. She raised one of the breakfast linens to her mouth and spit the cheese into it. Why had she tried to pretend nothing was wrong? She could continue this charade no longer. She dropped the soiled fabric on her plate.

"Please excuse me." She dashed after Mette and slammed open the door to the kitchen.

The servants all stared as Tatterhood bounded into the room. Mette turned quickly, almost dropping her tray.

"Where is my husband?" Tatterhood hadn't entirely meant to yell, but it came out that way.

"Wh-what?" Mette stammered, simultaneously setting down the tray and trying to curtsy.

Tatterhood put her hands on Mette's shoulders. It took great control not to shake the girl, though she desperately wanted to. "Where is Trygve? Where is the prince?"

"I don't know," she whimpered. "Why should I know?"

"Just tell me where he is. What did he say to you?"

Mette was almost in tears. "I've only been here three days. I've never even talked to the prince."

"Did he visit you this morning?"

The girl did not respond. She looked like a rabbit, frozen in fear.

"Did he?" Tatterhood yelled.

One of the other serving girls curtsied before her. "With all due respect, Princess, Mette shares a room with me. The prince could not have visited her. I've been with her almost every moment since she's been here."

"The prince never spoke to her," the other servants confirmed.

Tatterhood's eyes jumped from servant to servant, reading the sincerity in their faces.

She released Mette as if she were a burning hot pan. The girl sniffled and seemed to shrink away.

The other servants stared at Tatterhood. She breathed in and out, trying to control her rage. She trusted these people, these people who had worked for her family for years, and if they said the girl was innocent of wrongdoing, she had to believe them.

But oh how she wished the girl had wronged her, for then she would no longer need to blame herself for Trygve's departure.

She knew she needed to apologize to Mette, knew she should, but could not bring herself to do it. Not to this woman that Trygve desired, not to this woman that he had partially turned her into.

A throat cleared. Tatterhood turned reluctantly toward it.

Her father stood in the doorway. He held her wooden spoon.

She walked toward him, head bowed.

He put his arm around her, and did not even berate her for her treatment of Mette, though she surely deserved it.

"What has happened?"

Tatterhood could not speak.

Her mother came and put her hands on both of their shoulders, then led them back into the dining room. As the door closed, the words of a servant drifted through: "Tatterhood's not normally like this."

Her father gave her the wooden spoon and she clutched it to her chest.

"What happened between you and Trygve?" he asked.

"Trygve does not like being my husband." She swallowed. "And I think he has run away."

She let them hold her for a minute, and then they sprang into action, assembling the servants and courtiers and sending them to scour the castle, the city, and the surrounding areas. Tatterhood joined in the search herself. But during the entire morning, no one found a trace of him.

Tatterhood went to the stables. The stable master put his hand on her shoulder. He had kind eyes, eyes that understood, that had been through this before. But she could not bear his kindness, not right now.

"I need a little time alone."

The stable master sent all the stable hands away.

She beat at the hay with her wooden spoon. Little pieces of hay broke off and flew into the air. Several guards had seen the prince wandering the gardens in nightclothes during the early morning, but no one had seen him leave the castle grounds.

Tatterhood beat a new bale of hay. Her father had offered to send out the guard, all the way to King Varg's kingdom if necessary, to bring Trygve back. She had turned him down. She would force no man to be her husband. She did not want a man, anyway, who cared only about her appearance.

She set down her spoon and leaned with her back against the hay. Her stomach was a little queasy. For some reason she had assumed she wouldn't have the same physical troubles as other women. She put her hand on her belly, which had not yet begun to grow. There were no outward signs of the baby. Would Trygve have left if she had told him?

At least she had what she needed from him: an heir. She did not doubt her ability to rule the kingdom without a king by her side.

She stood, not bothering to brush the hay from her tattered dress. She walked through the stable, and a horse whinnied at her. She stopped.

It was Sunset.

She ran her fingers through the mare's immaculate silver mane. Sunset pushed her muzzle against Tatterhood's chest, so Tatterhood found a brush and groomed the horse. The steady, rhythmic action calmed her in a way that beating the hay had not.

How strange for the prince to leave Sunset behind—it would be like her abandoning Storm. She would never do such a thing unless under great duress.

Tatterhood set down the brush. Sunset snorted at her.

"Sorry to cut it short," Tatterhood said and stepped outside the stable.

"Sunset is still here," she said to the stable master. "Did Trygve take one of the other horses?"

He scratched his chin. "I don't know, Princess. There's been a lot of horses out and about, what with looking for him."

She waited while he called back the stable hands. They went over all their charges—every single horse—but not a one was unaccounted for. All the horses absent from the stable had been used by someone trying to find Trygve.

So Trygve had left on foot. Maybe he had bought a horse in one of the villages on the road, but why if he could take his own steed?

"I am sorry," said the stable master. "I should have checked earlier."

"It's not your fault." Her belief that Trygve had left her had probably made the people searching for him less likely to notice any details that contradicted that conclusion.

She returned to their rooms, examining them in more detail. Trygve had left his sword.

The laundry master brought in a dozen laundry girls and boys. They determined that the only clothes missing were his night-clothes.

Tatterhood could understand him leaving, but to leave in his nightclothes, without sword or horse? Maybe she had judged him too quickly.

CHAPTER 4

Tatterhood felt guilty for reading Trygve's letters, but he was not here, and now that she suspected foul play, she saw no alternative.

In the letter he had received from his father, it said, "There have been reports that the lhoosh has returned. It was spotted near the castle. I doubt it will make the journey to you, but take care, my son, take care."

A lhoosh. Tatterhood had never heard of such a creature. She spent several hours with the keeper of books, but to no avail. She left the woman searching the rather small castle library and spoke to the court singer, who knew of no reference to it in any of his songs. She wanted to ask the local witch, Bergljot, but the woman was taking her annual summer trip to the islands, and would not return for at least another week.

Tatterhood sat in the garden where Trygve had last been seen. She took off her shoes and stuck her toes in the dirt. Most creatures left some sort of trace, but she could taste no magic in the air.

No matter. She would find Trygve. If he'd left of his own will, she'd whack him with her spoon and then leave him be. But if he had been taken by a lhoosh—whatever that was—then she would get him back.

Since Bergljot was absent, she considered sending a rider to the next closest witch to ask for advice or assistance, but it was a full day's ride and the woman had an unusual obsession with poisonous plants. Besides, Tatterhood hadn't needed any help to find and rescue Ingridr's head. There was no reason to doubt her abilities now.

It was too late in the day to start on a long journey, so she retired and woke early in the morning. Bright light already illuminated her room, sneaking through the curtains. She dressed in a comfortable, worn dress with a tattered hood and filled her pockets with odds and ends from her rooms. She went to the kitchen and packed a bag of food and water. She asked Cook about Mette and learned the girl was only a year younger than herself. She was from a town near the edge of the kingdom, a day and a half's journey away, and had been eager to come and work at the castle.

Tatterhood found Mette's room and rapped on the door.

"Just a minute."

Mette opened the door and blinked, bleary-eyed. It took a moment, but then a startled expression covered her face and she dropped into a low curtsy. "My princess," she whispered.

Tatterhood took in a deep breath. It was always easier to break things than to fix them. And generally a lot more fun.

"Please rise, Mette," said Tatterhood, and when the girl did, Tatterhood lowered her own head and mumbled out her apology. "I am sorry for yesterday, and what I said and did. I was, well, worried about my own problems, and jealous that my husband had noticed you, but you had done nothing wrong, and I'm sorry for taking out my feelings on you, and I do hope you'll stay here at the castle because we really want you here and Cook says you're a great help and if Cook says it, then it's true."

"Thank you, Princess. I do want to stay at the castle."

They stood, a bit awkwardly.

"And I'm sorry for waking you up," Tatterhood added.

"I needed to get up anyway." Mette tucked a strand of hair behind her ear. "I heard you are going to rescue your prince. I wish you the best of luck."

Tatterhood nodded. "Thank you." And luck she would need, for the keeper of the books had stayed up all night searching but had still found no reference to a lhoosh, and it was hard to defeat something you did not understand.

In the courtyard, she embraced her parents.

"Are you sure you don't want me to send soldiers with you?" asked her father.

"I tend to do better alone."

"Take care of yourself," said her mother, and she glanced at Tatterhood's middle. So she had realized, too. She leaned in and whispered in her daughter's ear. "It's normally safe to ride a horse, or a goat, for the first few months, but after that you need to be more careful."

"I understand."

Tatterhood sat on her goat, adjusted her tattered hood, and placed her spoon on her lap. She rubbed the wooden handle, thinking about Trygve. She couldn't use magic to find a person, though she had tried multiple times. People were just too complicated. But if she knew an object well, it could lead her the right way.

After their wedding, when they'd returned to her kingdom, Tatterhood had given Trygve a ring as a sort of late wedding present. She had helped the goldsmith forge it, spent hours learning how to set in the emerald. She focused on the ring, remembered the feel of it in her fingers and the way it slid onto the prince's hand. She continued rubbing her wooden spoon, thinking only about the ring, until she felt a slight tug on her body.

She nudged Storm, and they rode into the forest, following the direction of the tug. There was no path before her, no trail or map, yet she traveled toward the ring on the prince's hand. For three days she followed this guide. Sometimes they went at the pace of a goat, and sometimes, when she held the wooden spoon just right and the wind touched the tattered hood over her hair, the forest sped by in a blur.

The sun had set at the end of the third day when she arrived at a clearing next to a large lake. The ring tugged at her more strongly now, like a rope wrapped around her middle. The last two nights she had gone to sleep at this time—it must be close to midnight—but the twilight would linger for a while, and she was close now. As she walked around the lake, leading Storm beside her, she felt pulled toward the water itself. Then, in the rushes, she saw a form floating in the water, one arm outstretched.

"Trygve! Trygve!" she yelled as she dashed into the lake.

The cold water shocked her legs. A tree branch cut into her face. Tatterhood tripped, soaking her dress up to her chest. She forced herself through the murky, muddy water and then stopped.

It was not a body. It was a man-sized log, floating in the water. And what she thought an arm was just a branch.

Tatterhood climbed out of the lake, shivering as her wet dress clung to her skin. There was still a bit of light in the sky, but not enough to search for a body. She picked up a rock from the ground and focused on the candlestick next to her bed, willing it to switch places with the rock. It did. She tried using her fire striker, but while she managed to create a few sparks, her hands kept shaking and she could not light the wick.

She cursed the sun and its decision to sleep.

Who would be awake in the castle at this time? Surely a light would be left in the kitchen for the scullery maids. She imagined herself walking into the kitchen at night, tried to remember where the lights were placed and what they looked like. She had not paid enough attention. But then she thought of Cook's face, pock-marked and wise. Cook always held a lantern to make sure no dirt or crumbs were left in the kitchen for mice to find.

Tatterhood focused on the lantern, willing it to switch with the useless candle. She had to think not only of the object, but also its location: the magic only worked if she thought of the item within a few paces of its actual position. She imagined the lantern in various spots around the kitchen. In a moment, she held it in her hand. The sudden brightness made her close her eyes. She would apologize to Cook later.

She continued her trek around the lake, using the lantern to look for Trygve's body. Time and time again she waded into the water, her search growing more and more desperate as the tug continued.

"Trygve! Trygve!" she called until her voice was hoarse. But no one responded.

Finally, she returned to the clearing where she'd started. She had completed a full circuit around the lake and there had been no sign of Trygve, no sign but the tug toward the water.

She collapsed on the shore, covered her face with her dirty, cold hands, tried to accept the evidence before her. Somehow, the prince had made it to this lake, and somehow, he had died. She did not want to believe it, but what else could she do?

Her dress was muddy—much muddier than normal—her body cold, and her stomach empty, but the thought of food made her sick. She lay flat on the ground with her face on the soil, still feeling the tug of the ring. But the sky was black now. The stars and the sliver of moonlight mocked her. She could not hope to find her husband's body in the lake; it would wait until the sun returned.

Storm pushed her horns against Tatterhood's back until she sat up. Storm grabbed a chunk of her dress in her teeth and pulled her toward the water, but Tatterhood did not follow: there was nothing she could do—nothing at all. Storm bit off a chunk of Tatterhood's dress, chewed, swallowed, and walked ankle-deep in the water.

"You want me to go in the lake?" Tatterhood asked.

The goat did not respond. But perhaps, after so many days following the ring, she also felt the tug.

Tatterhood left the lantern on the ground and stepped into the water, holding her wooden spoon. Storm pushed her deeper in, causing her to stumble toward the center of the lake.

"Come with me?"

Storm made a guttural sound that from a human would be a snort.

"Wait for me?"

The goat climbed out of the lake and chewed on a plant.

"Very well."

The water rose from her ankles to her knees, from her knees to her waist, and still she walked toward the center of the lake, almost blind in the darkness. Her purpose calmed her. Her goat said she should go into the lake, and so she would go. Fish and other creatures brushed past her body, but she had no fear of them.

The water reached her shoulders, and Tatterhood began to swim, slowly, steadily, until she reached the center of the lake, or as close as she could tell in this darkness. The tug of the ring continued, but the direction changed. It pulled her down.

Dead bodies floated—that she knew. Perhaps the ring had fallen off in the center of the lake and Trygve still lived.

With that hope inside her, Tatterhood took a deep breath and dove, kicking herself deep, deep, deeper into the water. Below, she saw a yellow-green glow, so she swam toward it. Something clear pressed against her spoon and her face, but she kicked herself through it. Suddenly, she found herself falling through the air. Her body hit the ground. She instantly leapt up, her wooden spoon at the ready.

She turned in a circle, making sure there was no imminent danger. She lowered her spoon slightly. She was standing in a strange bubble of air, twice her height, and extending several paces in each direction. Above her and on the sides of the bubble she could see the lake. On one side of the bubble was a rock face, and in the rock face stood a large wooden door, covered with troll carvings, and glowing with a strange yellow-green magic.

She rubbed the carvings on the door, which depicted trolls, some with two heads or three eyes or five arms. For trolls, the stranger they looked, the more successful they tended to be. How peculiar that trolls had taken her husband—trolls always left a trace. They despised the sun and preferred to bother humans during the long, cold nights of winter. After retrieving Ingridr's head from a band of trolls, she had been certain the creatures would leave her family alone.

Tatterhood tucked her wet gray hair back into her tattered hood. The first moment with trolls was vital, for it was then that they were most likely to rip off your head or a leg, or even bash your skull. She took a deep breath, raised her wooden spoon with her right hand, opened the wooden door a crack, and slipped inside.

The trolls were eating a feast. For humans, a meal is a civilized affair, but for trolls it is a savage dance. To avoid becoming part of the meal, Tatterhood immediately joined in. Three trolls were ripping apart a deer, so she screamed a fierce battle cry, grabbed onto a leg, and pulled with all her might. The deer came apart with large amounts of blood.

Tatterhood had eaten raw meat with trolls before, but today the idea made her nauseous. It would not be good for the baby. She swung around her wooden spoon in her right hand, the deer leg in her left, weaving in and out of the trolls, roaring when they roared at her, ducking and twisting when they punched. A particularly nasty three-headed troll came at her so she whacked it in the groin with her spoon and threw the deer leg into one of its mouths.

After several hours, the feast died down and the trolls collapsed on the floor. Tatterhood sat on the ground with them. After a minute, the troll she'd hit in the groin noticed her. "You— not a troll. What are you?"

She stood, her spoon raised. She kept most of her attention on the three-headed troll, but stayed aware of the others. "My name is Tatterhood. I'm human."

"Hmpff," said one of the troll's other heads. "You sure? You don't look a human."

Another troll came up to her and sniffed her hair. "She don't smell a human."

Tatterhood chuckled. Trolls always thought that humans smelled so fresh and clean, but with a few days of travel, any human could smell as bad as a troll.

The trolls began to argue amongst themselves about what sort of creature she was. She knew that if their discussion continued for too long, it would pivot to whether she was edible, and trolls had a favorite way of answering that question. So she yelled, "Yaaaaah!"

The trolls stopped talking and stared at her.

"I'm looking for a human. A man-human."

"No humans here," several trolls muttered.

"There's humans a walk south of the lake," said another.

Tatterhood felt the tug of the ring, but with all the commotion, she couldn't track its exact location. But Trygve was close, she knew it.

"Have any humans been here the last few days?" asked Tatterhood, hoping none of them had eaten Trygve. "Any of you seen a human at all?"

A three-armed troll in the back stood. Tatterhood thought it was a female troll, but could not be sure without closer inspection. "I saw a human. In the woods at night."

"Did you eat it?" another troll asked.

"No," said the troll. "But I got a human hand."

The troll raised one of her arms. The troll's hand was missing. Attached to the troll's arm was Trygve's hand—the hand Tatterhood had taken in marriage, the hand that had held hers just a few days ago, the hand that had caressed her in bed. The troll used Trygve's hand to scratch her warty green nose. Trygve's ring was still attached to the finger.

CHAPTER 5

Tatterhood marched through the trolls, whacking her spoon at the ones who tried to grab her. "That hand belongs to me!" she roared at the troll.

A puzzled look covered the troll's face. "Humans have two hands."

"Is she a human?" the trolls once again began to debate.

"It's not for my arms," yelled Tatterhood. "That hand was promised to me, and by no right could be given to you." With a certainty, Tatterhood knew Trygve would not give up his hand willingly, no more than her sister had wanted to lose her head.

"The man wanted it," admitted the troll. "But the lhoosh said I could take it, as long as I kept the ring on."

At the word "lhoosh" the trolls reached for their clubs. If Tatterhood wasn't mistaken, they feared the creature.

Tatterhood wondered at the type of creature who would get rid of the ring. Had the lhoosh known Tatterhood could track it? There was no magic in the ring, though perhaps there was a part of her in it, since she'd helped make it. Or maybe the lhoosh had sensed Tatterhood following, but it would take a deep magic to do that. And what sort of creature would cut off Trygve's hand rather than simply remove the ring? And why give it to a troll?

Tatterhood could feel the unrest growing in the room. A fight could erupt at any moment, and she needed to get all the information she could before it did.

"What is the lhoosh?" she asked. "Does it live around here?"

"Not here, not here at all," the trolls seemed to rumble.

"Is it big?" asked Tatterhood.

"Not big," said the troll with Trygve's hand. "Your size."

"Is it a witch? An animal? A spirit?"

"Yes."

"Yes to which question?" asked Tatterhood.

"Just yes," the troll roared.

The other trolls stood up and began punching and hitting each other. Trolls never gave useful information—she should not have pressed them.

Tatterhood withdrew a metal chain from her pocket. She focused on a small bag of gold coins in her closet, and the bag switched with the chain.

Tatterhood opened the bag of gold for a moment—just long enough to let the troll see its contents—then cinched it tight. The troll leaned toward her greedily.

"Oh, you want this?" said Tatterhood. "Well, I'll trade you for it. Say this for . . . for"—she pretended to ponder—"for that human hand."

The troll growled. "But then I miss a hand."

"You have two other hands. But you don't have a bag of gold. And you can always get a new third hand." Tatterhood thought of the village to the south of the lake. She did not want to send the trolls upon them—they likely had enough trouble as it was. "Human hands are small and weak. A bear paw would be much better."

The troll nodded and reached with one of its troll hands toward the bag of gold. Tatterhood whacked the hand with her wooden spoon.

"Give me the hand first," she said. "Then you'll get your gold."

"Gold first." The troll grunted and tried to grab Tatterhood, but she once again used the wooden spoon to knock the arm aside. If she gave up the gold first, it might take hours of fighting to retrieve the hand.

Tatterhood made the gold disappear by switching it again with the chain. "It's gone, unless you give me the hand."

The troll roared. Tatterhood again switched the chain with the gold. "It's back," she said. "Now give me the hand."

The troll spit on Tatterhood, but she did not flinch. Instead, she spat back at the troll.

"You are not human," the troll declared, then used one of her other hands to rip Trygve's hand off her own arm.

Tatterhood snatched Trygve's hand and dropped the bag of gold on the ground. "I am a human," she said. "Just a very ugly one." Magic *had* played a hand in her birth—if her mother had not eaten the ugly flower she would probably not exist—and while it had certainly impacted her appearance and abilities, her core being, her values, and her concerns were all human.

While the troll stooped down for the bag of gold, Tatterhood sprinted toward the door to the bottom of the lake. "Look! That troll has gold!" she yelled, pointing back at the creature. The other trolls rushed toward the gold and began savagely bashing each other with their clubs and ripping each other's hair.

Tatterhood felt a twitch of sympathy for the troll with the gold, but she pushed it aside. Trolls always found some excuse to fight, and she needed to make a quick escape so she could find Trygve.

She slipped out the door and closed it tight. She tucked Trygve's hand in her pocket—it barely fit—and jumped through the magical bubble into the water. She swam as fast as she was able to the edge of the lake, where her goat slept next to the lantern. The silly animal hadn't even stayed awake to keep watch for her.

She plunged her fingers into Storm's soft, thick hair, needing its familiar comfort. The hair was a bit patchy right now, as the goat had shed some for the summer, but in a few months, it would all grow back. Storm lifted her head and bleated at her, then fell back asleep. Tatterhood had gotten Trygve's hand, but she was no closer to finding Trygve himself. Her body shook with cold, starting with her hands and moving to her teeth. The sun's early morning rays did nothing to warm her; it was hours before she normally woke, and the air was chill.

She took everything out of her wet pockets, trembling as she did so. She set the hand in the bowl of the wooden spoon.

With a bit of concentration, she switched her dress and tattered hood for a warm, dry set from her rooms. It felt much better to be out of the wet, muddy clothes, but still cold possessed her body. She stumbled through the forest, gathering sticks and branches, which she piled together.

As Tatterhood used the lantern to light a fire, she almost burnt her hand. She threw more small branches in the fire than necessary, impatient to add larger wood. She looked at her husband's hand, sitting limply on the spoon. How could he have been so foolish? If Trygve had told her about the letter, they could've prevented this entire mess, done something to protect him. And even if the lhoosh had still managed to capture him, at least she would know something about the creature and its whereabouts.

Tatterhood rubbed her arms and shuffled her feet back and forth. She was still cold. She took three larger pieces of wood and leaned them against each other. She put the final piece in with a little too much force and they all toppled over. One landed on the tiny flames, threatening to put them out.

She pushed at the pieces with a stick, repositioning them to give the fire some air. The flames licked the larger pieces of wood until they caught hold on them. The fire reached upward, growing. Tatterhood had hoped, with time, that the way she and the prince felt about each other would grow. In some ways it had. She felt fond of him, and thought he felt at least a bit fond of her. She ran her fingers through her wet hair, remembering how it had turned red. Of course he would find other women more beautiful than her—every woman in the land possessed more beauty, and yet for the most part, it had never bothered her. What bothered her was the way he only desired her if she was not herself, and the way, on their wedding day, he refused to even look at her gray face until she changed it.

The fire's warmth finally penetrated her body, but it couldn't reach her heart. She added more logs. She dried her wet hair, leaning it as close to the fire as she could without letting it burn. It would smell thick with smoke tomorrow, but she rather liked the smell.

Maybe she would find Trygve, but maybe she would not. She had no leads, no clues left to follow, only the word "lhoosh." She tucked her mostly dry hair back into her hood. While she sought her husband, a part of her hoped she would not find him. Her life had been much simpler before she married him.

Tatterhood pushed those thoughts aside. She was tired and not herself. The sky was already glaringly bright, but she would take what sleep she could. She added more wood to the fire to keep it burning, and curled up with Storm near the flames. Right before drifting off to sleep, Tatterhood tucked the prince's hand close to her body. She did not want any bugs or birds to bother it.

When she woke, Trygve's hand did not look very well (it was easiest to preserve body parts while attached to a body). The sight and faint smell made her vomit what little was in her stomach.

She built up the fire and gnawed at a piece of stale bread in her pack, and then she foraged in the forest. Substantial problems could never be solved without substantial food. She almost never used magic to switch items for food, because she had to switch for a specific food item (a particular roll, with its exact lumpiness and taste), not a general one (the rolls Cook normally bakes). She picked wild carrots and mushrooms, a bit of thyme, and some mallow leaves. On the way back to the fire, she surprised a rabbit. She caught it with her bare hands.

She sorted through the pile of items that had been in her pockets and chose an ugly bracelet. She made it switch places with a small cauldron she kept under her bed. Her maids, her parents, and, of course, Trygve frequently complained about how much stuff she kept in her rooms, but if she wanted to switch something, it helped to see it often and be in charge of its whereabouts. Her habits were useful in times like this. She filled the cauldron with water and placed it over the fire.

It didn't take long for the stew to be ready. She ate slowly, hoping her stomach would not lose its contents. Then she held the prince's hand and stared at the soup. The prince liked soup. True, he preferred venison to rabbit, but if one were trekking in the wilderness one could not complain.

She put the prince's hand in her pocket, picked up her wooden spoon, and half-muttered, half-sang a little nonsense tune. Storm was eating bark off a tree, so Tatterhood peeled some bark off and threw it into her cauldron. She thought for a bit, then yanked out a few of her goat's hairs. Storm cried out in pain, rammed her horns into Tatterhood's backside, and went back to chewing bark. Tatterhood pulled several dozen hairs from her own head, twisted them together with the goat hairs, and tossed them in the soup. She switched the lantern for a small knife, which she used to shave a bit of wood off her wooden spoon and into the pot.

She took the cauldron off the fire and used her wooden spoon to stir the soup as it cooled. It took a good hour—maybe longer—but some things could not be rushed.

Tatterhood didn't know exactly what she was doing—she had never heard of anything like this—but she must try to save the prince's hand. It was better to follow her gut and act than to wait and hope for the best.

She picked up a rock and switched it for a quality goatskin wine flask that Trygve's father, King Varg, had given him. She almost drank the wine, but stopped with the flask to her lips. She remembered the townswomen talking about how a strong wine could hurt your unborn child. With regret, she poured it on the ground. She cut open the side of the flask with her knife, then switched the knife for a heavy-duty needle and thread. She placed the prince's hand in the flask, filled the rest of the space with soup, and stitched it up as tightly as she could.

Tatterhood cleaned the cauldron and switched it for an ugly pebble in her room. She considered sending the prince's hand back to the castle so she wouldn't have to lug it around, but she worried that if it was not with her then the magic would not preserve it, so she placed the twine of the flask around her neck, like a large and heavy necklace. She and Storm made their way to the human village. It was not as close as the trolls had made it out to be. She arrived, feeling quite nauseous, as the people finished their work for the day.

The townspeople were wary of her, but she shoveled some manure for one woman and chopped down a tree for another, and soon enough, her appearance no longer bothered them.

"Has anyone heard of a lhoosh?" she asked, but no one had. She weighed different options in her mind. She could always write to King Varg, but by the time she received a reply, Trygve could be dead. She could try to find a real witch to locate him, but had no idea if one lived nearby. But there were other creatures, creatures who lived everywhere and knew plenty about deep, dark secrets. It would be a risk, but could help her find him quickly.

"Has anyone been troubled by a nattmara?" she asked.

An uncomfortable silence followed. People shifted back and forth on their feet, looking down at the ground.

"What do you have to do with the nightmares?" one woman whispered.

"I'm going to catch one."

CHAPTER 6

O ld Man Bjarne was a large, tough man, not the sort you would expect to be plagued by nightmares, but in his youth he had fought in many battles, and seen—and perhaps done—terrible things. Nattmaras preferred easy prey. Like ants, they would return again and again to where they found nourishment.

"Sleep somewhere else tonight," Tatterhood told him. "I will catch a nattmara and, if I can, convince her not to bother you again."

Bjarne agreed to sleep in the house of a neighbor, and Tatterhood prepared to sleep in his bed. She paid a villager to keep Storm in a barn, and hung the flask with the prince's hand around the goat's neck for safekeeping. If Storm stayed with her, she would scare off the nattmara in order to protect her.

As night fell, Tatterhood examined the room. Old Man Bjarne had a small window, about the size of a hand, and it was shuttered up at night, but when it closed the poor workmanship of the wood left a small gap. Nattmaras could enter the tiniest crack or crevice by turning into sand. Tatterhood positioned the shutter to make the gap a tad larger—enough to make it easier for a nattmara to enter, but not so much as to raise its suspicions.

Tatterhood moved to the base of the bed, where Bjarne had placed nails. When a nattmara approached a person to feed on their fears, it always climbed onto the foot of the bed, and sometimes painful objects could stop them. But Bjarne had not used very many nails, they were spaced too far apart, and they were dull and worn. No wonder they did not stop the nightmares.

She lay on the bed, her wooden spoon in hand. Tatterhood had only been visited by a nattmara two or three times, when she was a young girl. And of course, it had fled when she woke up screaming. She had never experienced a nightmare as an adult. Tatterhood did not often entertain her fears—typically, she attacked things she feared with her wooden spoon—so she was not the most filling sustenance for a nattmara.

After hours of pretending to doze, Tatterhood realized her mistake: you could not fool nightmares. They fed on the sleeping, and must be able to recognize true sleep. She relaxed her body, cleared her mind, breathed deeply. She hoped she could force herself to wake, without scaring off the nattmara, at the moment she tasted fear.

Her fingers unbent, and she considered repositioning the wooden spoon, but the thought slipped from her mind.

She was in the woods. Bones hung from the trees. The wind blew at them, rattling them. A sudden gust hit the bones, smacking some of them against Tatterhood's face. She stepped away from the bones and rubbed her stinging cheek.

Birds flew above the trees—large birds, not quite like any she knew. In the distance, through the trees, the birds dove, attacking something. Though she did not want to travel in that direction, something pulled her toward them. She walked into a clearing. The birds pecked at a body, but of what sort of creature she could not tell.

Fear seized her and she ran to the still form. It was Trygve. His eyes were gone. Pecked out. Traded for two red, bleeding masses.

She ran at the birds with her wooden spoon, trying to club them out of the way. Her spoon turned into a twig. She focused with all her might, but she could not use magic to get her spoon back. The birds turned on her, pecking at her arms, her hair, her legs. She stumbled backward, trying to ward them off with her twig. One monstrous bird swooped down and used its talon to rip off her hand.

Tatterhood screamed. She had never seen birds behave in this way. They never acted like—

A nightmare had come.

She swallowed her realization, forcing herself to experience the fear and pain of the birds attacking her, seeing the blood spurt out from where she'd lost her hand. She had to stay in the dream longer or the nattmara would flee.

The birds attacked her belly. She forced her right eye—her real eye—open just a smidgen. The room was almost entirely dark, but she could make out a figure with the form of a woman wearing a nightgown. The nattmara sat on Tatterhood's chest, riding her like a man rides a horse. She had pale white skin and long, shiny black hair.

Tatterhood forced her eye shut, letting her fear surge as the nattmara continued to give her a vision of the birds. She let the fear continue, let her breathing remain frantic, let herself feel the terrible things happening to Trygve and herself as she grasped her fingers tight around the real wooden spoon. Even if the nattmara sensed her waking, if she continued to feed it with her fear, it might not flee.

The birds pierced her belly with their beaks and Tatterhood reached upward with her left arm—her real arm, not her dream arm—and seized the creature by the throat. Tatterhood opened her eyes. The nattmara reached out with her long black fingernails and scratched Tatterhood's face.

Tatterhood yowled in pain. She used her right arm to ram the head of the wooden spoon against the creature's neck. At the same time she used her left hand to seize the nattmara's upper right arm. Tatterhood pulled the creature down toward her left side as she rolled onto her left shoulder. She pushed her right foot against the bed to give herself momentum and swung herself on top of the creature.

She sat on the nattmara's chest, pinning it down with the weight of her body, pressing against it with her spoon and her hand. Her nose filled with the smell of birds and trees and blood and bodies—all the elements of the dream.

The nightmare possessed substance without true substance, weight without true weight. Tatterhood feared she could fall through the nattmara and lose her entirely. She willed it not to change into sand, hoping her grasp prevented the possibility of escape.

"Now I ride you," said Tatterhood.

"If you're riding me," the nattmara shrieked, "then why are you the one who is afraid?"

"I'm not afraid," insisted Tatterhood. As the words left her mouth, she knew they were a lie. She leaned her face close to the nattmara's. "You are afraid too."

"You're learning," said the nattmara. "Now let me go!" She dug her fingernails into Tatterhood's legs.

Tatterhood moved her hand back to the nattmara's throat. "Answer my questions, and you go free."

The nattmara stopped scratching, which Tatterhood took as agreement. She slid her hand back to the nattmara's shoulder, brushing the creature's night black hair in the process. The hair felt moist, like the skin of a toad. A chill ran down Tatterhood's back.

Tatterhood swallowed. "What do you know about the lhoosh?"

"The lhoosh? She has been gone for a long time. My older sisters knew her before, but I did not."

"Why has the lhoosh returned?" asked Tatterhood.

"I know not," said the nightmare. "I care not. She has come back, and brought plenty of work for me and my sisters."

"How can I find the lhoosh?"

The creature laughed—if it could be called laughter. It was the rattle of wind in the trees on a lonely night, the sigh of a woman about to die, the glee of a child eating something it knew it should not. The laugh made Tatterhood feel a deep, wintry cold, especially where her skin touched the nattmara.

"The lhoosh has something of mine." Tatterhood adjusted her knees, making sure her legs were firmly around the creature's chest.

The nattmara squirmed against Tatterhood's body, trying to get free, then went limp again. "If you go after the lhoosh, your nightmare will come true."

Tatterhood's heart thudded painfully. "The birds?"

"You humans are too literal. The lhoosh will destroy not just Trygve, but you too, and the one growing inside of you."

Tatterhood tensed. How did the nattmara know about her baby? Her first impulse was to flee, and her second to bludgeon the creature with the spoon, but she resisted, staying firm on the creature's chest.

"How do I know about your child?" asked the nattmara. "I can taste your fear for your baby. It's a very savory taste, even more delicious than when you watched your husband ripped to pieces."

Tatterhood choked on her own saliva. There was a reason people did not seek out the nattmara. "You can read thoughts."

"Only those tainted by fear. But so many are." The nattmara bent her legs, pushing her body up, away from the bed.

Tatterhood was almost thrown off. She wrapped her left arm around the back of the nattmara and rammed her right forearm into the side of her jaw. She would not let the nattmara go—she could not—or she would lose any chance of finding Trygve.

Tatterhood was stronger than the creature, but not by much. The nattmara shrieked and scratched, then twisted her face and bit down. The nattmara's teeth broke the skin on Tatterhood's arm. Cold, clammy fear washed over her, a wave strong enough to carry her away. Tatterhood clenched her jaw and stared into the creature's eyes. Finally, the nattmara stilled. Tatterhood did not relax her grip.

Tatterhood panted. "Tell me how I can find the lhoosh, and I will let you go."

She yanked a moist hair from the nattmara's head. The creature shrieked and tried to bite her again.

"If you lie to me, I will find you, and I will rip every hair out of your head and never let you go."

The nightmare licked her lips. "You want to find the lhoosh? She always moves her dwelling, never keeps it anywhere for long. But she stays long enough for her current victim to die. Go to the river—it's not far from here. Travel down it until you find a thousand-year oak. The lhoosh's fortress is within reach of the oak's long branches." She smiled, a cruel, heartbreaking smile. "You will go, and you will know with a certainty that you have found the right spot. But you will not be able to see the fortress or ever find a way inside."

"What do you mean?" Tatterhood demanded.

"The lhoosh is untraceable. I found your husband by tasting his fear. But you will never find a way in." The nattmara laughed again, sending a shock of cold through Tatterhood's body, like jumping into an icy river.

The nattmara performed the same move Tatterhood had earlier, grabbing her on one side and pushing her on the other, causing them to roll off the bed. As they crashed to the floor, Tatterhood lost her grip.

The nattmara hissed as she leapt toward the shuttered window. "You will never see Trygve again." She melted into sand and slipped through the crack.

Tatterhood shivered. She felt hollow inside, and not just from the cold the nattmara had left behind.

After a few minutes, she got to her feet. Her back ached from the fall and she rubbed it. It would bruise, she knew. But there was no pain in her front, in the place where her baby grew. How very fortunate. She needed to be more careful in the coming months, maybe get in fewer fights.

She pressed her hands to her face. They were freezing cold.

She went to the door and pushed it open. Several townspeople, including Old Man Bjarne himself, startled and stepped backward. They must have heard her fighting with the nattmara, come to the door, but been too afraid to enter.

"I'm fine," she said. "I don't think the nattmara will come back to this house again." She could make no promises for the rest of the town.

She went to the barn. Storm greeted her by licking her face and nibbling her hair. Tatterhood put the flask with the prince's hand back around her neck. She sat in the hay and held Storm close until her body stopped shaking from the cold. Then she set off in the partial darkness toward the river.

CHAPTER 7

Tatterhood and Storm moved slowly through the forest. Branches scraped her legs, mosquitoes bit her skin, and a cold wind cut through her clothing, but she would not stop for shelter. She could not. She kept her wooden spoon in hand, wary of attack. But nothing disturbed them. Nothing but the bugs and the branches, the cold and the darkness, the fear and the panic of arriving too late to save Trygve.

The light rose and she continued downriver, searching, all the time, for a thousand-year oak. She trusted the directions of the nattmara. Some creatures wove falsehoods, but that did not seem part of a nightmare's character. A nightmare took a truth—a frightening truth—and grew it bigger and more terrifying until it took over a person's soul. And perhaps in the growth there was a falsehood, for often fears aren't quite as terrifying as they seem. But at the heart of a nattmara's work was a truth—she worked with something real.

After several more hours of walking, Tatterhood spotted a clearing. Everything but the river was silent—no hum of bugs or chitter of birds. Storm plodded toward the clearing, understanding, without direction, where she needed to go. Exactly in the center stood an oak tree, wider and taller than any tree Tatterhood had ever seen.

A tree who has seen so many years, who has watched so many rulers rise and fall, gains a certain sort of power, perhaps even a magic. The lhoosh must be drawing on this natural magic for her own spells.

Tatterhood stood and led her goat around the oak. It would take four, maybe five adults to wrap their arms all the way around the tree. She put her hand on the tree, felt its bark. While the tree had a strength, a natural force to it, there was no trace of any other magic. Her mind recalled the soldiers seeing Trygve in the gardens. There had been no trace of magic there either, and yet the lhoosh must have used magic to spirit him away.

Tatterhood walked farther from the trunk of the tree, dragging the bowl of her wooden spoon against the ground. The nattmara had said that the lhoosh's fortress was within reach of the oak's long branches, so she stood under the edge of each one, looking for some sign of a fortress. How could a fortress be invisible? How could it leave no trace? There was no indication that anyone had climbed in the branches, no evidence of anyone walking on the ground.

She returned to the trunk of the tree, bothered by the lack of magic, the lack of lhoosh and fortress and prince. Yet there was this silence. An unnatural silence.

Tatterhood placed both hands on the tree. She felt its bark, then pressed her nose against it and breathed in its scent. Like a bolt of lightning, the force of the tree vibrated through her. She fell to the ground. In that moment, she knew, without a doubt, that the fortress was here, her husband was here.

The nattmara had been correct about the location of the fortress. Tatterhood pushed herself off the ground, hoping the nightmare was wrong about the rest. Yet while Tatterhood could channel a little bit of magic, she was no enchantress who could lift deep spells of hiding. And she had never been able to find people using magic, never at all, only objects she had a strong connection to. She had tried endless times as a child playing hide and seek, and never found anyone. And once the baker's daughter went missing, and all Tatterhood's attempts to help did nothing. The little girl had been found dead in the forest a week later.

But she had nothing else to do but try. She could not give up now, not when Trygve was here. She thought of the prince. She had seen him, touched every inch of him. Surely that knowledge would help her find him.

Trygve's hand hung in the flask around her neck, on top of her chest. Surely his hand wanted to reunite with his body. Surely it called to the body with all its might. And the body must long for its return.

And Tatterhood carried a part of Trygve inside of her. Their baby. Their baby belonged not just to her, but also to him. Surely that was connection enough.

Tatterhood thought of everything she liked about the prince. His laugh. His smile. The warmth of his body. She liked fighting him in the training yard. She liked the way the soldiers looked up to him, and the way he laughed and joked with them. She liked the way her mother smiled when Trygve entered the room.

She sat on Storm, rubbed her spoon, and concentrated. She felt nothing. No tug, no pull—no difference from the other times she had tried to locate a person.

Tatterhood tried again, remembering every detail of his face, his hair, his body, the way he spoke, the way he walked, the sound of his voice, the smell of his skin.

Yet still she sensed nothing.

The nattmara was right. She could not find her husband. He had been captured by an untraceable creature that even a nattmara could not find directly.

She whacked the ground, beating it with her wooden spoon until her arms ached with pain.

Tatterhood set the spoon aside and stumbled to her knees. Perhaps she could find a powerful enchantress and convince her to weave the spells to find Trygve. But in her heart she knew there would not be enough time. The lhoosh would kill him. She should've gone to someone with real skills in the first place, instead of attempting a fool-brained quest to find him on her own. She didn't even have enough magic to be a witch. Over the course of her childhood and adolescence, seven witches had evaluated her. Even with guidance and days of attempts, she couldn't do basic things like start a fire or summon a breeze. Each witch declared her impossible to train, her skills so paltry as to be mere tricks.

Tatterhood sniffled. She would not cry—she would not do it, not even though she was pregnant. But she had never failed at a self-appointed task before, and her inability to find the prince made her miserable.

She looked at her hands, at the dirt in her fingernails, and laughed at herself. Because to tell the truth, she was more sad at failing her task than at losing Trygve. What a terrible, wretched person she was, to care more about her own failure than about her husband, as imperfect as he was.

Tatterhood beat her spoon against the ground again and again, and then stopped mid-swing. She realized her error. Yes, she had sought for Trygve, but she had only thought about the things she liked about him. If you wanted to find something, you couldn't wish only for one aspect of it. In order to find her husband, she had to seek for, and truly want to find, all of him.

She thought of the dozens of little annoyances, the incongruities of character, the parts of Trygve that caused her pain. There were little things, like the way he insisted on brushing his hair, any time they went anywhere, even down the hall. There was the way he shined his boots when he didn't want to listen to her, and the way he always volunteered to sit by visitors to the kingdom and then made little effort to include her in the conversation. But these were trivial compared to the fact that he valued beauty so highly, and as a result, found her so lacking. She balled her fists. She had changed herself, time and time again, so he would desire her, so he would lie with her with passion. But he had never truly desired *her*, something the magic revealed when it changed her hair red.

Tatterhood ached, and not only from smashing her spoon against the soil. How could she pretend to want Trygve back, when he had wounded her so? How could she want someone who consistently found her inadequate, who did not understand the essence of her being, and would not value it if he did?

No one would blame Tatterhood if she failed to save Trygve—not her parents, not her sister, not his father, King Varg. They would grieve and blame the lhoosh. And rightfully so.

But Tatterhood would always know she might have saved him.

She touched her belly and imagined the baby growing inside. A little, imperfect human. Yes, the baby could survive with only a mother, but she wanted her child to know its father.

Tatterhood held up the flask with her husband's hand inside, considering its weight. In order to find Trygve, she needed to want all of him.

"Storm," she called.

The goat pointedly walked away.

"I'm calling you, Storm. This is important."

The goat paused, but did not turn.

Tatterhood dashed to Storm, ran her fingers through the long, shaggy brown hair until Storm licked her face.

"I need your help, Storm. One last time."

The goat let her lead her back to the tree. Tatterhood sat on her back and stroked the wooden spoon, nudging Storm to walk in a circle around the thousand-year oak tree. Despite all his failings, Trygve had tried to be a good husband. He had never wanted to hurt her. And it must have been hard for him, leaving behind his kingdom, his family, his friends—everything he knew—so he could marry her. Could she not at least give him a few moments of forgiveness?

She considered the prince, giving the attributes she liked and despised an equal measure of attention. This time, instead of treating his characteristics as points causing either pleasure or pain, she considered them without judgment. Like a painter creating a portrait, she filled her thoughts of Trygve with both light and shadow, because together light and shadow make a person human.

Storm walked around the thousand-year oak, again, and again, and again, not bothered by the repetitive nature of the task. Tatterhood hummed a little tune and for the first time she found herself wanting Trygve—wanting all of him. She felt the slight tug of her husband, so she kept riding around the tree, again and again, thinking of every little detail about him. Her mind was a canvas, and she would capture an exact likeness. The pull to her husband grew, but it did not call her elsewhere, so she continued her journey around the tree.

A shimmering appeared in front of them. Storm stopped, and Tatterhood tasted a bit of fear. Sometimes it was good to be afraid, she decided. It would keep her alert.

"Come, Storm," Tatterhood said, and prodded her forward.

CHAPTER 8

Tatterhood found herself in a cool, dank, stone room. Had she located the lhoosh's fortress? Only a small bit of daylight entered, through a small hole above her, and she waited as her eyes adjusted to the relative darkness.

There was something in the corner, on the floor. On top of it rode three nattmaras.

Tatterhood slid off Storm and bounded across the room, wooden spoon in hand. She almost screamed a battle cry, but if the lhoosh was not already aware of her presence, she did not want to alert it. She smacked the first nattmara on the arm with her wooden spoon. In a human, the strike might've broken a bone, but nightmares weren't true creatures of flesh. The nattmara melted into sand, scurrying away, across the floor, up the wall, and out the small hole of light.

Storm charged the second nattmara, chasing it across the room. It transformed into sand immediately before climbing up the wall.

The final nattmara still rode her husband's chest. It stopped, turned, and cackled at Tatterhood. Its long black fingernails caressed Trygve's cheek. Tatterhood swung her spoon, but the nightmare dissolved into sand and fled.

Breathing heavily, Tatterhood crouched next to her husband. He was naked. Attached to his left arm was the troll's greenish-brown hand. The lhoosh had bound him in chains. Cuts and bruises covered almost every inch of his body. Even his lips were scabbed, caked in blood which had dried a blackish red.

But Trygve must be alive or the nattmaras would not have come. There were other sorts of creatures that fed on the dead—all varieties of death feeders, small and large—but nightmares restricted themselves to the living.

"Trygve. Trygve." She found the pulse on his neck and let out a deep breath of relief.

There was a vile-smelling chamber pot next to them. She used her foot to push it farther away.

Keeping her hand on Trygve, she looked around. There was no sign of the lhoosh. The room was a strange sort of prison, made not of stones connected by mortar, but of a solid piece of rock, probably carved by magic. There was no door, no way in, and no way out. Storm ran around, her hooves clattering against the stone floor, butting her horns at the walls, looking for a weakness, but there didn't appear to be any. The lhoosh must use magic every time she entered or exited.

Tatterhood turned her head upward. She had been wrong before—there was not one hole for light, but three. Each was only the width of a man's hand and would not help them escape.

Tatterhood had entered through the magic of the tree, her ability to find objects, and her intuition to travel in a circle. But inside the fortress, she sensed heavy spells keeping them in. There might be only one or two enchantresses on the entire continent who could break this sort of spellwork.

She turned to the four chains and shackles binding Trygve, one on each arm, one on each leg. She grabbed hold of one of the chains and focused on one of the new curtains in her bedroom, willing them to switch places. They did, and she easily pulled the fabric off Trygve's leg. Which meant she now had chains hanging in her bedroom. When she returned to the castle, maybe she could discreetly remove them before her mother noticed.

She repeated the procedure on the chain on his other leg, and then on his right arm, saving the troll-handed arm for last. You could never completely control a body part that was not your own, something she had learned when dragging a troll-headed Ingridr around the countryside.

With care, she approached Trygve's troll hand and switched the final chain. The hand spasmed, but did nothing more.

She looked over the prince's body and wondered if he was in a state to fight. What if he could not even walk? She could probably get him on Storm, but then she'd have to deal with the lhoosh alone.

It would be better to send him back to the castle, but she didn't know if she could. She rested her hand on his shoulder. In the past she'd discovered that she could only switch like items. A stone could be switched for a candle or a bracelet for gold: they were all inanimate objects. But it was impossible to switch an object for something living. An animal had to be switched for an animal, so most of the time she switched her goat and her horse. She'd never managed to switch a person for anything before, but she might as well try.

She focused on her horse, Snowdrift, standing in her stall, and willed it to switch places with Trygve. Nothing happened. She thought of Snowdrift in all her normal locations, but still nothing happened. She tried again with the prince's horse but failed, and she didn't know if it was because she couldn't switch a person and animal, or because the animal was not where she expected it to be.

Back at the castle, there was an old sow that never left the pig pen. Tatterhood had switched her for Storm before, when her goat became too unruly and needed to spend some time with the pigs. She focused on the sow, willing it to switch with Trygve, but nothing happened.

Tatterhood smacked her hand against the stone floor. Once again, humans were too complicated for her.

Or maybe she could only switch a human for a human. But who did she know well enough to switch him for and how would she know their location? And was there anyone she could trade without guilt? There were several who had sworn their lives to defend the royal family, but she probably didn't know them well enough to switch, and even if she did she would not force them into this situation, where they had a high likelihood of being tortured and killed. She could not live with that on her conscience.

She prodded Trygve on the shoulder and said his name, "Trygve, Trygve, Trygve."

He blinked his eyes and stared at her.

"Tatterhood?" he said, like a man clinging to a raft in the sea, unsure if he has spotted land.

"It's me."

"Thank the stars." He tried to sit but did not have the strength, so she put her hands under his arms and helped him.

Trygve reached out, as if to embrace her, but stopped. He put his knees to his chest, perhaps to cover his nakedness, and hid his troll hand behind his body.

"Are you all right?" she asked.

"I'm fine," he said, but his voice shook. He turned his face away.

He must feel ashamed. Ashamed that he had been captured. Ashamed at the terrible things the lhoosh had done to him. Tatterhood did not know the full extent of the lhoosh's actions, but with his wounds, she could guess. But it could've happened to anyone—it was not his fault.

"Tell me about the lhoosh."

Trygve shuddered, as if experiencing physical pain at hearing the creature's name.

She waited for a response, but none came. "Is there a way out? A door I can't see?"

"There is nothing. It's impossible." He hid his face in his knees.

Tatterhood thought she heard a sob come from him. She wanted to reach out and comfort him, but did not know how. How do you offer hope to someone who is a shadow of his normal self?

"There's always a way out. We just haven't found it yet." She removed a water pouch and the rest of the crusty bread from her bag on Storm's back. "Here." She held it out to him. "It's all I have with me."

He grabbed the bread and shoved it in his mouth, eating without any of his normal, polite manners. The troll hand tried to pull the bread away, but Storm growled at it and it lowered. Tatterhood wanted to remove the hand and give him back his own, but it was a lengthy, painful process, not something to do when the lhoosh could return any time.

Trygve needed to tell her more about the lhoosh, but he seemed so beaten down. She remembered how long it had taken for her to feel back to herself after her experience with the nattmara—and three had fed on Trygve at the same time, and before that he had been tortured by the lhoosh. She gathered the curtains she had pulled off his limbs, wadding them into a ball. Perhaps with clothes he would be more himself.

She thought of the clothes in their rooms, but it was difficult, as Tatterhood never paid much attention to his apparel. She had memorized her own tattered hoods and dresses, and other outfits in case she needed them, but Trygve was taller and wider than her.

Of all his many clothes, she only knew the outfit he had worn on their wedding day: polished black boots, finely tailored black pants, a shirt made of green brocade and gold and silver embroidery, with a long black coat with silver clasps. She focused on the clothes, forced herself to remember them in detail until the curtains in her arms disappeared, replaced by the rich garb.

She held out his clothes, but he didn't take them. He kept his knees folded up in front of his chest.

He swallowed his last bite of bread and drank the rest of the water. "I didn't think you would come for me."

"Of course I came for you. You're my husband." It was better not to tell him that she almost hadn't, better not to tell him that she almost gave up.

"Well now you're stuck here with me. The lhoosh will be happy."

Tatterhood continued to hold out the clothes, but Trygve made no move to take them.

If there were any hope of escaping, it would be by working together. And even if, by some small chance, she could save them on her own, Trygve would only find peace if he faced his nightmares and overcame them.

How could she stir him to action if he wouldn't even take his clothes? How could she give him a glimmer of light? She would not give him false assurances—he would see through that. Her head throbbed with fatigue as she tried to think, and her limbs ached with exhaustion. Too many nights with little or no sleep, too many impossibilities to face. But she had found Trygve, and that should've been impossible.

She sat down beside him without touching him, careful to give him his space. She fingered the flask around her neck.

"Trygve," she said.

Tatterhood waited for him to raise his head or look at her, but he did not.

"I have something important to tell you." She hesitated, then placed her hand on the prince's back. He tensed at her touch, and she wanted to rip apart the lhoosh for hurting him so much that a simple human touch unnerved him.

Trygve's back relaxed a little.

"You're going to be a father," said Tatterhood. "I am with child."

He turned to her, took her hand in his human one at the same time as he struggled to keep his troll hand on the ground. "Are you really?"

"I don't show yet, but yes, we're going to have a baby."

"A baby!" he exclaimed. His lips crinkled into a smile. With the bruises and cuts on his face, smiling must be painful. "A baby," he whispered. Despair returned to his face as he looked around the room. Storm started pushing against the walls with her horns again, looking for a weakness.

"We need a way to escape," said Tatterhood. "If we don't make it out, you'll die. I'll die. And our baby will die." The nattmara had allowed Tatterhood to see things that she normally kept locked up, and she knew, at this moment, that she needed to share those parts of herself with her husband. "I am afraid," she said. "I don't want us to die, but I don't know what to do, and I need your help. I don't care what the lhoosh did to you—it doesn't change who you are. I need you, Trygve."

He lifted his human hand and touched her face. "I have never seen you afraid."

"Normally I hide it." She resisted the impulse to turn away and held his eyes. "I never wanted you to see my fear."

He tentatively touched a few strands of her hair. "Do you think we can escape, even though you are afraid?"

"I do," she said.

"Then I will do what I can to help you." He picked up the clothes and raised his eyebrow. "You want me to fight in these?"

"They're the only clothes I could manage to summon," she admitted.

"Then they will suffice."

Trygve stood and began to dress. The bruises and cuts made the process look quite painful, and watching him felt uncomfortable, almost invasive. Tatterhood had seen the prince dress and undress so many times, but this was different. She turned around, giving him his privacy.

"I'm ready," said Trygve, and Tatterhood turned back to him. The clothes transformed him, made him a different man than he had been a moment before. This was the man she had married, always crisp, always well-tailored. Trygve's approach to clothing was the opposite of Tatterhood's: he gave his apparel great thought, admired fine workmanship, and dressed to assert his own view of himself to the world. Clothed in his wedding outfit, he looked strong and confident, brave and ready to fight.

For a moment, Tatterhood could see into Trygve's soul. Fine, well-crafted clothing was part of Trygve's essence, just as her tattered hood and dress were part of her own essence. It surprised Tatterhood that she had not realized this before—surprised her that she had cared so much that he did not understand her, when clearly, she had never understood him.

Trygve's face still looked battered, but in a rugged, attractive sort of way. Perhaps he was a handsome man, as her maids always said, and perhaps she could admire his beauty even though she did not desire it for herself.

The only incongruous part of him was the troll hand. But really, that was a minor thing, and she feared that if she addressed it now, she might not survive an encounter with the lhoosh.

The prince ran his human fingers through his hair and grimaced.

His comb. He needed his comb.

Tatterhood took a pebble from her pocket and switched it for the comb that Trygve kept next to his bed.

"Thank you." As he took it, he held her hand for a moment.

He used his comb to carefully, methodically fix his hair. Strange that he would give it so much attention, at a time like this. The way he brushed his hair had always annoyed her, but doing so must help him tap into his essence. She could not fault him for that.

"Now tell me about the lhoosh." Before he could object she said, "I know it's hard, but it might be useful. I read your father's letter—have you encountered the lhoosh before?"

Storm tried to bite his boots, and Trygve pushed her off. "The lhoosh came to my father's kingdom when I was a lad. She had once been an enchantress, but to gain more power she melded her soul with that of a magical creature. Yet her appetite for power was not satisfied. She decided to strengthen herself through torturing others. She prefers to do it to grown men because . . . " He stopped, staring at the comb in his hand. He passed the comb back to Tatterhood. His chest rose and fell before he continued talking. "On occasion, she has also drawn strength from a woman or a child. When she's finished, she leaves the remains of the body for people to find.

"My father sent his soldiers and several witches to try to capture or kill the lhoosh. But her magic makes her virtually untraceable. They even tried traps, using a solitary man as bait, but she would not enter a room or a section of the forest if she sensed any kind of weapon there.

"I was thirteen years old and decided to solve the problem by myself. I traveled across the land until I found an enchantress and begged her to stop the lhoosh. She said she would not do it even if I gave her half the kingdom, which I couldn't even promise because I was not the heir.

"I told her that there must be a price she would accept, that she must want something. So she sent me on a quest to retrieve a golden feather. I set off by myself—it was not my smartest idea—and it took me three months and tricking a dragon, but I did it.

"I brought the golden feather back to the enchantress, and she kept her end of the bargain. She used her magic to find the lhoosh and bind her in her own invisible fortress, so she could harm no one else."

It surprised Tatterhood that he'd never told this story before. True, he was not the bragging sort. If they escaped, she would need to spend more time listening to him. Surely he had other stories from his youth.

"If the lhoosh was bound," said Tatterhood, "then how did she escape?"

"I would need to speak with my father to be certain, but my guess is the enchantress who cast the binding spell died."

"I thought spells lasted beyond death."

"Normally they do," said Trygve, "but some types of spells must be fed magic to maintain them. Or maybe the lhoosh managed to weaken the spell from the inside."

"So she escaped and came after you for revenge?"

Trygve nodded, and he seemed to shrink a little. "I should have kept a weapon on me at all times."

"She sounds powerful enough that she probably would've captured you anyway." Tatterhood considered her wooden spoon. If the lhoosh could sense weapons, she might not enter the dungeon and they could be stuck here forever. She switched it for a small wooden spoon, made for eating. It made her feel vulnerable, but at least she could get her normal spoon back at any time. "You said the lhoosh melded her soul with a magical creature. Do you know what sort?"

"No."

"Well, we'd best create a plan."

But at that moment Storm bleated in fear and ran in a circle. A blast of wind blew through the light holes and the stone walls themselves seemed to tremble.

"The lhoosh is coming," said Trygve.

CHAPTER 9

For a moment Tatterhood stood riveted in position—paralyzed by her lack of plan, the possibility of failure, and her only vague knowledge of the lhoosh. She pinched her arm. Now was not the time for inaction.

She turned to Trygve. He could help her, but not if the lhoosh killed him immediately. The sort of creature who would cut off a man's hand rather than remove a ring did not value human life. "You will know when to fight. Don't let her realize you're a threat until then."

Trygve was pale, but he did not have the beaten look he'd worn before. "Take care of yourself, my dear. If you need to leave me so you can save yourself and the baby, then do it."

"It won't come to that." No matter what happened, she would not leave Trygve behind, not when she was just starting to understand him.

Trygve squeezed her hand and sat down on the floor, in the same spot where he had been bound. The lack of chains, his clothing, and his open, alert eyes made him look much more capable than before, but hopefully the lhoosh would not perceive him as a threat.

Storm bleated and took a defensive position in front of him.

The walls continued to tremble, but still the lhoosh did not enter the dungeon. Either she was actually bad at magic and couldn't navigate her own fortress or she liked to build up fear and suspense.

The key for defeating—or surviving—any creature was to understand it, and, to a certain extent, to act like it. She had been
able to do so with both the trolls and the nattmara. She would
need to figure out the lhoosh, and quickly. At least the fact that
she avoided attacking armed men meant she feared her own mor-
tality. Some creatures were practically invincible.

Tatterhood tightened her fingers around the small wooden
spoon. It did not reassure her, did not have the same life in it as
her much larger spoon.

She swallowed. Her mouth was dry, but she had given her husband the rest of the water. Why wouldn't the lhoosh just come?
She shifted her weight back and forth between her feet, as if
she were a peasant preparing for fisticuffs. They would need to
kill the lhoosh. She had already come after Trygve once out of
revenge, and if they escaped she would surely pursue them. And
Tatterhood was no enchantress—she had no way to bind her.

A light flashed and a section of the stone wall liquidized. Tatterhood glimpsed the room beyond—it was packed with animal
traps, building supplies, and other items she could not make out.

A silver-cloaked creature walked through the entrance: the
lhoosh. The wall re-formed behind her. It was a rather showy
spell, which probably meant she could do simpler things like
walking straight through the wall. And if she could walk through
walls, how to stop her from fleeing when they attacked?

The light from the ceiling holes hit the lhoosh, illuminat-
ing her features. Her silver cloak was long and elegant, with no
adornment or embroidery. Like a nattmara, she had the shape of
a human but the poise of a predator.

The strangest feature was her face. It was like the lhoosh had
layers—two parts on top of each other, semi-translucent. In the
light, her face looked human, with beautiful, flawless skin. But
beneath that layer was the face of a creature, a monster, with wild,
red eyes and fangs. The lhoosh took one more step forward, out
of the light, and the layers switched places: the creature face on
top, with the beautiful, human face visible beneath it.

The lhoosh stopped suddenly, noticing Tatterhood.

"Welcome," said Tatterhood, extending her hands with graciousness, in the manner her mother used for greeting foreign dignitaries. Her mother had taught her to control her face, to never reveal her emotions no matter how repulsive she found her guest, something which took great control with the creature before her. This creature deserved death for what she had done to Trygve and so many others.

"What are you?" asked the lhoosh coldly. "And what are you doing here?" Her eyes took in Trygve on the floor.

"It was a very nice tree," said Tatterhood, trying to buy herself time and learn more about the lhoosh. "And that's a very nice man. But I think he looks better dressed than in chains."

The lhoosh smiled in a calculating way that accentuated her fangs and revealed her teeth. Her teeth had been human, once, but now had designs chiseled into them. The indentations were dyed with colors. Red, like the blood of man. Purple, like the blood of dark beasts. And orange, like a consuming fire.

Perhaps the grooves in the lhoosh's teeth were part of the ritual she had used to bind herself to the creature of power. Or perhaps they were another ploy to intimidate. But Tatterhood would not cower.

The lhoosh lifted her hand. Instead of fingers, the creature had claws. Sharp, pointy claws—the clear source of the cuts on Trygve's body. The lhoosh began to mutter, and Tatterhood forced herself to remain still. She could do nothing to prevent the use of magic, nothing at all. And if she let her fear show, the lhoosh might kill her or Trygve.

The lhoosh snapped. Snakes shot out of the walls, wrapped around Tatterhood's arms, and transformed into heavy chains.

At least this was a threat she could handle. Tatterhood smiled. "Oh, these are lovely, quite lovely. But I can make them prettier."

She swapped out the chains for the rest of the curtains in her room.

The lhoosh snapped. Another dozen snakes shot out of the walls, binding Tatterhood as they became chains. The weight of the metal pulled her down. Her knees crashed into the stone floor. That would leave bruises. She bit her lip, stopping herself from crying out. She must not show pain.

"What a fun game!" Tatterhood exclaimed. She switched some of the chains for the curtains in Ingridr's old rooms and the rest of the chains for her parents' curtains. It was a good thing her mother had replaced all the curtains in the castle so they all matched—before there had been a hodgepodge that she would never have been able to keep track of. Of course, if this lasted much longer, the palace would run out. Free of the weight of the chains, Tatterhood stood, pulling off the fabric.

The lhoosh twisted her face in rage. Both her creature and human faces distorted for a moment, as if attacking each other. She stepped closer to Tatterhood and snapped again.

Two more snakes shot out of the walls, this time near Trygve. Storm intercepted them, biting off their heads before they could form into chains. Trygve crouched on the balls of his feet, ready for action, but did not stand.

The lhoosh stepped closer, but not close enough for Tatterhood to grab her. Tatterhood dared not approach her, for if she made any aggressive movements, the lhoosh might flee.

"You have a powerful creature," said the lhoosh. "How did you force it to stay in goat form?"

"Oh, I don't know," said Tatterhood. "She likes it that way." Better not to mention that Storm was truly a goat. A talented, opinionated, and sometimes challenging goat, but nothing more.

The lhoosh stepped closer, but not quite close enough. "What is it you want?"

Tatterhood stared into the lhoosh's two layers of eyes—a human blue and a demonic red. In that moment, she realized that the lhoosh was afraid of her. Yes, she'd summoned chains, but she hadn't actually attacked Tatterhood. The lhoosh was trying to understand her, just like she was trying to understand the lhoosh.

"I want to know why you kill people," Tatterhood said truth-fully.

The lhoosh became very still—as still as death. Trygve yelled "Watch out!" and pushed her to the ground. Tatterhood barely got her hands out in front of her face to break her fall.

A burst of fire shot out at the spot where her head had been. She could feel the heat from the flames, even with Trygve on top of her, shielding her body.

Tatterhood panted. Her chest shook. She could be dead. She should be dead. She had misjudged the lhoosh, said the wrong thing, and would've died for it, if not for Trygve. How had he known? He must have seen her anger many times, and been able to tell when it hit a boiling point.

Tatterhood lifted her face a little off the stone floor, looked up at the lhoosh. The flask with Trygve's hand still hung around her neck, pressing uncomfortably against her chest.

"I see," said the lhoosh. "You didn't just track the ring. You gave it to him." She smiled, and the grooves in her teeth looked like they were dripping blood. "You're his wife."

The lhoosh held out her hand and summoned a sword. A strange buzzing filled the air, and the blade dripped with sweat. It was a long, slightly curved, single-edged saber. There was no guard or knuckle protector on the handle, probably so she could hold it with her clawed hands. The lhoosh strode toward them, swinging the saber down at Trygve.

Tatterhood twisted her arm back, grabbing a fistful of Trygve's coat. She needed to switch it for something—anything. What could save him? "Please work," she mumbled, thinking of her father's chainmail in the great hall.

There was suddenly pain on her back where Trygve was pressed against her, and the sound of a sword hitting metal. The lhoosh shrieked in rage.

Storm ran around the lhoosh, making a fuss, standing upright on her back hooves and ramming the creature with her front hooves and horns. Both Trygve and Tatterhood took the opportunity to get to their feet. Trygve looked a bit strange with the chainmail on top of his fine green shirt, but it wouldn't hurt for him to have an extra bit of protection right now.

The lhoosh raised her hand toward Tatterhood, ready to perform a spell that would surely kill her and Trygve both. Tatterhood raised her hand in return, as if to do some equally terrible spell. The lhoosh froze in place.

"What are you?" shrieked the lhoosh.

Tatterhood reached out with a wisp of magic, pushing it toward the lhoosh. But instead of exploring what the lhoosh desired her to look like, she nudged it to discover what the lhoosh feared. Desires and fears were connected, like two sides of a coin. Tatterhood turned the magic back on herself, letting it change her appearance.

"I am what you fear," said Tatterhood. She did not have a mirror, so could not see how her face had changed, but her hands looked like rotting purple claws.

Both layers of the lhoosh's face—human and creature—flickered, like a candle flame blown by the wind. The lhoosh turned and fled toward the wall.

"Grab her, Storm!" Tatterhood yelled. She must not escape, not now—she must not get through the wall.

Storm bit the lhoosh's silver cloak, pulling her to a stop right in front of the wall.

"What do I look like?" Tatterhood whispered to Trygve.

"A death watcher, from the legends."

Just as a nattmara fed on fears, a death watcher needed to feed. But it did not normally kill, feeding instead on that which was already dead.

But why would the lhoosh fear that Tatterhood was a death watcher, following her, a living soul? There *were* stories of death watchers pursuing other magical creatures of death, like death gobblers. Maybe the lhoosh had bonded with a death gobbler to gain access to its magic . . . Perhaps, because death gobblers fed on death, the lhoosh tortured people, consuming their life force in the days leading up to their deaths, in order to fuel her power.

Tatterhood dashed toward the malignant creature.

The lhoosh lunged toward the wall, and it trembled as it had before. Storm bit into her leg and held on even as she tried to kick her off.

The lhoosh tripped, falling partway through the wall. With a bang, the four stone walls around them turned to ash and drifted to the ground.

They were in what appeared to be the basement of the lhoosh's fortress. It was part storage room, part series of traps.

The lhoosh snapped her fingers and a dozen furry creatures appeared. They were about the size of Storm, but moved like cats, with teeth the length of human hands. One attacked Storm, distracting her from the lhoosh, and the others rushed at Tatterhood and Trygve. Tatterhood switched the little spoon for her normal large spoon.

"It's good to see you, friend," she said to the spoon as she smacked the bowl against one of the toothy creatures, then the back end against the other. She jumped after the lhoosh—she would not be distracted, she would not lose her quarry.

The lhoosh leapt across piles of wood furniture, kicking chairs at Storm, tapping devices that threw rocks around the room as she headed toward a stone staircase. But Storm would not be deterred and jumped from one thing to another, dodging barriers, ducking beneath the saber, pursuing the lhoosh without faltering. People always underestimated goats.

Tatterhood took a different path to the stairs, trying to cut off the lhoosh's escape. The creatures kept coming at her with their giant teeth, but she kept her spoon and her body in constant motion.

Trygve hollered in pain and Tatterhood glanced back at him. He was using his troll hand to defend himself against the creatures. One bit into the hand. He tightened his fist around its head, crushing it with an inhuman strength. He flung the creature away.

"I need my sword," yelled Trygve.

Her stomach sank. How had she forgotten to give him a weapon? She took his comb out of her pocket and switched it for his sword. She hefted it and threw it across the room in Trygve's direction. It was the best she could do.

She turned around in time to see the lhoosh kick Storm. The goat fell against the floor with a thud. Tatterhood yelled an awful yell. She charged the last few steps to the staircase, arriving at the same time as the lhoosh.

The lhoosh swung her saber. Tatterhood ducked, blocked, feinted with her wooden spoon.

Storm rose, shook her hair, and rejoined the fight. Her hooves pounded against the floor, making short, sharp sounds, and she screeched as she rammed her horns into the lhoosh's back. Tatterhood stepped farther up the staircase, blocking the exit with her body. She smashed her wooden spoon against the sword. There was no reason for a pretty fight, a fair fight—no rules but winning against a magical creature like the lhoosh.

Tatterhood shoved her spoon forward, like a spear, into the lhoosh's ribcage, and heard a rib crack. The lhoosh raised her non-sword hand, perhaps to cast a spell, but Tatterhood hit it with the spoon, and then blocked the saber. Storm pulled on the lhoosh's leg, making the creature lose her balance.

She spared a glance a Trygve. He was fighting six of the creatures at once, keeping them away so Tatterhood could engage the lhoosh.

They parried. Tatterhood was better, especially with her wooden spoon and with Storm darting in between them, interfering with the lhoosh's movements. But how to end the fight? Tatterhood needed to kill the lhoosh for the terrible things she had done to Trygve, for all the men she had tortured to death. She needed to kill the lhoosh to prevent her from harming others.

Tatterhood could bludgeon the lhoosh to death with the spoon, but it would be slow and brutal for both of them. Or she could switch the wooden spoon for her sword in the castle.

The lhoosh swung her saber and Tatterhood barely managed to block with her spoon. The strike had so much force behind it that Tatterhood lost her balance and fell backward onto the staircase. She lost hold of the magic making her look like a death watcher. She looked up at the lhoosh. Before, both of the lhoosh's layers—creature and human—had been visible, but now she could hardly see the human at all, as if the creature had consumed it. Now there were only demon red eyes and fangs, fangs that could surely rip her apart.

The lhoosh struck her again and again, with a supernatural strength that could not be matched by a human. First Tatterhood rolled to the side, next she managed to block the saber, but only because Storm slammed her horns against the lhoosh at the same moment. Tatterhood's heart pounded painfully in her chest. Now she could only defend, not attack, and the lhoosh was using her longer weapon to her advantage. Tatterhood swallowed, but her mouth was dry. Even with her wooden spoon, even with Storm's help, she would lose. She was not good enough, not against whatever fed the lhoosh's powers.

Tatterhood blocked the lhoosh again, but the effort caused her arms to shake with pain. The lhoosh kicked Storm off the stairs and Tatterhood drew in a ragged breath. She should have let the lhoosh escape and found a different way out of the dungeon. She should never have tried to fight her. Now she would die. Her baby would die. Storm would die. The lhoosh would kill Trygve—they would all perish today. And she could do nothing to stop it.

But maybe she didn't have to do this alone.

"Trygve, I need you!" she shouted.

He slew another creature with his sword and jumped toward Tatterhood, over two more of the animals. At the same time, Storm shakily rose to her feet.

The lhoosh dropped her saber, raised her claws, and began muttering.

Tatterhood focused on a wisp of magic and turned it on her face, visualizing for herself what she desired to be. She changed her face to a troll. The lhoosh's hands twitched, perhaps as part of her spell. Tatterhood switched her face in rapid succession—to a nattmara, to a death gobbler, to one of the big-teethed creatures, and then to mirror the lhoosh's own face.

The lhoosh stopped muttering and stepped down one stair.

Tatterhood let go of the magic, allowing her face to return to its natural gray appearance. She jabbed her wooden spoon forward, into the lhoosh's chest, and Storm rammed into the lhoosh's legs, knocking her off balance.

The lhoosh muttered something and the saber rose through the air, to her hand.

Trygve hollered as he reached the bottom of the staircase. The lhoosh swung around to block his sword and Tatterhood bludgeoned her on the back. Trygve feinted, stepping to the side, and the lhoosh lost her balance for a moment. Tatterhood kicked her, forcing the creature the rest of the way down the staircase.

Tatterhood and Trygve fought as a team, coordinating their strikes against the lhoosh and her toothy animals. There was something intimate about fighting together like this. The human in the lhoosh appeared for short moments, but mostly, the creature layer blotted it out entirely. The lhoosh's strikes were inhumanly strong, yet together, with the help of Storm, they gained ground.

Tatterhood smashed the lhoosh's right wrist at the same time that Trygve slammed his sword against the lhoosh's. The lhoosh lost her grip on the saber.

Tatterhood tackled the lhoosh, pinning the creature to the ground.

"What are you?" gasped the lhoosh. She looked more human now, less creature. The layers on her face quivered back and forth.

"I'm a girl with a tattered hood. That's all."

Storm bleated.

"Watch out!" yelled Trygve.

Tatterhood kept holding the lhoosh down, but she shifted to give Trygve room.

He plunged his sword into the lhoosh's heart.

The lhoosh's magic fought back against him, pushing against the sword, swirling around it in a rage of wind, battering Trygve's body. But he did not flinch, he did not falter. Tatterhood held the lhoosh's body down with all her might as she watched her husband with admiration.

The lhoosh's body went limp.

The death creature part of her fell away, dissolving into dust until all that was left was the corpse of a woman, a woman who had once been beautiful.

Trygve removed the sword and helped Tatterhood to her feet. "We did it!" he exclaimed.

The walls of the magic fortress began to crumble with an ear-thundering crash. The lhoosh must have bound it so strongly to her magic and her life force that when she died, it could not stand on its own. Storm bleated in alarm, then led them up the stairs and through cracks in the walls. Shimmering pockets of magic flashed through the air, destroying the fortress. Trygve sheathed his sword and took Tatterhood's hand in his human one as they dashed out, into the shadows of the thousand-year oak.

CHAPTER 10

Too much wild magic flooded the area. Hopefully the tree could contain it, repurpose it for something good. If Tatterhood were a trained witch she might stay here and use the magic to make reattaching Trygve's hand easier, but it was too volatile for someone with her limited skill and knowledge to handle.

She touched the chainmail Trygve wore and switched it with the black coat from their wedding day. Then they jogged upriver, using the same path she and Storm had taken in the night.

Once she judged they were far enough from the wild magic, Tatterhood stopped, panting. Trygve breathed deeply for a minute, then cleaned his sheath and sword while she filled her water pouches at the river. Storm wandered off, probably to eat something.

Tatterhood and Trygve sat on the ground, not quite touching as they drank their water. She studied his profile. She did not know what to say after an experience like theirs. In some ways she still hardly knew this man she called her husband.

Trygve reached with his troll hand to scratch his face, but stopped right before it touched his skin. He forced the hand down to the ground. It was already healing itself from the bite of the lhoosh's toothy creatures, much faster and better than a human hand would. A look of disgust crossed his face as he considered the hand. "I suppose it's a memento of the whole experience. A little worse than a scar, but nothing I can't live with."

"If you want to keep it, go ahead, but I did get *your* hand from the troll."

"You rescued my hand?"

"I was trying to rescue you."

"Can you reattach it? The same way you fixed Ingridr's head?"

Tatterhood shivered, remembering how much it drained her to sew Ingridr back together. But it was a small price to pay—she could do this one more thing for her husband. "There might be a little scarring." Tatterhood removed the flask from around her neck, switched a stone from the ground for her knife, and carefully cut open the goatskin. "Sorry about ruining your flask. But since it was a gift from your father, the bond between you two may have helped preserve your hand."

"You put my hand in soup?"

Tatterhood shrugged. "It worked." She lifted out his hand and rinsed it off in the river. It had kept quite well and did not smell of decay.

She refilled their water pouches. Then she made a pile of objects and switched them, one by one, for the additional things she needed: a sharp saw, a needle and thread, and a pile of clean cloths. Trygve did not stop pacing until Tatterhood told him she couldn't do it unless he let her focus.

Storm wandered back and Tatterhood asked her to sit on top of Trygve's legs. Tatterhood had him hold the wooden spoon in his human hand.

"This will hurt." She wadded up a piece of fabric. "You may want to bite this."

He studied her face. "You're nervous." The surprise in his voice was evident. "If you don't want to do this, or if it's too difficult, I will be fine as I am."

"I will do it," she said, forcing the fabric into his hand. He placed it in his mouth, then held on to the wooden spoon again.

Tatterhood set the saw on his skin, right at the edge between the troll hand and the arm. As she pressed, Trygve gasped. She sawed as quickly as she could, not looking at his face, afraid that his pain could undo her. When the troll hand finally came off, she gave it to Storm, who carried it away to dispose of it.

She poured water over the prince's arm, preparing it to receive the hand. She was not a fine seamstress, and had ruined many of her mother's embroidery projects. Of course, she always struggled to create beautiful things. Sewing someone back together was much more practical, so it was easier to focus on neat, even stitches.

She sang a little nonsense tune as she inserted the needle into the skin and muscle. A weight pressed against her chest but she kept stitching, kept singing. Her body got colder, slower, as she made her way around the wrist, but she willed herself not to shake as she put in the finishing stitches. A trained witch or enchantress could probably do such a thing without drawing so much from herself, but Tatterhood did not know how.

Tatterhood massaged Trygve's arm, starting from the shoulder and moving down to his hand. She willed the arm to remember the hand, to accept it again. She willed the blood to flow between the two. She slowly bent each one of Trygve's fingers. She was short of breath but she continued to sing until she could do so no longer.

She took back the wooden spoon and collapsed against a tree, completely spent. After reattaching Ingridr's head it had taken several days for Tatterhood to recover.

Trygve only had eyes for his hand. He wiggled his fingers, then bent them carefully. He sat next to Tatterhood and used his reattached hand to caress her face. "You are a wonder." He leaned close and kissed her cheek, but she was too tired to even muster a smile at his excitement. Instead, she focused on breathing.

Concern covered his face. "You're so pale. Are you ill?"

"It wasn't quite this bad when I fixed Ingridr's head. Of course, I wasn't pregnant."

"If I had known what it would do to you, I would have kept the troll hand." Trygve cupped his hands around her face. "How can I help you? What can I do?"

"I need food, and quickly."

She closed her eyes, not even waiting for his response.

"Watch over her, Storm. Do not let anything disturb her," she thought she heard him say.

The next thing she knew, his hands were on her arms. "Wake up, Tatterhood, wake up."

He had killed and roasted a rabbit, and found some small wild carrots. He brought it to her, helped her eat and drink.

She had almost finished eating the rabbit when a growl came from Trygve's stomach.

"Oh—I'm sorry," she said, realizing he had not eaten any himself. "You must be starving."

"I'll eat later."

"No, you can have the rest," she protested.

"You have done so much for me. Let me do this one thing for you," said her prince.

His sincerity stunned her, so she ate the rest of the rabbit.

"What else can I do?" he asked.

"Hold me."

Trygve took her in his arms and suddenly the ground did not feel so hard. Storm nuzzled up to Tatterhood's other side, and they slept.

When they woke, Tatterhood switched an ugly pebble for the cauldron and they prepared a meal together. They stayed in that spot, next to the river, for a full week, eating and sleeping and stretching their legs as they both regained their strength.

By the week's end, they both agreed that a bath was long overdue. To clean themselves, they dipped rags in the cold river and scrubbed their bodies. Trygve's skin had partially healed from the cuts and bruises inflicted by the lhoosh, and he would probably only acquire five or six scars from the experience.

After their makeshift baths, Tatterhood tried to brush her hair. She yanked and tugged at it with a comb, but it was filled with so many knots and snarls that she made no progress. She might need to cut it off near the roots and let it grow again.

"Can I help you?" asked Trygve.

Tatterhood paused and considered. Sometimes one of the maids would brush her hair, so it couldn't hurt to let Trygve. "If you'd like to, you can."

He combed slowly and methodically, starting at the bottom of her hair, and working with much more patience than she possessed. She liked the way his fingers brushed against her back and her neck.

After a few minutes, he asked how she had found him. She described the three-day journey to the lake, the trolls and the nattmara, and finally, unlocking the mystery of the tree. She left out her doubts about wanting to find him—after all, her desire to find him had been stronger than her doubts, or she would not have pressed forward—but she did explain how she had to seek all aspects of him, both the things that gave her annoyance and the things that gave her joy.

"When we finally got into the dungeon, Storm and I scared away the nattmaras and I removed your chains. You know the rest." She turned to look at him. "Are you done with my hair yet?"

He chuckled. "You do realize there are snarls the size of my fist? I'm only halfway finished vanquishing the knots."

She smiled. "I guess I shouldn't rush epic battles against monsters. I'll try to hold still." She turned back around so he could continue.

They sat in silence and Tatterhood watched the tranquil trees as he combed and combed. A brown beetle climbed slowly up the nearest trunk and disappeared into the branches.

Then, unbidden, Trygve spoke. As he combed, he told of how the lhoosh had come when he was walking on the castle grounds. She had used a spell to silence him, which also left him gasping for air, and then another, very painful spell to whisk him away.

His voice choked and he had to stop several times as he described how the lhoosh had tortured both his mind and his body, the way she'd humiliated and hurt him until he almost lost his sense of self.

Tatterhood's hands clenched. If the lhoosh weren't already dead, she would kill her.

"I keep wishing I had done something different and prevented all this," said Trygve. His brushstrokes had slowed, but not stopped.

"It's no use laying blame on yourself," said Tatterhood. "Regardless of what you did or did not do, what happened to you is *not* your fault. You can't hold yourself responsible for the actions of such a creature."

He finished brushing her hair, so she turned to look at him. His face almost made her weep. She had only seen such vulnerability on him once before, when she first found him in the dungeon.

"You are very brave," said Tatterhood.

"I wasn't brave. I could do nothing against the lhoosh, so eventually I stopped trying to fight back."

"But you survived. And that takes bravery." She traced the line on his wrist where she had reattached his hand. She would need to remove the stitches soon, but even so, it would scar. "I wish I could do something to take away your pain."

"It is enough to have someone to listen to me."

"Thank you for trusting me enough to share what happened." She intertwined her fingers with his. "I hope our baby is as strong and brave and true as you are."

"Thank you, Tatterhood."

They sat in silence for a long time, holding hands and watching the trees.

The next day they decided to return home. They tried to both sit on Storm, but she was not large enough to carry two people, and it was a long journey back to the castle.

"See you in a few days, Storm," Tatterhood said. The goat made no sign of hearing her.

She tried switching Storm for her beautiful, white horse, but it didn't work, so instead of thinking of Snowdrift in her stall she visualized her in different spots in the fields. Finally, the switch occurred.

Snowdrift was already saddled, which meant she had not been grazing: one of the stable hands had been taking her for a ride. Tatterhood chortled. The poor girl was probably now sitting atop a very upset Storm.

And surely the entire castle was in an uproar, what with the endless number of items Tatterhood had switched and the lack of curtains in the royal rooms. She expected a lengthy lecture from her mother when they returned.

Tatterhood mounted her horse. She sat in front and Trygve behind. He wrapped his arms tight around her waist, and she did not want him to let go.

"Do you remember the day we met?" she asked. "Our wedding day?"

"Yes."

"I switched my goat for my horse. And you still wouldn't talk to me."

"I was a fool."

She shrugged. "No matter." She directed a bit of magic toward Trygve, let it explore his desires, and turned it on herself.

She raised her hands to look at them. They were still gray. Her fingers trembled. She took a chain out of her pocket and switched it for the mirror next to her bed. She stared at her face—her own face. No blond hair, no red hair, no changes in any of her features.

"What's wrong?" asked Trygve.

"The magic's not working." Fear clenched her chest. She had thought that access to magic couldn't dry up, that it was something she couldn't run out of, but maybe she had been wrong. Maybe she had used too much in fighting the lhoosh and healing Trygve. Maybe she was running out and could only do simple things like switch objects.

"Did you try to use my desires to change your appearance?" he asked.

Tatterhood nodded.

"Well that's why you didn't change. I want you to look exactly like yourself."

She turned her head and looked over her shoulder at him. "But I'm ugly."

"You are rough edges and frightening cliffs. You're feisty and muddy and gray. And you're never sorry for who you are." He paused, considering her. "You are complete. You don't need beauty."

Tatterhood sat there, stunned.

"When I was captured, I clung to the memory of your face, knowing you were the only person who could rescue me, and knowing I did not deserve you."

Tatterhood swung her leg over Snowdrift so she sat sideways in the saddle. Trygve wanted her—he desired *her*. Not some false image of what she was not, but herself, her essence.

She wrapped her arms around Trygve and kissed him with such passion that they almost fell off the horse.

They steadied themselves. He ran his fingers through her hair, down her back, and around her waist. "You've never kissed me like that before."

She traced the embroidery on his shirt. "I bet I could do it again."

"I bet you can't." Trygve's eyes glinted with his challenge.

Tatterhood kissed him again. This time they did fall off the horse, and it was quite some time before they decided to get back on.

As they began the long ride back to their kingdom, Tatterhood enjoyed the feel of Trygve's hands around her waist. She knew their difficulties were not over—there would always be troubles and annoyances. But at least now they were starting over with a greater understanding of each other. She had won the prince's hand in marriage months before, but only now did it truly belong to her.

The Little Mermaid

PJ Switzer

Dear sisters, who rise from the deep to mourn me,
I am here.
I am the breeze that ruffles your shorn hair.
I am the mist upon your cheeks that gives form to your tears.
Can you hear my voice, restored to its former glory?
Can you hear my plea for forgiveness?

Dear prince, who loves me but loves another more,
I am here.
I am the wind that fills your sails, pushing you home.
I am the zephyr that cools your brow as you hold your princess close.
Can you hear my voice, one you never heard in life?
Can you hear my offer of forgiveness?

Dear child, who might have been mine,
I am here.
I am the sweet breath of morning that stirs you to wake.
I am the gust of air that carries your cries to your mother.
Can you hear the lullaby I sing only for you?
Can you hear my promise of joys to come?

O my dears, though you think me lost,
I am here.
A daughter of the air, floating on the ether.
Master of my eternal destiny at last.
Be at peace, as I am
Seeking my immortal soul.

ÁSTHILDUR AND THE
YULE CAT

Sarah Blake Johnson

The Yule Cat prowled, searching for a child who had not been given new clothes. Green lights swirled and swayed overhead in the starry sky, and he bounded over the icy lava field toward the nearest farms and loped through the countryside and slinked through backyards. If he smelled fresh woolen sweaters or socks, he passed by the home. When there was no wool smell, he would circle the house, peeking through windows, but so far he had been disappointed, as the children were wearing new clothes, but not made from sheep's wool.

Ásthildur peered through a crack in the curtains in her front room. If she watched long enough, she was sure she would see Door Slammer or Candle Beggar or one of the other Yule Lads. It was Christmas Eve, and Candle Beggar would arrive tonight.

Instead, a giant, black cat walked up the street. She had always wanted a cat, but the Yule Cat was almost the size of a pony. His ribs showed like whale bones beneath his black hair. She had thought he was a made-up story, just to scare children.

The Yule Cat froze. This was the first time in over a hundred years that he had been spotted. The last time had not gone well, as dozens of men had come after him with shovels and spears. The girl's eyes were large, and a huge smile grew on her face. But she wore a new sweater, so the Yule Cat crossed the street and disappeared into the shadows.

For hours and hours he continued prowling. In the late morning, as shards of twilight appeared, he ate leftover skate fish scraps carelessly left in an open garbage bin.

The next Christmas Eve, the Yule Cat took the same route, but before he reached Ásthildur's house, he veered north and wandered through that neighborhood. Strong, fermented skate fish smell permeated the air. He couldn't remember the last time he had eaten anything besides scraps. It would probably be another Christmas season without any yummy children.

Ásthildur hoped the Yule Cat liked milk and fish. After her parents had settled into their evening, sitting next to the roaring fire and reading books, she put on her new sweater, new socks, new mittens, and new hat, just to make sure she wouldn't be a tempting tidbit. She slipped out her front door and placed a bowl of warm milk and a nice fillet of fresh fermented skate fish. Maybe that would lure the Yule Cat so she could see him again.

After an hour, the Yule Cat circled back toward her house. He pattered down the opposite side of the street. The smell of fish grew stronger, and his stomach growled. The Yule Cat didn't think, but bounded across a snow drift and up onto Ásthildur's front step and lapped up the milk. Light flashed as the curtain parted. The girl was there again, wearing a new knitted sweater.

The cat hated the smell (and the taste) of wool and any freshly-made clothing, so he grabbed the fish and leaped off the step.

Every year, after the Yule Cat searched for a child without new clothes, he visited Ásthildur's house. The third year, he feasted on lamb hot dogs and more skate fish. The fourth year, the door cracked open, and after they both looked at each other for a minute, he ate quickly, grabbed the last fish fillet, and darted away.

The fifth year, Ásthildur stepped outside and watched him eat while a light snow fell. As always, she wore a new sweater. She said, even though she wasn't sure if he could understand, "You could come every night. I set food out for you yesterday, but you only come on Christmas Eve."

Ten years later, the Yule Cat still visited Ásthildur's front step during Christmas Eve night. But this night, after he finished eating, he didn't leave. She combed through his hair with her fingers, and together they watched pink and green lights stream across the sky.

The Yule Cat finished eating the fillet of skate fish. He stretched, then padded over to where Ásthildur sat in a comfortable chair, knitting. It was Christmas Eve, and she looped the last stitch on a wool sweater for a granddaughter. Her silver hair sparkled in firelight. The smell of wool didn't bother him anymore, so he half-leaped into her lap, his head resting on the sweater, his back feet staying on the floor.

She set her knitting needles aside and rubbed behind his ears, and he rumbled a giant purr. "You're too large for my lap," she said, but continued to scratch his head.

After a moment, she bundled up, opened the door, and they stood on the front step. It was afternoon, and the sun had already set. The green and pink lights were already vibrant. Waves of blue and yellow joined the dancing lights, filling the sky. Ásthildur shivered as the strong wind blew. "Are you ready to roam tonight?"

The Yule Cat's stomach was full. Snow crunched under his paws and tonight he felt the cold for the first time. He leaned his shoulder into her thigh. It had been two centuries since he had eaten a child. Everyone always had new clothes, every single year. There was no reason to search. Fresh fish tasted better anyways. His aging joints ached. It seemed that he may not live forever, except in legend.

He ambled back through the doorway and into his home and waited in the front hall while Ásthildur took off her boots and mittens and scarf. He followed her into the kitchen where she gave him a small bowl of lamb. When she settled into her chair with a cup of hot tea, the Yule Cat curled up near her on a soft sheepskin rug in front of the flickering fire. They both closed their eyes and dozed.

PERFECTLY REAL

Robin Prehn

Over three weeks ago, I was fighting with my parents about their ridiculous expectations. Then I ran away and got caught in a storm. Days later, I found this castle and took refuge, though my first night was not at all restful. When I admitted I did not sleep well, a gorgeous guy—a prince named Johan—asked me, Isabella, to marry him. All under his mother's triumphant gaze. Then his mother, the queen, said she placed a pea—a *pea*—underneath my mattresses to test me.

Because I'm stubborn and perhaps a bit defiant, I agreed to marry Prince Johan. I deflected their questions about my lineage with a vague, "Oh, yes, I'm a princess." They clearly wanted to believe me, and as I needed to escape my parents' plans for me, I nodded and smiled and tried my hardest to play the role of a "real" princess—whatever that was.

The castle—a palace, really—burst into activity from that second until now. I'd dealt with fittings and place settings and wedding plans. Through it all, I managed to hold my tongue, for the most part. But I could feel myself wearing down, could feel the familiar resentment at my place in life burning in my chest. Johan rarely made an appearance, and although I caught glimpses of him here and there and he spoke kindly and carefully at shared meals, I spent most of my time with his mother, the queen.

At first, I thought maybe her outlook would be less oppressive than my own mother's. I hoped that I could find freedom just that easily: a hasty and impetuous run through the forest and an unplanned trip down a river during a storm. But after nineteen days, I was beginning to realize that although the prison looked slightly different, it was still restrictive. Today, they planned to outfit me with my royal clothes, the formal wear I'd use during official meetings, banquets, traveling, and so on. I didn't enjoy being dressed like a straw doll, and although I'd gotten a little better at withholding my impatience and even scorn, the restlessness was building.

I sat this morning in the sunroom, my favorite space in the palace. Though I rarely had the chance to escape, when I did, it was to find this oasis in the midst of the chaos. I perched on a padded lounge, watching as the early-morning sun built tree shadows across the wide lawn leading up to the forest. My mind drifted like the few puffy clouds, and for this moment, I felt peace.

A door creaked, and the queen's voice interrupted the stillness. "Here you are! Why are you not in the fitting room? The prince would like to see you in orange, our family's royal colors."

"I'm not a fan of orange." Then I remembered my manners, stood, and curtsied before the queen. "I apologize, your Majesty."

She nodded, her brown eyes narrowing a bit. "Did you not get enough breakfast this morning?" Without waiting for an answer, she beckoned me with her slender arm. "Come. We have much to do today."

I followed her without a word. After all, what could I possibly say? I'd already made my bed here, and to be honest about my feelings now would serve no good.

"When shall we contact your family?" the queen asked, her tone bordering on brusque.

She'd already asked numerous times, and I wasn't sure how much longer I could put her off. "They are still traveling, your Majesty," I murmured. I didn't want to talk about it; I didn't want to be pushed. In the rare moments when I allowed myself to think about my parents, what I mostly felt was hurt and lingering anger. Despite the distance between my home and this palace, surely I should have heard something about parents searching for their missing daughter, regardless of my status.

"They must plan to return at some point." She huffed. "I'm beginning to wonder—" She broke off, glancing at me as she hurried us through the corridors. "Which district did you say you were from again?"

I hadn't—not really. When Johan made his impromptu proposal and his declaration that I must be a "real" princess, I'd been astonished. But with my opportunity to escape staring me in the face, I couldn't let it go. "I am," I'd cried. "Of course, I'm a real princess." It helped that my clothes, torn and soaked as they were, revealed their high quality. I'd stolen them from the stable where I regularly used to meet up with Sofia, now a princess married to a prince from a far land. Sofia always kept an extra gown tucked away in case she mussed whatever she had chosen for that day's ride. We were close enough in size that I knew it would fit, and she had no need for it now that she was far away.

I took a deep breath as the queen slowed, indicating we were near a more public area where she did not want to be seen rushing along. She turned the corner with a purposeful but stately deportment, and I followed her up the marble steps toward the fitting room. She looked back at me, her delicate brows raised as she clearly awaited my response.

"Featherwick," I murmured. "I come from Featherwick." I'd had enough time here to know this was a safe answer. Featherwick was distant, small, unimportant in status and tactics, and the ruling family was a mere blip on the list of significant bloodlines while still holding "royal" status. It helped that it was true.

Her expression showed a brief hint of surprise before smoothing over. "Ah, of course. One of our minor royals. I met your parents years ago, when you must have been a small child. But now that I know, I can see some resemblance to your mother," she finished, coughing gently. Then she sped up, her slippers tapping out a strong rhythm. I hurried to follow, smirking a bit at the ease of that response.

Inside the fitting room, I took my usual spot—the place where I'd been measured for the wedding gown, my honeymoon gown, my everyday dresses, and even a nightgown. I pasted a slight smile on my face and tried to breathe.

"Here, Princess," said Shyla, the assistant seamstress. She wasn't much older than I, and I often wondered about her ringless hand. Why was she unmarried? In Featherwick, all maidens were expected to marry unless their skills offered more than their role as wife and mother. Was her ability to sew considered so great that she would not need to bind herself to a man? Perhaps I should have learned something other than horsemanship or arguing with my father.

After a few minutes of close scrutiny, the queen finally took her leave, and I relaxed a touch. When the other ladies-in-waiting retired to the corner of the room, as they usually did once the queen was gone, I gathered my courage. "How is it you're not married?" I whispered to Shyla.

She poked her finger with the needle and flinched, and I noticed her eyes flitting toward the group in the corner. "That was not the path chosen for me," she said, her voice low.

I frowned. "You *wanted* to be married?"

She swallowed. "I had promised someone that we could be— but it wasn't meant to be."

Only then did I notice the trembling chin, and I suddenly wished I'd held my tongue. "Could you not still—?"

"No," she said immediately. "He has been given to another. To Lady Nelda, actually." Nelda stood in the corner with the other young ladies, and only then did I recognize the undercurrent of tension between Shyla and Nelda. I assumed from her position as a lady-in-waiting that Nelda did not have any discernible skills. In Featherwick, this would usually mean that Nelda had no say but Shyla did; yet here, things were skewed.

My thoughts churned. I had left Featherwick and my home because my father had promised me to a man I did not, *could* not love. My father appeared not to care at all about my feelings and had instead focused only on his own gains from the match. I deeply resented being used as a pawn, and although he'd seemed to enjoy a healthy debate when I was younger, this time, he'd stood firm. "You *will* do this, Isabella," he'd ground out. "You must see how beneficial this will be for all of us. Your mother will no longer have to put in such long hours, and I will be free to retire. Haven't I done enough? This is your time to take on these responsibilities. Your sister already did her part; it's your turn."

And that, according to him, had been that. Here I stood, not even a month later, allowing a sweet, sad girl to dress me in an ugly orange gown. I'd run away so I wouldn't be used by others, so I could forge my own path. But even though I'd made the choice to marry Johan, was I truly building my own future? Or had I simply traded one cage for another?

Suddenly, the gown seemed restricting, even though I knew it was perfectly made for me. I fought to keep my composure as Shyla wheeled over the full-length mirror. When I saw myself there, I gasped.

Shyla smiled, obviously misinterpreting the noise. "It fits you so well," she said.

As if summoned, the queen glided in behind me. "Yes, it will do nicely. Well done, as always, Shyla. Thank your mother, as well."

I met the queen's gaze in the mirror, and suddenly I couldn't hold back. "I won't wear this," I said. "These colors are hideous!"

Her mask didn't slip, though I noticed her lips tighten. "You don't really have a say in this, my dear. Johan will want you in the royal colors, and indeed, we insist. If you are to marry him and be his bride, you *will* wear our colors."

"Fine. Then I guess I'm not marrying your son." As the dress wasn't fastened, I could pull it off with some ease, and I did so quickly before moving past her and running from the room. I heard noise behind me, but I knew the queen wouldn't run herself, and I'd surprised the others enough that I had a few moments.

Of course, only three weeks in the palace did not make me an expert, and I was soon lost. But I watched the angle of the sun shining through the various windows, keeping the slanting shadows before me as much as I could. Soon, I found a side door, and when I pushed it open, I was outside. I ran down a mildly sloped lawn until I reached a bench. Only then did I realize I was sobbing—and half naked.

"What will I do now?" I gasped. I wiped my face, but it had little effect on the torrent of moisture. I felt utterly and truly trapped. If I didn't go through with this marriage, then I would have to return to my parents and marry that horrid man. After all, what skills did I have to survive on my own? I certainly couldn't sew, like Shyla, and I'd never understood exactly what a lady-in-waiting did—not that this would help me avoid a marriage. I could ride a horse, but the only people I ever saw working with horses were men.

I'd spent a fair amount of time with the stable boy when I'd sneaked out with Sofia, the princess. When I was younger, I'd thought maybe I could marry him. He was good-looking enough, and we'd done a little exploring with kisses and caresses. Sofia had always seemed so shocked when she realized what I'd been up to with him. "Don't you think you should save this for marriage?" she'd asked.

"Wouldn't it better to know what I'm doing if I *do* get married?" I'd countered.

"You mean 'when.' And you'll figure it out; everyone does." She'd seemed so confident, so certain.

"You don't want a little practice first? Silvan has a cousin," I'd said.

Sofia shook her head. "Silly Isabella," she'd said, touching my cheek. "When you marry someone, you let your body follow your heart. It will all work out."

And maybe it had for her. She'd been married to the foreign prince only a few months after that, and although it was arranged in advance, she'd seemed content and pleased the last time I saw her. To my surprise, it wasn't as much fun spending time in the stables without her, and I'd let my exploration with the stable boy fade. My parents would never have allowed me to marry him, anyway; he could do nothing to promote their status, after all. The man they'd chosen offered them a path to a more dignified future. It mattered little to them that they were sacrificing their own daughter's happiness in the process.

The hopelessness of it all swamped me, and I slumped against the cool stone back of the bench.

"Are you all right?"

The quiet voice interrupted my bitter thoughts, and I realized my face was wet, my nose running, and I was wearing little more than a thin corset. I refused to look up. I felt a presence beside me, and then a handkerchief was pressed into my hand. "Here. I think you might benefit from this."

I managed to capture a bit of the snot from my nose and tried to turn away, but a gentle hand stopped me. "Isabella, what is it? What is wrong?"

Then I recognized Johan's deep voice. I didn't know what to say, so I focused on calming myself. Johan waited, not moving, as I tried to put myself in order again. "I don't like your royal colors," I managed to get out, my voice hoarse and rough.

"Few do," he said calmly. "If it helps, we rarely have to wear them. I think I see that outfit thrice a year, at most."

"I yelled at your mother," I blurted. "I refused to wear the orange gown she had made for me."

To my shock, he chuckled. "Well, she'll probably appreciate that—eventually. She likes strength."

Did nothing ruffle this boy? I turned to him, lifting my chin. "I don't like the rules that say women must do what everyone else tells them to."

"I wouldn't like it either, if I were a woman." He sighed. "Honestly, I'm not that fond of all the rules for *me*, as well. As a prince—oh, who am I telling?" He smiled. "Perhaps the rules you truly don't like are those for royalty."

I stared at him, taking in his calm demeanor, his handsome face with large brown eyes, long charcoal lashes, and his black curls. "Why on earth do you want to marry *me*? You don't even know me."

Johan studied me for a moment, and I felt my face warm under his scrutiny. I certainly didn't look my best. "Why are you here, Isabella?" He sounded both sad and a little frustrated.

I opened my mouth to give the same vague answer I'd been giving for the past three weeks when something stopped me. I bit my lip, looking at him. At this point, I had nothing to lose with honesty. I was trapped either way. If I had to return to my parents—if I wasn't "real" enough for Johan and his mother—I didn't want to leave without baring myself at least once. Somehow, I felt I owed Johan that much.

I searched to find the right words, then cleared my throat. "I had no desire to remain with my parents. They were in the midst of drawing up a marriage contract between me and Count Hapstorn, the leader of his royal family through circumstance rather than birth. I suppose it wouldn't matter how he got there, though. He was not someone I could see myself loving or even enduring, even if it meant I could eventually take my place as the ruler of our small district. My father's cousin would take over otherwise, and my father has never liked him. They put it to me quite clearly: perform your duty and marry the count. Since they gave me no other options, I chose to leave."

Johan blinked, and I saw true surprise flit across his face. "That's not what I expected you to say," he admitted.

"What did you expect?" I asked.

"I thought you were not a princess. I thought you'd been lying all along."

"You . . . ?" I stared. "Why would you allow me to stay, if that's truly what you thought?"

He shrugged. "I figured you needed to be away from your home. After all, you showed up here on a stormy night, and it was obvious that you'd chosen to leave, regardless of the dangers. I knew the truth would come out eventually, and in the meantime, you'd gain some comfort."

Words deserted me. He'd allowed all this to go on—the time with his mother, the fittings, the clothes, the food—for compassion and nothing more?

"Did you know that I required a wife?" he asked then, his voice unnaturally even.

I didn't hesitate to tell the truth this time. "Honestly, I paid little attention to other royal families. I will admit that my own troubles blinded me to anything beyond our palace gates. It is only my sister and me, and as the eldest, she got to choose between finding an appropriate husband to take over Featherwick's minor "throne" or looking abroad. Once she chose, it fell to me to fulfill the rest. When it became apparent that Hapstorn was the strongest choice, someone my father's cousin couldn't challenge, they decided for me. Your family is so far above our station, I never gave your struggles any thought. Indeed, I don't think anyone in Featherwick did." I glanced away, my eyes stinging. This level of candidness brought extreme discomfort; I had only ever expressed myself truthfully to Sofia, my dear sister, who was gone forever now that she'd married her faraway prince.

Plus, the level of vulnerability did not sit well with me. The last thing I wanted was for Johan to feel trapped like I had, especially now as I saw more of his strong character. "It's unbelievably kind of you to allow this to continue up to now," I rushed to add. "But please don't feel you need to move forward. I will find a way—"

Johan took my hand in his, his touch silencing me as he smoothed over my fingers with his own. "I have no doubt of that," he said with a smile. "It's obvious that you are quite capable of making your own happiness." Then his smile faded. "I have known since a very young age that my parents—especially my mother—expected me to marry a certain type of woman. A princess, of course, and a perfectly real princess beyond that. When I was a child, I considered running away, as well."

I couldn't hold back a breath of surprise, and Johan's full lips quirked into a smile. My own responded, as if compelled, and his scrutiny dropped to my mouth for a long second.

When his thick eyelashes rose, the heat in my cheeks followed. I slid my hand out of his, suddenly self-conscious. His smile grew, and he continued. "Months ago, my mother insisted I travel throughout the world, visiting all royal families of our status, seeking this perfectly real princess to be my bride. I did travel, but I had no intention of actually choosing a stranger to live with me. Instead, I found some flaw with every female I met, learning quickly to discern aspects that my mother would understand. When I returned, she despaired of me ever finding the flawless princess I so desperately sought." He grinned now, and I clearly heard the sarcasm in his voice.

"And then you appeared. Your bedraggled appearance couldn't hide the spark of your forceful personality. I insisted to my mother that you—and you alone—would be my bride." He laughed, a mixture of actual amusement and some chagrin. "Little did I know that you were a true princess. I assumed you were a beggar girl. Even though you claimed more, it never occurred to me you were telling the truth.

"My mother, of course, decided to test you—and somehow, you passed the test! Yes, I realize you *are* a princess, minor or not, but I can't imagine how you felt a tiny pea under all those mattresses—"

I couldn't hold back my laughter any longer. I laughed till tears trickled down my cheeks. When I could speak, I said, "I rarely sleep well. I have insomnia. The ludicrous number of mattresses on that bed made me wonder if there was some kind of strange tradition or even a jest in play. I shifted the mattresses, and I discovered the pea beneath it all. Although I couldn't ascertain the goal absolutely, I suspected I was being tested in some way."

Johan's own laugh rang out, rich and full, and the look of delight on his face silenced me. For the first time since I'd left my own home—perhaps for the first time ever, notwithstanding Silvan—something stirred in me, fluttering in my stomach.

"Oh, that is priceless!" Johan calmed himself down, shaking his head. "So you *are* a princess, but that seems a coincidence." Suddenly, he sobered, frowning darkly. "Why would you agree to marry *me*? You know nothing about me, and I could be just as unpalatable as the count." The stiffness in his carriage indicated I needed to explain my answer carefully.

Slowly, I placed my hand over his fist, soothing the tension there with my fingertips. "Obviously, I cannot—even now— know you thoroughly. However, you're closer to my own age, you have the warmest and kindest eyes I've ever seen, you allowed this to go on despite your beliefs regarding my status, you offered me your handkerchief and didn't flinch when I wiped my nose on it, and, in all truth, I like looking at you."

The strain seeped from his shoulders, and he relaxed his hand, linking his fingers with my own. "I like looking at you too, though I suppose I should encourage you to put on some more clothes?" He winked, and I remembered how little I wore.

"If your mother finds me with you like this, that will be that," I said, truly worried this time. "I already said I wouldn't marry you because of the orange—"

Johan waved that final thought away and smiled. "As much as I've been enjoying the view, we should definitely spirit you away before she discovers you." He pulled me up and, slipping off his tunic, placed it over my shoulders. "That's a little better, I suppose." He took my hand and again linked our fingers. "All right?"

A tingle ran up my arm. "Yes." We walked quickly across the lawn, and soon we were slipping through a side door tucked beneath a curtain of ivy.

"My room is directly above," he said as we rushed up a long flight of stone stairs. "Now you know how to sneak and find me," he added, winking.

"Of course, other than the fact that I have no idea where *my* room is from here," I murmured.

He laughed quietly. We came out in a corridor that looked like all the others I'd been in, but Johan pointed at the gilded door on our right. "My room." Then he pointed down the hallway to a blue door at the far end. "Your room."

I couldn't hold back a surprised gasp. "Your mother allowed us to be so close?"

He grinned and pointed at a third door, a gold double door, in between the two. "My parents' room."

"Ah." That made more sense. "I should go before she finds us." I didn't want to leave him, though. For the first time since I'd arrived—for the *first time*—I felt a sense of peace and promise. Johan was nothing like the count, and even if I had to wear orange, I could see being myself with him.

He also seemed reluctant, and after a fast look around, he pulled me to him. "May I?" he asked.

"Oh, yes," I said. And then Johan was kissing me, his tongue dancing with mine with a confidence and hunger that surprised me. I twined my arms around his neck and returned the fervor. It wasn't long, but I knew the color in my face matched his rosy cheeks when we separated.

"I'll see you at luncheon," he said, lifting my hand and holding it to his lips. "My princess."

I blushed again, but when voices echoed down the hall, I quickly pulled away and ran to my door. After going in, I couldn't resist a look back. Johan stood there, a slight smile on his face and a rich warmth in his eyes as he watched me. I closed my door when the voices got louder, then leaned my forehead against it.

I couldn't control the rules that governed my world, but for the first time, I realized that perhaps I could determine how I lived within those rules. I'd been running toward something, even though I hadn't known it. Something within me—something fierce and promising and fresh—opened up, and for the first time in many years, I felt hope.

I didn't fool myself into thinking that I could ever be the *absolute* anything for anyone. However, Johan seemed to be open to possibilities, to change, to a world where princes and princesses formed a partnership. And that did seem . . . perfectly real.

THE PIED PIPER'S REVENGE

Scott Cowley

T his is not a kidnapping, if anyone asks," the piper shouted above the noise.

But the children of Hamelin would not stop sobbing.

Irritated, the piper continued to play his hypnotic melody while leading the children away from the now-distant town at a steady gait. Little voices whimpered at him from all angles.

"Where are we going?"

"I'm hungry!"

"My feet hurt!"

Lowering the pipe, the piper glanced back at the pudgy boy with the sore feet. "Kid, if you laid off the cake once in a while, you might be in better shape." The response had its desired effect, and the boy kept walking—visibly shocked, but mouth closed.

The piper quickly shifted his gaze past the boy toward the town from which they had come. No one pursued them. This was going to be far easier than he thought, which was saying something, considering he hadn't put much thought into this plan at all. Kidnapping a whole town's worth of children during Hamelin's church service had certainly been one of the more impulsive things he had ever done, but at the time, he had been feeling less regard for rational planning and more regard for making the mayor of Hamelin regret his stupidity. *Good luck running a town where you lost everybody's kids because you were too cheap to pay the rat exterminator.*

Returning to his pipe, the piper led the children onward. He was going to need a real plan soon—one that hopefully came with a payoff. Part of the trouble, he decided, was that children were not like rats. They were like giant insufferable rats with feelings. Rats that stub their toes and cry and poke each other and get tired and are generally annoying.

Getting the horde of rats out of Hamelin had been the easy part of the extermination, considering he had just barely learned to walk and play simultaneously. Early on, he discovered he could even stop playing his tune and the rats would continue to follow for a few minutes. That was nice, but when they got to the river, he couldn't get them to just hurl themselves into it. He recalled the entire psychotic hour of his life spent yelling at the rats to do themselves in. He threatened them. He encouraged them. He even dared them. *"You'd better not jump into the river because I would hate that so much!"* At one point, he booted one in, hoping the others would take a hint. They did not. It was only when he finally set the example for the rats by wading into the river himself that they willingly followed him to their demise.

All this was beside the point now though, as the piper had no desire to exterminate children like rats. He was not a child exterminator. Being branded a child exterminator would definitely hurt the rodent side of his business. Plus, the market for child extermination services was undoubtedly small.

"Stop kicking me!" one of the girls screamed.

"You started it," cried another.

"No, I didn't! You did!"

How was it even possible to kick each other and follow him at the same time? The piper took a deep breath. "I don't care who started it. But both of you need to stop it, or I'll . . . I'll take you back your parents!" Not quite the potent threat he was going for.

The yelling turned into shoving, and the piper did his best to ignore the two girls and press on with his tune. It still bewildered him that a seemingly simple combination of notes could will the feet of the children to obediently follow him while their voices whined in protest. The whining was something the piper hadn't expected, and he wasn't sure how long his patience could hold out. What he really needed was beeswax for some makeshift earplugs.

I never have beeswax when I need it.

"Does anybody have any beeswax?" he shouted. Not that he could make out a positive reply among so many cries and sniffles.

It was hard to play and walk and tune out the sounds and think simultaneously, but think he must. For up ahead the path forked, and the piper realized he had no idea where he was taking everybody. Should his plans of going from village to village as a traveling exterminator be shelved just because he had amassed an entourage of stolen kids?

"Alright everybody, listen to me. We're going to take a rest for ten minutes, but stay where you can see me. That's an order."

"I'm hungry!"

"I'm hungry too!"

Other voices joined in the chorus.

"Yes, you'll all eat soon enough," the piper said. *This is going to be a problem.*

"I have to pee!" cried another child.

"Go behind one of these trees," he said, pointing.

"But then I can't see you!"

"You'll be close enough to hear my voice."

"Not if I put my hands on my ears, like this."

"Well don't do that."

"I can't hear you! I can't hear you!"

The other children laughed.

This one I could definitely take to the river.

The piper pulled the child's hands from off her ears and whispered in his most menacing voice, "Go behind a tree and come back when you're done. Don't make me summon the poisonous snakes. You know I can." The girl got wide-eyed and immediately darted off.

The piper figured there was a snake tune somewhere among the pages of the small codex he carried, but it didn't matter. The threat was as good as the snake today. The piper closed his eyes and began collecting his thoughts for a new plan of action.

Thunk!

Something struck the back of his head. The piper whipped around in a frenzy.

"Who threw that!?"

Of course, it was impossible to tell, for he was surrounded by faces who seemed oblivious to the projectile that had pelted him in the head. *I'm taking them all to the river. Amazed their parents haven't already.*

He needed to escape the situation before he did something brash, as if he hadn't met his brashness quota for the day already. He looked around until he found a suitable tree to climb. Up, up he went until he reached a perch that was effectively safe from disruptions—like flying pebbles—and gave him a good vantage from which to see the surrounding terrain.

As he munched a bit of cheese he had secretly saved for lunch, he soon realized that they were not very far from another village—perhaps only twenty minutes at the current pace. His brain conjured up a magically favorable scenario. Perhaps it was a childless village, tragically rendered barren by some child-eating beast, and they would happily buy the whole lot of children from him.

That must be the stupidest plan I have ever had. It's not even a plan. Think.

What could he do with a hundred little people? How many little people did he have anyway? Peering down, he counted. One hundred thirty. He smiled. *That's a lot of angry parents the mayor has to deal with.*

He considered extortion. He would arm the children, surround the village, and threaten to lay siege and burn everything to the ground or else be paid for protection.

No, THIS must be the stupidest plan I have ever had. Hark, 'tis the dreaded Hamelin Horde! They'll poke you with sticks, then eat all your pudding and wet your beds! He'd have better luck getting paid for the sheer entertainment of his child army. *Now there's an idea! A traveling act I could take from town to town. Mock battles, reenactments of historic events, singing, comedy!*

Reality set in like a storm cloud.

You're out of time. It's been ten minutes already. Get rid of the kids and cut your losses. Leave them at the town and just move on.

The piper couldn't help but feel depressed about not coming up with a more gainful solution as he scaled back down the tree to the ground. Some of the children had gone exploring in the forest nearby, and those who stayed were quick to voice their complaints.

"I want to go home!"

"We're hungry."

"This isn't fun anymore."

"Well life isn't fun," he countered. "It was never meant to be fun. It's just one big ball of pain and death and misery, and if you're lucky, you'll get the plague and a few sympathy meals before you go. But don't talk to me about fun. I stopped having fun a long time ago."

They looked at him with blank faces, oblivious to the woes of adulthood and entrepreneurship.

"We're almost home, and you'll eat soon enough," the piper said. The children seemed to perk up a bit, even if it was a lie.

He took a quick gulp of water from his costrel and played the tune loudly enough for those among the trees to hear. Before long, all had rejoined the group, and they started toward the nearby town.

"Are we there yet?" a boy asked.

"We just started walking. We'll be there in minutes."

"How long is that?"

"Long enough for me to call out the wild boars, so they can eat you so you'll stop asking questions," the piper said.

"Boars don't eat p—"

"Child-eating wild boars hate questions as much as I do. It'll be very painful, so be quiet." And so the boy was.

They soon reached the outskirts of a small, but bustling town that looked much like the one they had left that morning. The piper stopped the group and watched from a distance. He knew now would be a good time to leave the children and take off into the forest, but the itch of opportunity was dying to be scratched. He decided to let things play out a little longer.

"Listen up. I'm going to find out where our lunch is, so everybody stay here until I return. Don't go anywhere."

He walked toward the group of townspeople who had seen him and were now starting to congregate, but he suddenly realized that the children were still following him because of the tune's power. Quickly, he put the pipe into his bag, which he lobbed over a tree branch. Sure enough, they stayed with the pipe.

They're just like the rats, only I knew what to do with them this time.

With the children safely behind him, he mentally prepared himself for what would need to be a convincing act as he approached the townspeople.

"My fellow denizens," he began with a flair. "It is your great privilege today to experience the marvel of the Piper's People Parade—the most extraordinary troupe of children you have ever seen. We have come—"

"Hey, this lot is from Hamelin! I recognize that one there," came a voice in the crowd. Other voices muttered in agreement. Some village children began to whisper and point.

This is not going to plan, thought the piper, before realizing he hadn't had much of a plan to begin with.

"Yes, yes, of course they are," he replied, trying to maintain a broad smile. "What I was about to say is that Hamelin has finished the harvest already and has sent me with its own strapping youths to offer assistance to the neighboring communities. The Piper's Produce-Picking People Patrol at your service! For a price, of course."

The townsfolk murmured to one another in astonishment, which turned to contempt, and the piper was able to pick out bits and pieces of the conversations.

"Could it be true?"

"How do they do it?"

"We won't be done for another month!"

"This is just like Hamelin! Always gloating about something."

"They're insufferable."

"Tell him to hang himself."

Sensing he had struck some nerves, the piper spoke up. "Of course, if you're not interested, we'll gladly take our services up the road."

"Hold now, don't be in a rush. You've just arrived," said a man, who quickly turned and conducted a hushed, but rapid-fire conversation with a small group who finally appeared to nod in agreement. The man turned back to the piper.

"We of Oldendorf are most grateful for Hamelin's"—the man coughed—"benevolence, and we'll gladly pay for your kind assistance so that we, too, may speed up the harvest. We know you'll have no trouble gathering our burgeoning crop of brambleberries in the south fields."

Brambleberries? No trouble indeed, you sadistic psychopaths.

If the devil himself had created his own fruit, he couldn't do much better than the black brambleberry. Thorny briars meant slow and often painful picking. Those who bothered cultivating brambleberries at all sometimes let part of the crop go to waste out of frustration. Half the time, the fully ripe fruit still tasted sour.

The piper looked back at the children. The effects of the pipe seemed to have worn off. Some were starting to wander. Others were on the verge of tears again. He needed to salvage this quickly before the villagers realized they were hiring a bunch of captive and spellbound help. That could make for an awkward conversation.

"Easy enough," he said. "We'll be done in an hour. I'll take them there straightaway and you meet me with empty baskets."

"But we haven't determined your price yet," replied the man.

"We'll take the wages of your own brambleberry pickers, paid up-front of course." He wasn't going to fall into this trap again.

"Quite fair. But we aren't accustomed to stockpiling wages for random traveling brambleberry pickers," the man said. "You'll have to gather the berries while we gather the gold. You said it yourself that this should be easy enough."

The piper's own fatigue had worn down his willingness to protest. Seeing the profitable light at the end of the proverbial tunnel, and knowing he wouldn't be doing any of the work himself, he relented.

The next few minutes wrangling children proved to be the most challenging task so far. A few had ventured out of sight, so the piper had to figure out where they had gone. And this was difficult because the piper was determined to pipe as quietly as possible. Otherwise, he'd have a bunch of Oldendorf children on his hands too, which would make for another awkward conversation. In a few minutes, he successfully found one hundred and thirty Hamelin children. Give or take a few. It wasn't as though he needed an *exact* count—he wasn't holding hostages for ransom or anything. The promise of berries raised the children's spirits one last time, long enough to follow the piper around the outskirts of Oldendorf to the fields. Fortunately, there were no major hitches along the way and after the baskets were delivered, the piper was left to supervise the gathering, with the sun high above the brambleberry hedgerows.

"There is no such thing as a free lunch," began the piper. "But in this case, the lunch is as close to free as it gets." He saw their rapt attention wasn't on him, but rather on the rows of plump, ripe brambleberries. "We are here to pick, not to eat, but I know you must eat, so in return you must pick. I have only one rule you must follow, and if you do not follow it, there will be a terrible, terrible punishment."

"What is it?" asked a boy.

"It is too terrible; I can't talk about it."

"No, the rule!"

"Listen, boy. If you want to live to see your seventh birthday, you will be quiet and do as I say," the piper said with his most intimidating voice. Once satisfied, he continued speaking.

"Now then, when you are picking these berries—"

"I'm eight already," interrupted the same boy.

"What?"

"You said I wouldn't live to see my seventh birthday, but I already did. Do you even have a punishment?"

The piper's nostrils flared, his eyes grew wide, and he let out the most primal scream he could muster at the boy. He knew that had any adults been watching, they probably would have doubled over with laughter, but the boy and several children turned pale and stiffened.

"Much better," the piper said as he cleared his throat and refocused on addressing the group. "Now, if you want to eat berries, you may eat ONE berry for every THREE you put in your basket. Do you understand? Pick three. Eat one. Pick three. Eat one. Is that clear?"

The children nodded and immediately rushed over to the brambleberry bushes, plucking berries and shoving them all into their mouths with a voraciousness reserved for big appetites crammed into little bodies.

"STOP, STOP, STOP!" the piper yelled. "Stop it! I want to see three in the basket every time you eat one. Pick three first. Three berries in the basket, people! I'm warning you. Do it right."

The children, for the most part, got the message and slowly put three berries into the shared baskets rather than their mouths. The piper was pleased to see that their small hands had an easier time than adults in maneuvering the briars. The piper led them in methodical practice for several rounds. Three berries in the basket. One berry in the mouth. The rhythm seemed to have stuck, and the piper observed for a few more minutes until he was satisfied that they would carry on without the pipe's enchantment, or his micromanagement. He needed this because all the while he had been concocting a new plan for personal enrichment.

The piper hurried back into Oldendorf to find the mayor. He wanted to make a separate deal to exterminate this town's rats, knowing that if he played it right, the children would finish the picking, he would collect payment for it, and he would receive an advance for the extermination. He could leave the children behind while he took the rats out of town, and by the time the villagers learned the truth, he would be long on his merry piping way.

Negotiations took a lot longer than expected. The mayor of Oldendorf was not an easy man to find, and once found he received the piper with a good deal of hostility, presumably because he was a Hameliner. Of course, the piper considered breaking character, but that would have thrown the entire game. Instead, he chose to provide a demonstration of his capabilities. While instantly attracting rats out from all corners should have been the dealmaker, Oldendorf's mayor was equal parts astonished and furious at the thought that Hamelin had such advantages. The piper had to delicately rebuff the mayor's pressure for him to defect to Oldendorf before the mayor finally accepted his extermination proposal. The piper was even able to formalize an impromptu contract, something he had neglected to do in Hamelin. At the conclusion, the piper invited the mayor and his harvest overseer to accompany him back to the hedgerows where the children would be nearly finished with picking, and he would finally be paid his due.

As the trio approached, the piper was the first to notice that something wasn't right. Where were the children? Could they have finished and wandered off already? Rounding them up was going to be one more pain to add to the day's collection.

What they found in the brambleberry rows sent the piper and his fellow inspectors into a panic. The bushes were picked clean as intended, but on the ground lay empty gathering baskets. Each was stained with the unmistakable brambleberry mark, but there were no berries left intact. The ground was well-stained with berry pulp and juice, now left to the birds and beetles. But where were the children?

In a daze, the piper ran down the rows with the mayor and harvest overseer close behind, desperate to make sense of what he had seen. And now it was all coming into focus. Like a swarm of locusts, the children had devoured every last brambleberry once the piper was out of view. Then they had moved on to the rows of late strawberries. Completely wiped out. Then the raspberries. Eaten through. The bilberries. Gone. And at last, there they were—all the children on the ground between the hedgerows of unripened elderberries—squirming in audible discomfort with telltale signs of berry vomit. And the piper knew why. Elderberries were already toxic when fully ripened and uncooked, and the green berries were worse. Fortunately, the consumption of all the other berries had probably left them full, explaining why most of the elderberries were still on the bushes. Had they started with elderberries, there was little doubt that the outcome would have been far worse.

The piper had a new problem. He now had a bunch of sick kids who were evidently horrible at counting and had very little self-control. Two problems, really, for he would probably be hanged for his role in the berry crop fiasco on account of Oldendorf's ill feelings toward Hamelin. He could read his fate on the stony faces of the mayor and the overseer as their attentions turned from surveying the damage to sizing up the piper. The only real upside was that he was now untethered by thoughts of wealth and could do what he should have done long before now.

"Fellows, I do believe that our berries are all sitting there right behind you," he said, pointing. And as the two men turned to look, the piper took off sprinting between the hedgerows, away from them.

He hoped that he would have enough speed and stamina to make it to the visible forest glades and maybe hide in the trees until he could safely escape. But in less than a minute, he was overtaken, tackled, and pummeled several times in the head and body by the harvest overseer.

Exhausted and a painful wreck from the torso up, he lay there, pinned to the ground by the overseer.

"Good work. Tie him up until the others arrive. I know they heard us," said the mayor, tossing some cord. "I'm going to take a lot of pleasure in hanging one of Hamelin's own saboteurs."

"Please! I'm not from Hamelin! I beg you! This is all a mistake!" the piper cried.

"That's exactly what a spy would say," said the overseer, pressing the piper harder to the ground.

"No! Hamelin cheated me, so I stole their children with magic," the piper gasped.

"That's also what a spy would say."

"I can prove it!"

"That's definitely what a spy would say. Save it for the gallows," said the overseer, binding the piper's ankles together.

But the mayor, remembering that he had indeed seen the piper command the rats at will, was disturbed by this strange claim, and asked, "And just how would you prove it?"

"Get off me and I'll show you," said the piper, wheezing. The overseer held his grip and looked over at the mayor, who, after a small eternity, nodded his head. The overseer loosened his hold and pulled the piper to his bound feet.

The piper took his pipe from the bag that had been flung aside in the scuffle and loudly played the melody—simple and whimsical. Like clockwork, the child army began to emerge in methodical fashion from the rows of elderberries. They plainly looked miserable about it and weren't going very fast, as if the feet said "yes" while the face said "I hate you for this." They were now a grotesque spectacle of pale, moaning, stained, sickly faces that would have caused an unfamiliar stranger to swear these to be the wiedergänger undead, come back to torment the living.

The mayor gasped. "Stop them. Send them away!"

"I can't. They'll keep coming. But they're the same awful little children who came with me. Shocking, I know."

"Look!" said the mayor, pointing. "Now our children are coming, just like the others!"

It was true. The Oldendorf children ran toward them, some with buckets or brooms still in hand; their eyes were wide with confusion. And chasing after the Oldendorf children were a mob of townspeople, looking utterly bewildered by this strange phenomenon.

"They'll have your head for this," said the mayor.

"I'll make sure of it," the overseer chimed in.

"What's done is done," the piper said, wincing. "I can't pay you or bring the berries back, but I have an idea that doesn't involve a noose. Please hear me out."

And with the mayor's consent, the piper quickly recounted the day's series of events—Hamelin's duplicity, the impulsive kidnapping, and the unfortunate journey that brought them to Oldendorf. He ended by proposing a plan that he hoped would appeal to the mayor's sense of justice (along with his ego). He had no chance to gauge the mayor's favorability toward the idea because the mob of villagers arrived and, seeing what the piper had done, was ready to pull him limb from limb. Now all the battered piper could do was await his punishment.

The Oldendorf children and villagers were flanked by the awful army of Hamelin children whose wailing and whimpering for home were truly wretched.

The mayor stretched out his hands to signal that he was about to speak (and possibly to create a momentary barrier between the mob and the piper).

"Oldendorfers, you see how our berry crop has been ravaged at the hands of Hamelin's children, led by this man."

The mob cursed and yelled.

"I want my berries!" cried a woman.

"I must remind you," continued the mayor, "that by our law, the punishment of children goes no further than lashings." The mob grumbled. "On the other hand, this man is not so lucky. I know how much you enjoy a good hanging once in a while, and it would send a message to Hamelin that we will not allow this with impunity."

The piper cringed as the mob roared with approval.

"On the other hand," said the mayor, "The loss of the berry crop has happened before and as you know, it is not critical to our winter rationing." The mob grumbled some more.

"I want my berries!" yelled the same woman in the crowd. The mayor ignored her.

"On the other hand, we cannot let Hamelin go unpunished. The very fiber of our identity as Oldendorfers depends on this." Those in the mob nodded.

"On the other hand—"

"That's too many hands! Let's hang him!" yelled a gravelly voice in the mob. A cheer went up and the mob started to advance.

"Quiet!" The mayor shouted, waving his arms to keep them at bay. "Before you decide his fate, I give you one other choice— and I believe it may suit us better than killing this scoundrel, who I'm not even sure is a Hameliner . . . "

It was dusk in Hamelin. Those at home were gathered in mourning: what had begun as a glad day, free of rodent pests, had turned sour with anger and anxiety. The mayor had concocted a story about the piper trying to demand triple the pay after finishing his dirty work and then stealing the children in retaliation when he didn't get it (in reality, the mayor hadn't paid him a single guilder, saying he had taken longer than promised and should be grateful for the practice). Since the disappearance of their children, most of the townsmen had been out in companies, concentrating their search along the riverbank because they feared the worst.

From the forest outside Hamelin, there came a flutter of birds, seemingly disturbed by something in the trees. Then came the unmistakable lilt of a pipe, distant at first, but growing steadily louder. Those who were indoors came outdoors, and those outdoors took their torches and set out toward the sound to investigate.

The piper emerged from the woods, but this was not the piper they remembered. True, he seemed to be the same person, but now he limped slowly along and looked haggard and unnatural, his face a ghostly gray (courtesy of the ash the Oldendorfers had added as part of their conditions). It seemed that all his remaining energies were put toward maintaining his tune, and the people of Hamelin now saw why. Behind the piper, a throng of children with the same eerie ashen faces, looking even more terrible than the piper, lurched forward with every step.

"Wiedergänger!" gasped a woman.

One of the boys behind the piper raised his hands in ghastly fashion toward the woman and cried, "Mama, Mama!" whereupon the woman shrieked and fainted.

The piper stopped playing as the children continued to advance behind him. The townspeople were frozen in terror, not knowing whether these children were living or dead, whether to embrace or to retreat. Some of both occurred, along with some more fainting.

Suddenly the piper brought the pipe back to his lips and played a different tune. From the grasses and forest came the rats. Big rats. Small rats. Oldendorf had far more rats to deal with than Hamelin. Now they would be Hamelin's to deal with. As the piper stopped and the spell dissipated, Hamelin's citizens watched in disbelief as rats scattered and scurried into the town's recently vacated nests, holes, houses, barns, and fields.

The piper had saved his own life by bringing both Hamelin's children and Oldendorf's rats back with him, enduring a torturous return journey that consisted of alternating between child and rat tunes. All the while, he had been forced to listen to the children's sickness-induced groans, weariness-induced cries, and rat-induced squeals. With his bargain fulfilled at last, the piper scanned the crowd, hoping to complete one more task. Finally spotting Hamelin's mayor, the piper staggered slowly toward the petrified man until the two were face to face.

"It looks to me like you've got a rat problem," the piper managed. "And it's not going to be cheap."

ETHICAL WILL

Kaki Olsen

PART 1: SHIVA

L ena knew that Mom would have liked a quiet graveside service, but it was simply impossible given the circumstances. Oncology nurses who had been her comrades-in-arms during the battle against leukemia were now here for the war memorial. Actual comrades-in-arms in uniform or civvies came to remember the brave soldier who had died in her own bed. Family members were fewer in number, but the focus of attention.

Mom would have preferred that a few friends and immediate family cluster around the coffin, with their taciturn rabbi performing the ceremony with no flourishes, but the sheer number of people demanded a place in which to congregate. The memorial service was well-attended at the synagogue, and the respectful quiet that ought to have been maintained became an amplified cacophony of weeping, sniffing, and surreptitious murmurs.

In the memorial hall, Lena was fortunate to be wedged between Aunt Anna on one side and one of Mom's cousins on the other. They had both kept respectful silence since entering, and whenever the congregational noise swelled, Anna would tighten her grip on Lena's hand. It wasn't a very effective gesture of comfort, but it anchored her to something other than the oppressive crowd that had turned up in her mother's honor.

It was easier at the cemetery, where much of the noise was carried away on the wind and the crowd was punctuated with headstones. When the rabbi sang the Kaddish, Lena was able to focus on his soothing voice rather than the fact that lowering the casket into the grave gave her no peace or sense of closure.

Sitting Shiva was a welcome respite from the formality of the funeral, but it was less pleasant to receive the condolences. She endured kisses to her cheek and comments about how much her mother had loved her, but she inevitably felt some kind of shame for her anger at the dearly departed. When her mother's fellow soldiers told Lena how much Platoon Sergeant Hoffman meant to all of them, she gritted her teeth at the idea that "Hoff" would have preferred dying painfully from multiple organ failures to being the target of an IED somewhere in Afghanistan. Lena had been privileged to be with her mother at the end, but it had not given her any peace to witness the passing of the woman she had only sporadically been close to. No one who instructed her to call if she needed anything was likely to help if the horror of her loss woke her in the middle of the night. The visitors wanted to fix her grief with a hug and a pot pie.

Shiva lasted seven days, but after the third day, the stream of visitors slowed to a trickle. Friends and even a teacher paid their respects as the community poured out blessings and condolences, but the fifth day passed with even fewer appearances than the fourth.

A few minutes before sunset on Friday evening, they dressed in their best clothes. They dutifully prepared the foods because life and faith had to go on, even during Shiva. Aunt Anna lit the candles and recited the Kabbalat Shabbat prayers. It had been Mom's place to lead Kavod Shabbat, so it was only appropriate that her youngest sister continue her efforts.

"Lena," she said after they had wished each other a good Sabbath, "would you lead us in singing?"

She had been assigned this role since time immemorial and, her imperfect voice cracking even more than usual, she sang the hymn to invite in the two angels of Shabbat.

> *"Shalom aleichem*
> *malachei hashareit*
> *malachei elyon*
> *mimelech mal'chei ham'lachim*
> *hakadosh baruch Hu."*

The Talmud said that the angels who accompanied them to Shabbat would look upon the state of the household where they were invited. If the home was full of light and the spirit of Shabbat, a good angel would bless them that they would find the same spirit the following week. His counterpart was a malevolent angel and capable of pronouncing unhappiness on the house should he be displeased with their worship.

A friend had once compared this to Santa's naughty-or-nice tally, and Lena had always wondered if she was one bad thought away from invoking the malediction of the second angel. She had never openly tried to make this an unhappy place, but she had to wonder if her good intentions would be offset by the impatience she had felt on the day of the funeral. Maybe her irritation that cousin Eleanor had burnt the challah would give the second angel power and the good angel would be compelled to agree with his decision.

Still, because she could not help but hope for better things to come, she invited both angels in.

"Peace be unto you, ministering angels, messengers of the Most High, of the supreme King of kings, the Holy One, blessed be He."

As they asked that the angels come in peace, the candles flickered as though some unseen person had sighed in their vicinity, but they continued, raising their voices in unison.

"Bless me with peace, angels of peace . . . "

There was no way to know if they had earned a seal of approval, but the only spirit of unease at that Shabbat was the one that had lingered since they returned from the graveyard.

The reading of the will was something of an anti-climax. Mom had never put much stock in personal belongings, so she had seen to it that the house and her personal income would go to Lena. A few family heirlooms went to friends or family, but she made no mention of clothing or personal journals. Anna had proposed that they donate any books that the family could live without to a library in need and made a half-hearted attempt to decide what clothing they should send to Goodwill.

Mom waxed poetic about why Lena should always have a home to call her own and how the money she had left should be used for her education, but she had left one cryptic line at the end of the document.

It is my wish that Lena welcome my nutcracker into her life.

After the reading of the will, she returned to the family home. The antique nutcracker waited for her on the mantel, where it had been on display every day she could remember. He was over one hundred fifty years old, but so lovingly cared for that the paint still looked new. Lena accepted the bequest instead of finding a good ballet school to adopt it, but left it where it had been for years without giving thought to how else she could "welcome" the nutcracker.

"I have one just like this at home." Meg took the foot-high toy off the mantel. "Mom thinks they're the perfect way to decorate for the holidays without being smothered by tinsel or fairy lights."

The high school friends she hadn't seen much of since graduation two years ago had shown up on the last day of Shiva, just after Lena had returned from the lawyer's office. They all seemed more amused than anything by the gift.

"Yeah, but *yours* only comes out in December," Alison rejoined. "I've seen this on the mantelpiece forever."

"And as far as I know, it's been there since Nana Marie got it for reasons that aren't exactly obvious to the rest of us. Especially since it's, you know, a *Christmas* sort of decoration," Lena replied.

Meg shrugged. "Well, it's not what you'd usually find next to the menorah, but I don't think there's anything wrong with keeping an heirloom from the Gentile section of your family tree."

"I was going to leave it there until I couldn't stand the sight of it, but Mom wanted me to welcome him. How am I even supposed to do that?"

"Throw a party?" Erin suggested. "Buy sugar plums and gingerbread and whatever else they had in that fairy tale kingdom in Act Two. Spend all night on a sugar high, then put him back on the mantel until you're home for the holidays."

Lena felt almost guilty for being able to smile at that, but it was the first time she had felt amused by something in two weeks and she was supposed to accept consolation from members of the community. She didn't quash the urge.

"If it weren't for the fact that the Stahlbaums liked it enough to haul it to the New World, I think we'd have put it in a yard sale years ago," she admitted. "I don't know exactly how to make him feel welcome, but I can start by not putting him in storage."

"For now." Alison leaned forward with an appraising eye to determine how out of place he would be on a dorm desk. "I don't think he has to be up there until you're old and grey."

"Or year-round," Erin added. "Maybe he can just come out for special occasions. After all, the original showed up on Christmas Eve and you have no obligation to keep that tradition alive."

Particularly since she would not be celebrating December 24th unless it coincided with Chanukah. "I'm not taking him back to the dorms. I'll check on him at Thanksgiving in six weeks, and he can stand guard over the house until after exams. I don't think he'll be too lonely."

By the time they had finished eating the lasagna that Meg had made and done the dishes, the nutcracker had been returned to his place by the family portraits where Mom had seemed to think he belonged, and Lena put the doll out of her mind.

Until a quarter past midnight, that was.

At first, Lena wrote off the man sitting on her desk chair as a dream. It made no sense for her to be visited by a handsome stranger in a uniform that belonged in a Disney movie. When he didn't disappear, though, she sat up and stared a little more fixedly at the object of her hallucination.

He simply smiled, as if he had been expecting this reaction. In case he was an illusion, she didn't try to touch him, but she turned on the overhead light to get a better look.

Still half-asleep and not prepared for a vision who wouldn't go away, she blurted, "Can I help you?"

"It is not your place to be of service to me," he said formally, "but I hope you will consider me a friend and ally."

"You're breaking and entering." Instinct demanded that she arm herself, so she wrapped one hand around the edge of her alarm clock. It probably wasn't the most effective weapon, but Lena had never been the type to keep pepper spray in her purse, much less sleep with a knife under her pillow. "Or maybe you're not really here."

"I am here by invitation of your ancestor, one Marie Stahlbaum," he said. "My last hostess was your mother, Rebekah Hoffman, but it is your right to turn me away."

A text notification chimed, which heightened the weirdness of this midnight rendezvous. Lena had experienced her fair share of dreams that made no sense, but usually technology stayed out of them. A quick glance told her that Erin had decided to invite her to lunch on Monday. She had been expecting something less ordinary to accompany such an extraordinary conversation.

"I'm sorry," she mumbled, "but are you, you know, real?"

"I am not a figment of any imagination," he stated most solemnly, "but I am not part of your own world."

"And this couldn't have waited until morning?"

"If you like, I can come at an appointed time," he said. "I am, after all, your humble servant."

Taking a chance on this being more than a vivid dream, she checked her events calendar on her phone. "What are you doing at five tonight?"

"I will be here if invited." He bowed his head as if she had just placed an order at an expensive restaurant. "If you would like to introduce me to the rest of your family, I would be honored."

"Introduce . . . " She scrubbed sleep from her eyes. "You haven't even introduced yourself to me."

"I have said I am a friend and ally and your humble servant," he reminded her. "I was a life-long friend of your mother and of her mother before that. I have known your family since before they spoke English and practiced your faith. I hope that you and I will be able to develop a close friendship as well, even if only for special occasions."

At that, she dropped her phone. He smiled placidly while she scrambled to retrieve the device and some of her composure. She now realized why that uniform of his had looked so familiar—she'd seen it sitting on the mantel all these years.

"You're . . . you mean . . . I'm sorry, but aren't you part of a fairy tale?"

"As are you," he replied. "You may call me Prince and I will return at five."

The lamp flickered as the candles had at Shabbat, and when her eyes focused again, the chair was empty.

PART 2: SHLOSHIM

In Lena's experience, princes were men of their word. All her expertise came from movies or fanciful stories and they had pretty strong opinions on the subject. If he was to be believed, he'd also been reliable for over one hundred years. She fully expected him to arrive at the appointed hour of 5 p.m.

When the doorbell rang, Lena assumed that the event was unrelated to her appointment and stayed where she was until her aunt's shout roused her: "Lena, you're keeping your visitor *waiting!*"

She scampered down the stairs to find her mother's imaginary friend kissing her aunt on the cheek as if he were an old college buddy. He had exchanged the military uniform for a suit and combed his dark hair with a severe parting.

"You didn't tell me he was coming," was Anna's opening remark.

"You didn't tell me you knew each other." Lena addressed them both. "I thought Mom inherited the doll."

It seemed strange that Prince had asked her to introduce him to her family, since apparently, he already knew everyone who remained. But maybe that was just some weird magical formality—Lena really didn't know the rules of this sort of thing.

"She did," Prince said, "but my loyalty is to the family as a whole."

"And I shared a room with your mom." Anna shrugged as if the answer should have been obvious. "One year, when Rebekah snuck out of bed, I followed. After that, he would bring me something to make up for the oversight."

"It was ungentlemanly of me to not extend you the same courtesy as your sister." He bowed and presented a box that looked wrought from spun sugar. "My people send their regards, their condolences, and their finest sugar plums."

To Lena's surprise, Anna swept one leg behind the other and curtsied. It was a startling move for someone who reserved dresses for weddings and funerals and had, once upon a time, faked stomach cramps to avoid dance classes.

"I hope you will take our thanks back," Anna said. "And I hope that our emissary will be able to visit your world soon. Meaning you," she added, glancing at Lena. "It's worth the trip."

Lena refrained from replying that until she had more answers, she wasn't willing to leave even the house with him, much less her dimension. "That will be up to me, thank you very much."

Anna glanced heavenward, probably lamenting Lena's surliness, but tucked the sugar plums into the crook of her arm. "I will leave you to it, then. Call if you need my input."

Prince offered an arm, but Lena strode ahead of him into the living room. Once she had claimed her usual spot on the loveseat, she gestured expansively.

"Sit anywhere you like."

Mom would have balked at her casual tone and her refusal of the gentlemanly escort, but she had never insisted that Lena act like some kind of debutante. She had just shared behavioral advice when the mood struck her and let Lena decide how to implement it.

Mom's friend apparently found this amusing instead offensive. "You are much like your great-aunt."

Grandma's older sister had worked in print journalism and had a flair for treating every conversation like an interview. "I'll take that as a compliment. Am I the only one who was left in the dark about you?"

After a moment in which he looked both startled and wary, he frowned. "My apologies. I did not mean to cause offense."

"You've caused confusion," she corrected him. "The family who kept this a secret are the ones who caused offense, but I'm not about to cut off all ties to my extended family just because they neglected this part of the family history."

"I am not surprised at the secrecy. As I understand it, when Herr Drosselmeier brought me to his goddaughter—your Nana Marie—he was the only adult who knew of my first visit. Her parents would have been alarmed at the uninvited guest, and her brother was not very imaginative. Those who kept an open mind believed, and they chose their confidantes well."

"Was my father in on it, too?"

"Your mother insisted that he know before they married, and he never begrudged us our friendship." There was a moment's hesitation. "I have not spoken to him in some years, but we parted on good terms."

The same could not be said for father and daughter. Dad had tried to reconnect when it became apparent that he was about to be the only parent she had left, but his efforts had not made up for the estrangement that followed the divorce. Since Prince seemed to have opinions on everything, she waited for him to nudge her towards reconciliation or attempt a lecture, but he said nothing for several moments and she didn't feel like making small talk about family relations.

"What other questions do you have?" he prompted.

"You're not going to tell me about my obligation to the Hoffman legacy or give me marching orders?"

"Your family's friendship has been a gift that I have repaid with my protection," Prince replied without responding to her challenging tone. "I hope to pass that protection on to you."

That sounded more like a greeting card than a genuine sentiment, but it grated on her nerves only a little and that was a good sign these days.

"I have questions you might not like to answer."

"I never said you were to ask me comfortable questions." He smiled for the first time since entering the house and suddenly looked closer to her own age, but that might have been a deliberate illusion. The toy who could turn into a real prince might have the power to alter perceptions as well. "I will do my best to give you whatever answers you are looking for."

"Then where were you when she went to war?"

He had probably expected something about the long battle with cancer, not the months Mom had spent in a different kind of life-or-death struggle.

"I was here on her orders."

"Why?" Lena blurted out.

The smile that had humanized him faded, and she recognized the look that followed as one from her own repertoire of guilt. "I tried to be what you might call a white knight. I would have fought in her place and let her come home."

Shloshim was a month of mourning, and gaiety was still discouraged. Lena hadn't felt much like getting back to normal things like enjoying life yet, but a disbelieving laugh escaped now before she could stop herself. "And you thought that was what she would want?"

He nodded, looking remarkably embarrassed by the memory. "I misunderstood her reasons for serving her country. That changed when she refused to leave unless the rest of her unit went with her."

"And you couldn't bring the whole unit? Some of them died over there."

"I know." His gaze never wavered, even if the memory was not a pleasant one. She appreciated the vulnerability, even if she wasn't sure that she accepted the answers. "The next time that I offered to bring her home was after one of her comrades was killed. She would not leave without her unit, and her unit would not think of leaving before their orders demanded it."

Lena was nodding before he finished the explanation. "She didn't like coming home when there was still work to do there."

"For that reason, I went where she commanded in turn. She said I could not fight a war for her, so she asked me to give her a different kind of peace."

I was here on her orders, he had said. He hadn't been running errands or defending them actively, so there was only one other reason that her mother would have sent him to her home address.

"You spied on us?"

"I looked after you," Prince said. "I never interfered in your home life, but she heard my first-hand account of your sports achievements, and for the dinner you helped prepare for Thanksgiving, I brought her—"

"An apple pie." Lena remembered it well; Anna had baked it because it wouldn't have been a holiday without Mom's favorite dessert and had been miserable when it went missing. "One went missing while she was deployed, and we all agreed that Cousin Mark must have enjoyed it himself."

Prince's mouth twitched, and he nearly smiled again. "He was wrongly accused, but she saw to it that I returned the pie plate like a noble thief and asked many questions about your happiness."

He was making this sound like a quaint children's tale instead of petty mischief while there was a war on. Had he involved them in that task, they could have done much more to support their soldier. Instead, they had made do with other means of communication and worried about what they should divulge about life back home. It had always felt inadequate, and harboring resentment years later was completely pointless, but Lena had too recently felt helpless to give her mother what she really needed.

"And it would have killed you to—"

Her voice had grown shrill on that half-finished sentence, and she fell silent, momentarily appalled by the outburst. He did not respond, nor did he look away, and it would have perhaps been easier if he had done so. Instead, she found herself balking at the severity of her own pain and broke eye contact.

"Will you excuse me?"

"I await your convenience."

Lena could have escaped the house at that point. The seven days of mourning in which others had come to her were over, and she had ventured into town. Nothing about Shloshim, the rest of this first month of mourning, forbade her from going anywhere she pleased.

It would make Anna unhappy and uncomfortable if she stormed out of the house, and when Lena returned, he would probably still be awaiting Lena's convenience. Then she would only feel worse for having run away from the problem. The freshness of her anguish would probably lead to more anger and would solve nothing. Moreover, she'd be immersed in a new round of guilt trips and take it out on anyone who crossed her path.

Welcoming this man had been anything but easy so far, but the only thing she could do to change that was to turn away from her frustration.

She locked herself in the bathroom instead of fleeing and shut her eyes until some of the pulsating anger had faded and the throbbing in her head eased. Breathing normally was still a challenge, but that was nothing new. The house had felt suffocating every time she had visited before Mom died, and no matter how few people were under this roof, it felt overcrowded these days.

In her current state, she couldn't promise anyone that she would be able to deal rationally with this new burden, but she could start small and resolve to not turn her back on this legacy.

Anna had joined Prince in the living room by the time Lena felt ready to articulate her needs, but she allowed Lena to be the one to resume the conversation.

"I am angry," Prince's new liaison confessed.

"We all are," Anna murmured. "You're entitled to feel that the world isn't right at this point."

The show of empathy was unexpected, but welcome.

"I'm entitled to be angry at you too," she said, turning first to Anna. "There was no reason to keep me in the dark. There was nothing to be gained from it and you could have at *least* mentioned something after the will was read."

Anna was quick to reply. "But that's not what Rebekah wanted. She wanted you to *welcome* him, instead of feeling some sort of obligation."

It wasn't her habit to speak to family in an accusatory tone, but Anna's response came close to attempting a guilt trip and it seemed justified. "But you won't rest until I'm his best friend as I was always meant to be."

"I won't be happy," her aunt confessed, "but it's none of my business what choice you make."

"Then why are you in on this conversation in the first place?"

"For moral support," Prince interjected. "In spite of what you assume, I suspect that she is here to see that I respect your wishes."

"And I want to *know* those wishes," Anna explained. "If I hadn't been here to show you I already knew about the nutcracker, I'm not sure you would have told me about meeting him. I don't think you'd *lie* to me, but I wouldn't have been surprised if this was your little secret for years to come."

"And I wouldn't have been surprised if you started pestering me about the bequest tomorrow," Lena said. Well-meaning meddling was something practiced by everyone in the Hoffman family. "You want me to be happy as long as you get some say in how that happens."

"Of course." Her aunt's shoulders hunched as if warding off a blow. "Your dad's not as supportive as I'd like, your mom just died, and I want to be the person you feel comfortable coming home to when life gets rough. I don't want you turning down anything that can help you."

"I don't *know* that anything you do will help me," she responded, squaring her shoulders in opposition of Anna's posture. "I don't need a bodyguard and I don't need a knight in shining armor. I especially don't want a babysitter."

Anna didn't relax, but the prince looked less at ease than he had the first time Anna had sided with Lena. She had never thought it possible for royalty to look nervous, but after generations of alliance, her inconvenient resistance seemed to be outside of whatever comfort zone he had.

"And I know that neither of you are trying to make it worse," Lena continued in a quieter tone. "But it's going to take me some time to make peace with the family legacy and make plans for what's to come."

"I understand," Prince said, and she could hear nothing suspicious in his tone. "I wish you to have peace and protection because I could not always provide it for your predecessor. That may not ever require me to stand between you and danger, but I will find other ways to be a friend to you."

The quiet acquiescence was enough to bring the conflict to a neutral ground, where Lena could put her anger on hold. After a few more breaths, she took her seat once more and clasped her hands demurely in her lap.

"I can't decide tonight how involved we'll be in each other's lives, but I want my mom's wish to come true. Will you visit me again soon?"

"Whenever you request it."

That seemed to be too broad a statement, but Anna nodded in confirmation. "He came when your mother asked for him during treatments and was here a few nights before she died. He will stay away as long as you command, but he will respond immediately when you need him. Everyone with this inheritance has learned that at one time or another."

That was probably meant to be reassuring, but it only reinforced the fact that Lena had lost many opportunities to understand her mother. It caused a phantom echo of painful guilt that was becoming too familiar for her emotional well-being.

"You are not the first of your family to negotiate the terms of this friendship," Prince said when Lena had no response, "and in the decades of our alliance, no one has had cause to regret the friendship. I do not believe you will be the exception to that rule."

"Then can we start there?" She lifted her eyes from her lap and held his gaze for a few moments. "I'm not ready for a comrade-in-arms and I don't know that I want a protector, but I could use a friend right now."

"If that is all you will ever require of me, it will still be my honor to fulfill that role," he said as though taking an oath of fealty. "Perhaps we could meet here again?"

Lena couldn't exactly ask that he drop by with a therapeutic pizza every Friday, but she could agree to a periodic check-in.

"I will be returning to school next week," she said. "Can I ask that you visit on Saturday after Shabbat ends? How would I even do that?"

An expression crossed the prince's face that almost looked like displeasure to Lena, but it was gone as quickly as it came. "I think you would be more comfortable meeting me here, don't you think? Call out to me for help in any fashion and I will come."

She wasn't sure she wanted to come back here to meet him again instead of just meeting back at school, but she figured she could deal with that question later. If she called to him from elsewhere, and he didn't come—well, that would be his loss, not hers. She also wasn't sure what to do with a mythical knight in shining armor, but this was a peace offering in her mother's memory, and she could play it by ear for Mom's sake.

"I look forward to it."

By Saturday night, Lena was absolutely certain that any meeting with Prince would have to be on her own terms. She thought it bad form to invite a strange man into her apartment without giving her roommate some kind of explanation, so evening found her on a park bench with her talisman stowed in the backpack pocket normally reserved for a water bottle. Mom would have probably disapproved, but it was more inconspicuous than carrying him around like a favorite teddy bear.

Once she had verified that she was quite alone, she set the nutcracker on the bench next to her. There was no set phrase; he could come whenever invoked, but tradition seemed to mandate that she say something more formal than "Get over here, would you?"

"It would be my honor to meet with you, Prince."

It was something of a relief when he materialized, not in a puff of smoke or shimmering of light, but as an ordinary-looking pedestrian approaching from the nearest footpath.

"It would be my honor to meet with you, Lena," he said. "May I sit?"

"Of course."

As soon as she moved the nutcracker serving as a placeholder on the bench, he sat with unusual grace and let a broad smile unfurl on his lips.

"The kingdom sends its regards." He produced a box from the folds of his military-style jacket. "It also entrusted me with the latest delivery."

The box was nearly identical to the one that Anna had received, and the smell was just as enticing, but she felt a frown forming. "What *is* it with you and sugar plums?"

That drew a chuckle from him. "It is not by my choice," he assured her. "Your family has made many friends in my kingdom over the generations, but your great-grandmother caught the interest of a young nobleman. Though the courtship was unconventional, it was a delight to witness. I supported the union, but it was not my place to give my blessing. That belonged to one of my most trusted advisors."

Was he saying what she thought he was? That she had some sort of fairy blood? It had been more of a shock to discover that the family trinket was her personal bodyguard, but it still took a moment to decide if this was distressing news. As far as Lena knew, there hadn't been any ill effects, but she couldn't think of a single benefit she'd reaped. It didn't give them immortality or long life; Mom was proof of that.

Pushing that aside, she glanced back at the box clutched in her hands. "But that doesn't have anything to do with . . . "

"The nobleman's mother has been my right-hand fairy for many years, and her principality is known for its—"

"Sugar plums," was Lena's guess.

"Precisely." He nodded to the box. "When her son chose this world, she began sending these as a reminder of her love for your family."

No matter what the nobleman's choice, she was at least part fairy and that raised as many questions as it answered. Why she didn't have supernatural powers or a summer home in the fairy kingdom, for example. She remembered the man in question from her very early childhood, but other than the fact that he had lived to the age of ninety-eight, she couldn't think of any other remarkable things about him.

"Should I be sending something back?"

"That is not necessary."

She tried a sugar plum, since the previous package had stayed, untouched, in Anna's possession, and found the candy to be rich, but somehow insubstantial. Her preferred junk food was a Symphony bar, but she wouldn't turn up her nose at anything of this caliber.

"Do you like them?" he asked, with a twinge of apprehension in his voice.

It was doubtful that Hershey's had a factory anywhere in a fairytale kingdom. This would have to be something she enjoyed on principle, like her paternal grandmother's corn chowder.

"I can't say I have much experience," she said, "but I suppose they're not the only thing about our friendship that is an acquired taste."

As if consciously trying to put her on more familiar ground, he asked a very parental question next: "How was your return to school?"

She had gotten through the week by taking class notes on autopilot and politely declining social invitations. She had woken up crying every night and found that her roommate had sympathetically taken over all of her usual chores. Under other circumstances, she would have resented the babying, but it felt oddly comforting to be left in someone else's care.

"It's been hard," Lena said. "I'm not expecting much of myself for a few days, and my professors have discovered their ability to have flexible deadlines. I don't know how long either of those things will last, but it's a first step."

"As is our meeting," he responded. "I am sorry for your troubles and would like to propose a course of action."

He was a prince and probably used to being hearkened to without questions. Lena, however, wasn't his subject or beholden to him.

"You hardly know me and you want to tell me what to do?"

The question came out in a less challenging tone than she had intended, but at the implied offense, his grin faded somewhat. "You did call upon me. In light of your recent bereavement and current challenges, I would like to discuss how our encounters might be of service to you. Your compliance is strictly voluntary."

"All right." She waved a hand. "Propose away."

He glanced at the nutcracker still clutched in her lap, then met her gaze. "I understand that in your faith, ethical wills are often passed on."

His unexplained knowledge of a somewhat old-fashioned Jewish tradition was nearly as much of a surprise as the news of her fairy ancestry. "Y-y-yes," she stammered. "People hand down wisdom and philosophies that they have lived by in hopes that the next generation will learn from those things as well."

He nodded. "Your mother did not leave such a document, but she left you the emblem of our alliance," he said. "I believe she would desire for you to take advantage of the protection that I may be able to provide you. Her wisdom was in choosing the battles that felt most important. Perhaps you may consider if battling against your family legacy is as important to you as finding a way to have peace through your grief." He paused before continuing cautiously. "You might think it presumptuous, but I would like to be of service to you."

She still wasn't sure if she wanted any kind of long-term relationship with this man, but she was sure that she still needed to rely on her mother's advice.

"I suppose we could try that," she agreed. "Can I still reserve the right to call off the alliance?"

"That is your right," Prince said, "but I hope our meetings will not reinforce your desire to have nothing to do with me."

"I hope so, too," Lena said without hesitation this time.

They parted ways half an hour later, Lena tucking the nutcracker back into her bag while its counterpart retreated down the path. She glanced up in time to see a shadow detaching itself from a tree and falling into step with her new ally. A few paces later, another shadowy figure did the same, and by the time he rounded the bend, he was accompanied by six others.

Spies, she thought first. *Or maybe guards? Is he afraid of me or is this standard procedure for everyone?*

She immediately reached for the zipper pull again, intending to call him back and ask for an explanation. After a moment, she decided to provide him the chance to come clean and introduce her to his friends at the next opportunity.

His next visit was no different, though. He arrived by the same footpath and picked up his Fairy Secret Service or whatever they were at the end of their time together. He made no mention of it and for all she knew, he didn't think her able to see them.

On the third visit, however, she blocked his access to the bench as soon as he appeared. "Should I get some chairs for your friends?"

Prince didn't look surprised by her question, but frowned thoughtfully. "They would prefer to stay at their posts," he said. "It is prudent to establish a defensive perimeter at some distance."

"Defensive perimeter?" Lena echoed quietly.

"In case of an attack," he clarified.

"So, they really think I'm a threat to you?" She had a yellow belt in tae kwon do and a smart mouth, but this was a man who, according to the book and ballet, had led an army in defense of her ancestral home. His statement was laughable, but acting on that impression would be offensive.

"You?" This time he arched an eyebrow and cocked his head to one side. "Why would they think that?"

"You just said they're here in case of an attack."

"Yes," Prince said. "It is only natural for them to guard an ally of the kingdom, so they will keep an eye out for any adversaries."

Lena glanced at the usual positions of the guards, but they were still hidden from view. For all she knew, magic had a hand in that, but his disclosure of their purpose explained nothing about their presence.

"I don't get it," she admitted. "Why all the secrecy?"

"It was for your comfort." He inclined his head deferentially. "If you prefer, I can conceal them more effectively."

"But you won't ask them to leave?"

"No. There is every chance that they will be needed."

"But they weren't there at the house." She hadn't recognized every visitor, but she would have almost certainly noticed such furtive figures.

The prince went still for a moment. "At the house?"

"Yes, you know, at the house—where we met before. Is this campus really more dangerous than my hometown?"

Prince shook his head slowly. "The risks are the same," he said, "but you are correct that they were not at your house."

"Then why—"

"And nor was I."

That sentence cut all sound from the world for a moment. After a moment, her pulse began pounding in her ears and the wind picked up, but her mind remained blank.

"But you came," she protested. "You showed up and brought sugar plums. Anna can back me up on this."

His expression turned grave and his shoulders sank a few inches. "Let us sit down."

At the sound of words that almost always preceded disaster, the pounding of her heartbeat struck up a duet with a ringing in her ears. "As long as you promise to tell me the truth," she said.

"I always have spoken the truth to your family," he responded solemnly, "and I intend to continue to earn your trust."

No sooner had he sat than she felt the urge to be on the move. The only force that drove away the sudden fear was restlessness, and she paced the length of the bench four times before feeling settled enough to ask the next vital question.

"What do you mean, 'Nor was I'?"

"I mean," Prince said, "that you and I first met in this park. I have not entered your house since the days when your mother was alive, and I blame myself for that."

"I sat with you in my house," Lena blurted out. "Who was *that* if not you?"

"If my suspicions are correct, it was a sorcerer who changes his form as often as he changes his clothes," he answered.

If that was true, Lena couldn't be sure who she'd been meeting with; she had been duped at least once. Immediately, her mind stoked an ember of fear into a flame.

"If that wasn't you, how did he do such a convincing impression?" She hadn't met him before, but she hadn't been the imposter's only audience. "He had Anna convinced."

That earned her a somewhat apologetic frown. "I must hazard a guess, but it may be that it is partially my fault that he was able to do so. Your mother would have said he did his homework," Prince said. "He must have been watching and waiting for the right moment and with his long association with your household, he must have learned a great deal. When he lacked information, he could avoid giving a direct answer. The sorcerer who has long been my enemy was always very fond of half-truths."

Apparently, it was not time for her heartbeat to resume its normal pace. She couldn't fix generations of danger with a bit of healthy anger, but she *could* start doing damage control on her present circumstances and that required a greater understanding of her enemy.

"Does he ever take the form of Anna?" she demanded shrilly.

"As far as I know, he has never been able to assume the form of someone within your family," Prince murmured in a tone that might have been soothing under other circumstances, "but he apparently dared to take my form. No doubt he hoped you would prefer him to me once the truth was revealed."

"I don't prefer one of you over the other, but it seems I can't trust myself to know the difference."

He stood at attention then while she assumed a defensive stance. "If you can do no more than trust your mother's judgment, I will learn to be content with that," he said. "I, like my compatriots, only wish to provide you protection."

So far, he had been unable to do that by his own admission. The defensive perimeter was now like a fire extinguisher being aimed at a pile of ashes, but he still hadn't put the danger into words.

"Against what?"

"Against whom. I blame myself because he was once one of us and I thought him long dead. Had I not been so arrogant, he would have never contacted you or your aunt and he would have never been permitted to begin overpowering your household. I knew him as a dissident in my kingdom, but Marie knew him as the Mouse King."

Now that they knew the Mouse King had tried to approach Lena, the prince and his guards had all sorts of safety regulations. They began with "I will only visit when invited" and included "Do not let anyone cast a charm within your residence." Lena asked questions about the Mouse King's longevity and powers until she ran out of ideas, but began the next visit by challenging his impression that the King was a current danger to Lena herself.

"He has already found a way to insinuate himself into your life," Prince answered without hesitation, "and if he successfully enters into your existence, he will come to have control over your actions and perhaps, with time, even your thoughts."

"I wouldn't let that happen." She had trusted the imposter because there were no alternatives, but now she had enough reason to stay on alert. "I would know better."

"He would let you think so, but he is far from a novice at this kind of manipulation," Prince replied. "He did not attempt anything more than talking you into an alliance because you might have recognized anything more as a danger, but do not believe that he would be willing to stop at that. The only absolute safeguard is to cut off contact with him altogether."

They ended that visit by agreeing that Anna had to be told and the house had to be magically sealed off.

"It's for your protection," Prince said over dinner at the student union in October. "On the only known occasion that the Mouse King has come in contact with you, it has been on that property and by the invitation of someone in your family. He is already bound—"

"But he appeared as a mouse in the stories," Lena argued. "The book said he had seven heads."

"He had seven *faces*." The distinction made the prince grimace. "He could take seven forms."

"But he chose to be a mouse?"

"He was trapped in that form by the same spell that compelled me to appear as a nutcracker," he said. "Marie helped break that curse, but she also helped to unleash him."

"Glad you don't victim-shame," she deadpanned, setting down her fork.

"She was brave and loyal and succeeded in defeating him that night," he countered solemnly. "For that, I have honored your family for the long years since. She succeeded because his power was divided between directing his troops and dueling with me, and because I was foolish, I believed that the defeat was permanent." After a few heartbeats of silence, he continued speaking in a subdued tone. "I apologize for that lapse in judgment."

In her current mood, Lena neither acknowledged the apology nor pardoned him. "So, he has re-established his domain in my house. Why now?"

"Because the link between our worlds was made vulnerable at the time of your mother's passing," he explained. "I am unsure if this is the first time that he has attempted such a feat, but it succeeded this time and for that, I am guilty of negligence."

"You are." She pushed her plate away, appetite suddenly gone. "What does it mean for me? If I return home, will I be trapped?"

"You will be in danger, but not beyond my power," Prince said. "By agreeing to meet with me here, you fortified the alliance that was yours by birthright. You are under my protection wherever you go."

"Except you will not visit except by invitation," she reminded him. "That was part of the agreement."

"Unless I am coming to your defense." He didn't shrug, but he tilted his chin as if challenging her to disagree. "Peril will demand that I act."

"And how will we define that peril?" The Mouse King's original infraction of telling her borrowed stories from her mother's deployment was manipulation, but not much as far as threats went. "Will you be my Secret Service agent or annoying older brother?"

He was silent for a few moments of contemplation. "If you are in physical or magical danger, I will respond immediately," he said. "In other circumstances, I will come when invited. Is that all right?"

Lena nodded. "So, what has to be done to seal the house?"

He seemed to relax at her acquiescence, or at least his posture seemed less battle ready. "The first move would have been to remove from the house all physical ties to our kingdom," he said, "but Anna took the sugar plums and you brought the nutcracker with you, so that is done. I will take care of the binding spells and set watchers."

"Which means that if there's no physical tie allowed in the house, I'll be unable to go home?"

"Until we have found a permanent solution," he confirmed. "It is currently too dangerous."

"So, my family's legacy means exile?" Lena had felt more at home on campus for the last year, but her house was the last place that she associated with Mom, and that wasn't to be taken lightly. "Unacceptable."

"Unavoidable." Once again, he straightened his shoulders and leaned forward. It had taken less than a minute to erase the progress that had been implied in her accepting his help. "At the moment, you have no heir to pass this legacy to, and I have no wish for this to be the last generation of Hoffmans for me to protect."

"It seems to me that you haven't done much to protect *this* generation." She allowed herself to lean forward as if she were ready to charge him. "I'm not agreeing to banishment from my own home."

"I'm not asking you to forever, just temporarily." He held his stance for a minute longer before looking away and standing. "I will hold him at bay, but you must agree not to confront him without allowing me to put some defensive measures in place. You would be able to visit your home without being as much under his power as the house itself is."

That seemed more reasonable; keeping her out of the house would allow Prince to work without setting this many conditions, but he wouldn't keep her from still using home as one of her havens.

"All right," Lena agreed. "If Anna accepts this as well, what happens next?"

Lena knew beyond a shadow of a doubt that there would be consequences, whether in the form of increased protection or a proper lecture. She doubted if Prince would dare to put her under house arrest, but he would not be happy about her decision to break one of the fundamental rules. This wasn't picking a fight, though, just testing the water by crossing her own threshold for the first time in weeks. She'd resisted the urge to visit there in all this time, but the pull of home kept growing stronger until she decided she just had to go peek. It would be fine; the prince was far too quick to assume everything was dangerous. Nothing would go wrong, she kept telling herself until she almost felt convinced. And if the prince was angry at her for it, she even had a menorah to retrieve in case she needed an explanation for this errand.

Anna had insisted on coming along as backup or moral support, but Lena had firmly instructed her to stay in the car. If there was anything amiss, Anna would be more valuable as a getaway driver than as an escort. Anna was about as enthusiastic about being sidelined as she was about risking a visit to the house, but she eventually agreed that Lena should be allowed to put herself through this.

Before she could lose her nerve on her own doorstep, she jammed the key into the lock and twisted. She half-expected to find something visibly altered now that her family's old enemy had been in control of the premises, but other than the scent of slightly stale air, home was just as she remembered it. The only sounds were caused by the heater and fridge, and even her breath seemed inappropriately loud in such quiet. She nevertheless moved cautiously and left the hallway lights off, but turned on a lamp as soon as she reached the living room.

"I did not expect to see you here," the man she had first thought of as the prince commented from Mom's favorite armchair. "On the other hand, I should have known that you would come when I called to you."

Lena had been waiting for this ambush since she unlocked the front door, but it did not lessen the shock any. Her bookbag fell from her shoulder with a thud and she immediately gripped the edge of the table.

"I'm sorry." Her ersatz nutcracker chuckled, maintaining the ruse that he was the prince. "I wished to welcome you home without doing permanent damage to your peace of mind. It has been so long since we spoke."

If he was going to pretend, she would too. She crossed to the bookshelf and retrieved the menorah she would need for the holiday with relative calm, but when she finally spoke, she kept her voice steady and her smile fixed in place.

"I called for you," she admitted, "but when you did not come, I assumed that our bond was not strong enough to reach beyond these walls."

He stood and approached, reaching a hand towards her. Lena immediately turned and headed for the kitchen as if she had something to accomplish other than getting beyond his reach.

"It will change in time," he promised at her back as she casually got a glass of water. "This is a difficult time for you, and our bond is not as it should be. Perhaps while you are home, that will change."

Over your dead body, Lena thought, not trusting herself to look him in the eye.

"Perhaps," she echoed. "I will be back soon, and we will see how things go then."

For a moment, his expression darkened, but he almost immediately affected a mournful look as though disappointed in her. "I *had* hoped that this would be a friendship to be enjoyed on the holidays."

"I know," was the only thing she felt comfortable saying.

"It would pain your mother if you trusted me so little," he continued. "Perhaps, if you came here every time you were in need of my assistance, our bond would grow strong enough for me to answer your call whenever it occurred."

That was undoubtedly part of his end game and Lena couldn't say what that would accomplish, but she didn't want to know. He was a treacherous rat, but he was a treacherous rat in a very small cage and that was how she liked it.

She turned just before he would have laid hands on her and was able to back away. "As you said, it has been a difficult time."

"Then perhaps you should stay here after the semester resumes." He arched an eyebrow, inviting her into the discussion. "What better place to heal is there than home?"

"How about your kingdom?" She watched for any sign of suspicion or a hint of doubt, since this would seem like a huge step forward for someone who had resisted an alliance at first, but he was as flawlessly uncaring as ever. "If I have inherited your allegiance, I hope that I have earned the right to go there as my ancestors did."

"Once we are better friends, perhaps," he suggested. "My loyalty to you is not in question, but I am not sure that you would find yourself welcomed in my realm just yet."

She didn't know her mother's prince very well yet, but she knew that he would have never made her welcome conditional. He had already tried to manipulate her into cooperating and this most recent lie immediately set her teeth on edge. "I understand," she lied. She stepped around him to retrieve her bag and strode to the door. "We will speak more of this over the break."

"Why wait?" He had moved across the room with almost silent ease and blocked her access to the doorknob. "If we break down a few of the barriers between us, perhaps our friendship will not be confined to this house."

"I don't want to rush into this." It was a feeble lie that she suspected he wouldn't tolerate more than once. "I'll learn to trust you in time . . . "

"You have no reason to mistrust me."

Lena fell back a pace at his ingratiating smile, and he stepped forward, driving her farther from her escape route.

"Why not give me the benefit of the doubt?"

"Because I know."

The words were out of her mouth before she even thought to censor herself, and she clenched her jaw. The Mouse King leaned forward, encouraged by her discomfort, and it was a struggle to stand her ground.

"What, precisely, is it that you think you know?"

She had said too much, so she opted for a half-truth. "I know that things are not as simple as you're making them out to be," she said. "I don't know why that is, but I don't want to make any promises until everything's on the table."

His hand latched onto her upper arm with such speed that the air rushed from her lungs in surprise. His grip, which she had assumed would feel slimy, felt no more extraordinary than a friend's hand on her shoulder.

"If you truly *think* that, this is no time to put distance between us," he said in a rat's hiss. "It's for your safety as well as mine."

His touch wasn't forceful enough to hurt her arm, but a pressure behind her eyes caught her attention and flourished into a dull, throbbing pain. Time seemed to stand still as the pain became stronger and all the while, he stared intently at her as if measuring her ability to suffer.

"I have to go," she suddenly blurted out, wrenching her arm away. "I will . . . you and I will . . . "

She couldn't find a single thing to say in the end, but she managed to reach the door. The pain didn't fade as she put distance between herself and the house, and by the time she reached the car, it had been joined by a churning in her stomach. Anna immediately shifted gears and peeled away from the curb as if driving a getaway vehicle. Lena kept her gorge down, but just barely.

"What happened?" her aunt asked once they were outside the city limits.

"I almost told him." Shutting her eyes against the glare of sunlight helped, but the pain now pounded against the inside of her skull with each heartbeat. "I think he realizes something's wrong—"

"But he didn't tell you who he was?"

"No."

"And he didn't hurt you?"

He probably didn't even leave bruises, but she couldn't risk causing a panic by checking her arm for marks; the sudden headache was the clearest evidence that she had been subjected to gut-wrenching terror. "He didn't."

Anna's grip on the steering wheel relaxed slightly, but her voice remained tense. "Summon Prince."

"I think his watchmen will have tipped him off," Lena said.

"He promised to only come when summoned."

"Which means he'll probably exercise some kind of ultimate override on the family contract." She rubbed restlessly at her temples, more out of weariness than any belief that it would do some good. "I'll summon him as soon as I get home."

The headache began to subside by the time they returned to her apartment and Anna accompanied her back inside. True to his word, Prince had not invaded against her will. True to Lena's word, she summoned him immediately.

"You permitted him to touch you," he said without preamble. "There are still traces of his sorcery on you."

"Traces?" Anna squinted at her arm as if looking for some kind of neon marker. "Traces that he can use to come here now?"

"I think not." Prince handed over the sugar plums as an afterthought, as though the tribute were the last thing on his mind. "I recognize his power, but it is not strong enough for him to wield it from afar."

"Which is another reason against her going back." Anna folded her arms. "If she keeps her distance, he shouldn't be able to do anything, right?"

It was the first time that she had seen a glower on his face. He had too much respect for her mother to be angry with Lena in most situations, but he seemed to think that her breaking their agreement about the house was an extenuating circumstance.

"Correct." He looked as if he wanted to add more but clenched his jaw instead.

Lena appreciated the restraint in not belaboring the point, and Anna nodded in satisfaction.

"I will have to study how to best rid you of his influence, but I hope that you have satisfied whatever need drove you to contact him and that you recognize the danger."

The headache throbbed more emphatically at that moment, and Lena could only respond in a whisper. "I do."

Prince left, having given her a potion to help with sleep, but Lena awoke the next morning with a dull version of the previous night's headache. She doubted if painkillers would touch it, but she took some just in case. By the time she got out of classes, all that was left was a cramp in her neck.

It flared up three days later without explanation or warning, but only lasted an hour. The following day, with no exams to take or essays to hand in, she left the lights off and only awoke when her phone buzzed with an incoming text alert.

Anna had only written two words: *Summon him.*

Her alarm clock claimed it was just after midnight, so she responded, *I will in the morning. Want to tell me why?*

Summon him now. Anna was almost certainly glowering at the phone and it wasn't like her to answer this quickly late at night. *I'm on my way so we can talk about what you've been up to.*

After shooting off a quick reply, Lena stretched muscles that felt as stiff as if she'd been holding still for a full week. Her stomach cramped in protest of her long day in bed, and she headed for the kitchen. She wasn't about to dress up for the conference, but no one would fault her for bringing a bowl of cereal.

The stench of spoiled food hit her as soon as she opened the fridge. The jug of milk was distended, and its contents were beginning to separate. The leftover chicken from Sunday dinner was looking slimy instead of marinated, and a slight fuzz of mold was creeping along the corner of a half-eaten sandwich she'd made for lunch. None of this should have been possible—the fridge was in perfect working order and they had not lost electricity. None of the food should've spoiled . . . unless something more sinister was at play. Even more puzzling, Laurie's food looked like it had been there less than a day.

From the force of the knock on the door, she guessed that Anna had arrived first. Lena shut the fridge door tightly and answered her insistent pounding empty-handed.

"You're going to wake Laurie up."

Anna stepped aside to let Prince past, and he entered with all the caution of someone expecting to find an active shooter around the corner. "Please leave," he said.

As much as she disliked having male visitors after curfew, Lena suspected Laurie would have an even stronger reaction to finding herself alone except for an intruder.

"No way. If you're coming in, I'm staying here."

"I'll stay inside with him," Anna said, "but Lena, we have to check something, and you shouldn't be there for it. Here." She grabbed Lena's jacket from the coat rack and thrust it into Lena's hands.

Lena pulled the proffered jacket over her shoulders as they shut the door, but she didn't have long to wait before they emerged.

"It's safe to go in." Prince's voice was low and reassuring.

"Are you sure?" She glanced towards the kitchen. "I think the Mouse King has done something to the food."

Neither of them looked surprised by such an absurd statement, but Anna reached out to draw her into a quick embrace. "It's not the food," she said. "It's the time."

Lena pulled away and powered up her phone's display. It was still the middle of the night, but her eye caught the date.

"That can't be right."

"How's your headache?"

She honestly hadn't thought about it since the text had woken her up. "Better," Lena said cautiously. "But what do you mean the *time?*"

"What do you remember of the last ten days?"

"Midterms, a paper, lots of homework . . . " She shook her head. "Five days ago, I went home. I took yesterday as a sick day."

"Any lucid dreams?"

At Anna's query, she vaguely remembered a recurring one in which she attempted to reach out to the prince but couldn't get a response. The dream had been terrifying, but it was probably nothing more than a byproduct of the fear she'd felt in her own home.

"Well, maybe a few," she said, "but nothing important stands out."

Anna turned to stare at Prince, as though daring him to act. His head had bowed when she mentioned going home, and for the first time since she'd met him, he seemed to slump.

"With your permission, I'd like to see one of these dreams."

The request seemed odd, but nothing raised an alarm in her mind. Her lie that she remembered nothing important had been a white one and he wouldn't find anything incriminating.

"How?"

While the Mouse King had seized her upper arm, Prince took hold of her wrist where he could feel her pulse. Darkness nibbled at the edges of her vision, but a memory of the dream returned. She watched with detached interest as she futilely demanded that he come to her aid.

"What? Am I that easy to abandon?"

She felt a momentary flash of hot shame at seeming so needy, but in the same way she couldn't blame the prince for not responding to her dreams, she could not think of this as a real interaction. Where the dream normally ended, however, some other memory unfurled. She recognized classrooms and the quad by the sciences building, but the scenes that played out were as unfamiliar as images on a surveillance camera.

"Stop."

He obeyed at once and she was left feeling as shaken as if she had just been violently ill.

"That wasn't me," Lena blurted out. "I've never seen anything but that first part before."

"That's what I thought," Anna said, looking just as unnerved as Lena by what she had not witnessed. "Your calendar isn't wrong."

This time, it took bracing her elbows on her knees and hanging her head to make the dizziness and nausea subside.

"How?"

"His magic left traces that I thought were an attempt to establish control over this household as well. I did not realize that the power was just enough to have a foothold in your mind."

"So, I'm possessed?" She choked back bile and clamped her jaw shut, but a moan escaped. No one responded, but Anna took hold of her hand. The dizziness subsided, but the unease didn't. The only thing that could be done was to start looking for solutions and hope that had been the worst of the news. That wasn't much, but action made her feel like less of a prisoner and she attempted to look resolute when she finally straightened her spine and shoulders and looked to Prince. "You said he had a foothold."

"A foothold, not control," the prince clarified, still keeping a solicitous eye on her.

"Which is why Laurie didn't bring it up?"

"Laurie said on Facebook that she was feeling lonely while her roommate was sleeping off the flu, but I don't know if the illness is what the Mouse King told her or if she just made an educated guess," Anna answered. "I also found a passive-aggressive note about cleaning out the fridge, but she's not the one in danger and he's only been messing with you."

Prince nodded in agreement. "It took him a few days to gain this much control, which is likely the source of those pains that you have been experiencing, but he has been holding you hostage for the last ten days."

She nearly swore, but the urgency of Anna's texts was finally clear. "Ten days. And this is the first time I've come back to myself?"

"You were always there," Prince said gravely, "but you have not been yourself."

"He *invaded* me," Lena said after another long moment of horrified contemplation. "I let him stay in that house and I let him *invade*."

"He would say he's a marauder," Prince said, "but we call him a plunderer. An enemy wants to conquer, but a plunderer wants to leave nothing but destruction in his wake. Nothing less would satisfy him."

This time, she bolted to the bathroom, but she hadn't eaten recently enough to bring anything up. The dry heaves turned into gasping for air. Once those had passed, she reached a claw-like hand out to turn the water on and noticed that her arm seemed suddenly shrunken and frail. Of course, if she hadn't eaten properly in ten days, she probably *had* started to waste away.

Anna's knock was timid this time and it took Lena several moments to compose herself enough to open the door. Her aunt guided her back to the living room, but no one spoke until Lena was seated and provided with a glass of water.

"He has a foothold because he was able to enter your mind once he had touched it with his powers," Prince said at last. "What he wants is to drive you out entirely, but you have resisted him too well. You have been resisting and it is because of this that he has had to settle for invasion tactics."

"Stop talking about me as if I'm Belgium!" The water slopped over the edge of the glass as her hand shook. "I'm not something to be overrun."

"You're not," Anna said, "but if he's an invader, there's a good thing about that."

"Which is?"

Anna and Prince wore identical looks of resolve, but it was her ally, not her aunt, who answered. "Invaders can be driven out."

The rules and regulations for her safety didn't change, but by the following morning, Prince had placed additional wards around her. She didn't ask what they were, but something about his efforts cleared some of the fog from her brain, and time proceeded at a normal pace.

She panicked a few days later when she lost track of five hours, but Prince responded to her summons and assured her that it had been the enemy at the sentry line, not marching through the avenues of her mind. She only sounded the alarm when the lucid dreams returned for two nights in a row and he returned to reinforce whatever spells he had placed on her apartment. There was, he said, not much else he could do without spiriting her away for a few days.

"You're really a masochist," Laurie commented one Thursday in late November. "No one in their right mind would spend Thanksgiving break on campus when they were in driving distance of home."

It wasn't the first time Lena's roommate had made this argument, but this was her last-ditch effort to save Lena's long weekend.

"My aunt will be here." Lena reiterated her usual explanation. "And I'm in driving distance of an empty house. It's not the home I'm looking for right now."

"You're still welcome to brave my family."

"Not while Anna's here." She flashed a grateful smile across the living room so Laurie would know the offer was still appreciated. "It's my first major holiday without Mom, and I think it'll be good to keep things low key."

In previous versions of this conversation, she had spoken about getting a head start on end-of-term papers and studying for finals. Anna had been the one to insist on bringing dinner for two Hoffmans and a prince, should he decide to join them.

Laurie had even offered to stay behind at one point, but Lena had encouraged her to enjoy home comforts and let someone else do her laundry.

These were all cheerful fronts for the fact that she was currently in danger even far from her childhood home, but Laurie didn't need to know that. It didn't keep her from committing Lena to calling her if she felt at all in need of rescuing.

"If we burn the turkey and get sick of each other, you'll be the first one to know," Lena promised.

Anna arrived four hours later, just after Lena had conquered one of her assignments for the break. Lena hadn't exactly lied about needing to get work done, but this was going to be an unpredictable weekend and she wanted as much out of the way as possible. Anna set down two duffels before giving Lena a hug, but there were several things conspicuously absent from what she unpacked from the car.

"No food?"

"Prince promised to take care of such things," Anna explained. "I thought you'd have summoned him by now."

"Not until you got here," Lena said. "This is supposed to be family time, and you're not missing out on a single moment of it."

Anna's smile was slightly nervous, as if she were remembering their last "family time" at home. Before she could pose a tactful question, Lena added, "I'm on better terms with the true prince."

"Then we should go ahead and invite him over," her aunt suggested, heading for the side table where the nutcracker was standing guard. "If you will do the honors . . . "

On their first meeting, Anna had tried playing the role of peacekeeper, but that had been before the revelation that they had been ensorcelled in the process of welcoming an old friend back into the fold. She had not, as far as Lena knew, taken Prince to task for the oversight, but it had not escaped Lena's notice that Anna refused to greet the family friend with anything more than a tight-lipped smile at the door. So, the fact that she was now suggesting his presence meant that she too was on better terms with him again.

Prince rang the doorbell less than a minute later and presented Anna with a particularly large box of sugar plums before accepting Lena's invitation to enter.

"I apologize for coming with so little," he said by way of greeting, "but we will not be staying here long."

"You would have told us if it was safe to go home again," Anna commented. "Since Lena's planning to host here, just where are we going?"

"My home." His clear, blue-eyed gaze slid from Anna to Lena. "If that's all right."

"Will we be staying there long?"

"Only as long as you like," he assured her. "If you would like to bring your textbooks, you may, but we are not technologically equipped for anything more advanced than that."

"I'm not asking if you have wi-fi," Lena said as calmly as possible. "I'm asking if you mean to have us over for dinner or if you are taking us into protective custody."

"We wish to look after your happiness on this holiday," Prince said, "but the other matter *will* come up."

"Good," Anna said. "I'm pretty sure we'll both forgive you in time for that, but we're a long way from forgetting."

The comment brought the conversation to a standstill. It wasn't exactly an ultimatum, but it was something for which neither party was likely to apologize.

"What do I need?" Lena changed the subject.

"Whatever you like," he said. "We are at *your* service. If you do not wish to pack a change of clothing, we can accommodate your needs."

"Then I'll be just a few minutes."

He nodded. "I'll return when summoned."

They were ready to leave ten minutes later, once Lena had packed pajamas, underwear, a dress, two pairs of jeans, and three t-shirts into her backpack next to the Norton anthology that she would need for her British Literature paper and her notes for Biology.

On this momentous occasion of visiting the kingdom for the first time, she had wanted to upbraid a few "allies" for letting the Mouse King's plots go on under Prince's nose, but the state of siege was the more pressing concern and all she wanted to demand was help in breaking free.

"Are you ready for a plan of attack?" Anna asked while they were still able to speak privately.

"No." Magical blood or not, this wasn't something she could tackle on her own. That didn't mean she hadn't contemplated everything from throwing a ballet shoe if she ran into the false prince to looking up black magic on the internet, but she was no warrior and she was most likely in over her head. "But I'm ready to ask for help, forcefully if necessary."

Prince always responded to an apartment-based summons by ringing the doorbell and less than a minute after Lena had invoked that right, it chimed. An aristocratic-looking woman in a lavender dress stood at the threshold, and she bore enough of a resemblance to Mom for her identity to be obvious. The part of Lena that still waited for an intuitive connection scoured her memory for times this woman had made an appearance, but not even one came to mind. There was no need for clarification, though. Not given the means of arrival.

"You are my escort," Lena guessed. "Thank you for sending the sugar plums."

Her great-great-grandmother smiled and handed over another box, which resembled the one that Prince had brought earlier, but it seemed to glow softly in the afternoon light. The prince ruled the kingdom, but he had only been a courier to Lena, and the gift directly from its source reflected something of her magic.

Lena had never gone on a magical, mystical adventure before, but she stashed her keys in a purse and donned a coat in case the ambient temperature of a fairy tale kingdom involved inclement weather.

She returned to find Anna asking about how often their families had actually crossed paths. It was an odd kind of small talk, but genealogically, it was probably no stranger than "So, you from around here?" Lena decided to ask a more pressing question before they set out.

"I know who you are," she said once the conversation had come to a polite pause, "but I don't know what you'd like to be called. Prince calls you his right-hand fairy, the stories say you're the Sugar Plum Fairy. I've never had a conversation with a great-great-grandmother before."

The woman had looked somewhat wistful during her discussion of what nineteenth-century Germany had been like, but she smiled affectionately at this question. "I thank you for thinking of such things. Most call me Lady Sakharnaya of the Sliva Groves, but I see nothing wrong with you calling me Great-Great-Grandmother. And you?"

"Lena will be fine," she responded.

"Anna is the only name I'll answer to," her aunt answered. "It's a pleasure to meet you at last, Great-Grandmother."

Lena hadn't meant to sound so formal, but it had allowed them to speak as equals while they were still learning to see each other as family.

"What should I expect?" she asked once they had left the building.

"Dear child," the fairy said with a sigh, "that is the question of many of our kind as well. We know your family of old, but we expect you to be your own person and I, for one, am quite excited to discover what that entails."

Lena couldn't be sure that the fairy would still say so once she had heard her demands, but for now, she could agree that this journey was a risk worth taking.

This opinion was only strengthened when they reached the forest between worlds. Something indefinable had suddenly changed.

"I've been wondering if I'd be able to tell a difference when we crossed over," Lena admitted, "but this looks like Washington state, not a wonderland."

Great-great-grandmother had likely never been to the Pacific Northwest, but she smiled at the observation. "Our world is not as strange as you might imagine, and over long years of association, the flora and fauna of your world have occasionally come to ours. Some are merely the last of species you no longer know. Others have evolved after many years in such a magically powerful place."

"So the trees might talk or we'll play with dodos after dinner?" Anna asked.

Their escort did not answer immediately, but peered beneath one of the trees that stood sentinel along the path to a new world. After a minute, she plucked a black feather that had caught on a branch. "I often see birds in this part of the forest, and this was left by a visitor from your world. I have been told by my emissaries that they are called Labrador ducks."

"Which went extinct over a century ago, if I remember right." Anna was no ornithologist, but she loved a good museum. "Could they be brought back?"

"Only if that is their wish. It is a rare thing for us to turn anyone away, and they have been happy here. But that," she said to Lena, "is not what you meant by 'a difference,' is it?"

"No." She wasn't entirely sure how to articulate the sensation at first, so she put it in plain terms. "I feel a different kind of power, even in the forest. I can't imagine what the kingdom will be like."

The magic that Prince had brought to bear on her underfurnished and overpriced student apartment had given her reprieve from the headaches and allowed her to have some distance from the malevolent powers of the Mouse King. Escaping her world, however, felt like being allowed into a ballroom after weeks of being trapped in a closet.

"You cannot be touched by that sorcery here," Great-great-grandmother said as if she had spoken the thought out loud. "This is part of your ancestral homeland and it protects you. While you are here, we will decide once and for all how you may claim that power in your own world."

The Hoffman family had never been very gregarious. They visited each other but never felt the need to have elaborate family reunions or fifty-cousin Seders. It was, therefore, a bit overwhelming to be immediately treated as a long-lost sister by everyone she met in the fairy kingdom. A few of the flower fairies insisted that she wear a wreath like theirs and every actual blood relation claimed that she bore a strong resemblance to her great-great-great-aunt because of the family nose. Those who were around her age weren't the sort of cousins who would hug without permission, but they appointed themselves as her entourage, and Lena didn't protest.

Thanksgiving at the palace was beyond description. Lena's favorite dishes were served on plates of gold and eaten with silver utensils. Musicians played melodies that swirled like snowflakes in the background, while emissaries from every province of the kingdom paid their respects with stories of her family. It was a bit like sitting Shiva within a carnival, but every passing moment made it more difficult to remember the mortal peril that came along with her tie to this mesmerizing place.

Once the last plate had been cleared and the guests departed, however, they were left with the ruling council of a kingdom and two women rendered exiles from their family home by the kingdom's negligence. The servants and guests departed and the shift from gathering of friends to council of war was unstated, but unmistakable. Introductions had been made during the feast and it now was not only permitted, but mandated, that they turn their discussions to what had brought the Hoffmans so far from home.

"We have asked much of you in agreeing to the terms of our protection," Prince said. "In the past, this alliance has been a straightforward thing. You have recently been gracious with your allegiance and generous with your trust. What do you wish in return?"

The nutcracker had passed to Lena, which meant the answer was her responsibility, but she yielded to Anna with a nod and allowed the other Hoffman to speak with the confidence of someone who had overcome every temptation to change her mind.

"The Mouse King committed crimes against my family without your interference," she stated. "It is my right to demand that you make amends for that, if not to me, then to Rebekah's heir."

"You are a guest and an ally," Salam of the coffee-growers scoffed. Looking at him, and at the other counselors, it was like watching the childhood ballet come to life. It was so distracting she could hardly focus on his words. "It is not your place to *demand*."

"I disagree," Prince said.

Mother Gigogne, whom the prince had described as a compromiser and who did *not*, as far as Lena knew, have a troupe of clowns hidden under a giant skirt, nodded towards Salam. "Had she a seat on this council, she could command an army or demand our aid," she said. "Since she is under our protection, I believe she is merely entitled to defense."

"I disagree," Anna and Prince chorused. At his inviting look, Anna added, "We should be entitled to acts of restitution and that *must* include eradication of threats originating in your kingdom."

"But *is* he of our kingdom?" Soledad of the chocolate-producers asked. "He has been in exile for over a century—"

"But kept alive by drawing on this land's power," Prince concluded. "When he was near death, he survived because Marie's alliance with us tied her world to ours."

"Then he will continue to live as long as that alliance does," Anna concluded.

"But he could be bound," Great-great-grandmother proposed.

"We have attempted that in the past and failed," the prince said. "I concur with the Hoffmans that it is our duty to defeat him as we should have done in the days when Herr Drosselmeier doted on young Marie Stahlbaum."

"Is it possible?" Lena's question left silence in its wake, but was meant for the prince, not his waffling counselors. She kept her gaze on him alone, and he held hers until he was prepared to give his answer.

"If we sever his tie to this kingdom, he will be nothing more than a man," he said. "He will be as mortal as any other."

"But it would require you, Lena, to renounce your claim on this kingdom," Great-great-grandmother added quietly. "I understand that you have no reason to be loyal to us, but that is not a decision to be taken lightly. It would protect you from that sorcerer, but we could not intervene if you came under attack by another."

It was unfair to say so when she had been fed and fawned over so well, but the homesick anger that she had brought with her had a place here as well. "Would it mean that I renounce my family's ties to this kingdom forever or just for this generation?"

"You would be cut off while he lives," Prince said honestly, "and I am unsure of how long it would take for us to re-forge the link between our worlds. It may be within your lifetime or in a future century."

"But it would allow him to be defeated now," Lena said, "and we would be freed from his sorcery."

"If all goes according to plan, yes," he answered. "If you would like some time to consider . . . "

"I accept those terms," she interrupted.

In this place where joy and camaraderie had been on hand since her arrival, it was startling to see tears on the face of a few people. Anna was among their number, but she did not speak in opposition.

"It is more important to protect my family than anything else," Lena explained. "I am willing to sacrifice the happiness I have

felt here tonight if it means that the danger we now face will be
eradicated."

"Your mother's daughter," her great-great-grandmother whispered.

She wasn't really sure she was following in her mother's footsteps in this decision. She did, however, feel that she bore at least
one resemblance to Rebekah Hoffman. "I am no warrior, but I
hope I learned some of my bravery from her."

Anna's fingers wound through hers, and they waited for a response hand in hand. None of the counselors gave further input,
but every set of eyes was on Prince. By the time he spoke again,
his words carried the weight of a decree.

"In the name of your family's loyalty, it shall be as you wish."

Laurie returned from Thanksgiving break to find leftovers in
the fridge and Lena in apparently good spirits. She didn't seem
bothered when Lena had little excitement to report, but she also
hadn't been made privy to any of the powers and plans that were
centered around this two-bedroom apartment. She *did* comment
that Lena should have gotten more rest on her days off, but left
her alone after that.

Prince and his council had set a date for one week from her return to her own world. It seemed sufficient time to eradicate any
immediate threats that might interfere with the ritual and would
give Lena time to reconsider if she felt so inclined.

By the time the hour arrived, however, Lena was feeling as
restless as an outnumbered soldier anticipating some kind of ambush. She had been assured that she was anything but outnumbered, but there was no guarantee that this would go as anticipat-
ed, and her appetite disappeared entirely, though it was a case of
nerves and not sorcerous compulsion that kept her underfed this
time.

Anna was the one to answer the doorbell a minute after the summoning, and she entered the bedroom with Prince in tow. In addition to the usual sugar plums, he carried a silver knife, a small sack, and a tightly furled flag of some kind.

"You left nothing behind you in my realm?" he asked without preamble. Lena shook her head. "Then we may proceed."

They went to the bench where they had first met, but this time, Prince walked by her side instead of materializing out of thin air. They had first become allies there and it seemed only appropriate to do all important rites in the same location. The sack, when upended onto the lawn, contained soil and nothing more. Prince handed over the flag with the same ceremony that usually attended a military funeral. Perhaps the analogy was not inappropriate.

"In order to renounce your link to my kingdom, you must swear a blood allegiance to this world," he stated once the knife was laid between them. "It will not require much blood, but the power of the spell lies in your loyalty to one world before the other."

As her loyalty to his domain had been tenuous at best, she felt no real need to retain the connection. It did cause a pang to think that she was denying one of Mom's final wishes, but she was certain that Mom, of all people, would understand this being a matter of life and death. She looked away from the knife and tried to not think of how much blood he would need. Her gaze fell instead on the white flag with a golden rose at its center, which she had only seen flying on the ramparts of his castle.

"Why did you bring your flag? I'm not swearing loyalty to your kingdom."

"No . . . " He avoided her gaze. "But it is an important token for me." He shook his head and returned to the previous subject. "Are you ready to give your loyalty solely to your world?"

"All of my loyalty is to those here," Lena answered, "so it might as well be official. How do I do that?"

He was silent for a long moment before picking up the knife. "How do *we* do it? I have placed the kingdom in the hands of the counselors so that when I swear my loyalty to this world, the kingdom will not be left without a leader."

It took a moment for his words to dawn on her, but suddenly they did. *"What?"*

Before she could ask for further explanation, he sliced a thin line across his palm and pressed the wound against the small mound of earth. "By my life, by my being, by the beat of my heart, I will defend this world and those in it."

"What did you do?" Lena shrieked.

"Lena," Anna interjected, "you asked for the bond to be severed."

"My bond," she shouted. At a loss for anything else to do, she swept her hand across the mound of dirt, but she had no power of her own to cancel the vow. "I said nothing about cutting him off from his home!"

"It is the only way to ensure that the tie is severed," Prince said, extending the knife to her. "You must do the same."

"You have to take it back," she demanded.

"It is done." Blood oozed from his palm and color drained from his face. "Will you not swear the same allegiance to the world you are so eager to protect?"

His grand gesture was so unexpected and absolute that she still had not thought through any alternative options. There was no guarantee that, if she refused to complete the rite, it would invalidate this contract. He was here as leader and expert and there was no path to take but the one that led forward. She made an identical cut on her palm, but the tears that followed had nothing to do with the pain. They made no sense when she was severing a bond that she had barely discovered. The tears were for no one but the prince who had just sent himself into exile for her sake.

"By my life, by my being, by the beat of my heart, I will defend this world and those in it." She wept. "That now includes you." She pressed her hand into the soil.

He customarily reserved physical touch for greetings and goodbyes, but he gathered her into the kind of embrace that only family shared. "It includes both of us," he reminded her.

PART 3: SHNEIM ASAR CHODESH

P rince left for parts unknown looking like an ordinary man, and Lena could only think of what he had said in a council of war in a fairy tale kingdom: *The Mouse King will be as mortal as any other.* There was no mention of Prince getting a job or crashing on Anna's couch until he could pay rent. They agreed not to discuss the rest of their lives until the crisis came to an end, but she had to wonder if he had given thought to what would happen after the war. For all she knew, he didn't plan to survive that long.

Anna spent the next two nights at Lena's place curled next to Lena in bed; neither of them needed to say that they felt the need to stick together at this moment. The initial pain faded only slightly at first, but on the third day, they visited the empty house. No prince, ersatz or otherwise, paid them a visit, and the summoning yielded no results. They took it as a sign that either the prince's obligation to her had been severed or, worse, he was not alive to receive the summons. There was no sign of struggle in the house, but the magical equivalent of radio silence was ominous.

There was nothing left to do but try to move on with the life that had been interrupted by her own fairy tale. Two days before the semester resumed, Lena returned a few of her things to the house as a first step in reclaiming her home. She did a load of laundry and ate pizza there, as those seemed the most domestic ways to reclaim her homeland, but she made sure to set the nutcracker back in his rightful place on the mantel. Whether there was any power in it or not, it was undeniably the home's protector.

She still waited for some sign that all had not been lost on that night, but life went on without him as it had while her mother had been alive. She tried valiantly not to mind that, but the scar on her palm served as a reminder of her own guilt.

Life plodded on at times, but the normalcy of it became a source of comfort and reassurance. Months passed, college continued. There were days when she could laugh at things without putting them into the context of grief, and there were days when she couldn't face the prospect of leaving the sanctuary of her room. Slowly the pleasant days began to outweigh the painful ones.

September 3rd was to be a special occasion. She had survived shneim asar chodesh; the year of mourning rituals was behind her, and she had returned home for the installation of her mother's headstone, but the anniversary also meant meeting with Anna and a few others to remember what Platoon Sergeant Rebekah Hoffman had taught all of them. While the crowd at the funeral had overwhelmed Lena, the small group at this memorial was a kind of tight-knit family. They spent the afternoon together recounting the life lessons and tongue-in-cheek moments of wisdom that would have comprised Rebekah's ethical will.

Lena had hoped to see a familiar man with clear blue eyes and a military bearing there, but she had no such luck. Yet it was on that day that a box of sugar plums was left on her bedside table, and though she had sworn by her blood to have no dealings with the magical, she welcomed its unmistakable glow.

BREADCRUMBS

Jeanna Mason Stay

Every day was much the same for Gretel. She awoke, suddenly, to a piercing scream echoing through her nightmares, accompanied by the smell of gingerbread. She startled from bed, her heart pounding. She told herself that it was just a dream, but that was a lie.

To push the memories from her mind, she rose, headed down the narrow stairway into the kitchen, and began her day's work. She cooked porridge for breakfast over a little stove, made up frybreads in a pot. The oven stood neglected, used only when absolutely necessary; Gretel had no taste for baking and ovens.

She worked until the rest of the household awoke. Her father always came downstairs next, already fully dressed, ready to slip out and away as soon as possible. It had been over five years since her stepmother's death, since Gretel and Hansel had returned from the forest, but her father was still the tiny man he'd been then.

Gretel often wondered if it was the memory of his guilt that kept him from looking her in the eye when he mumbled his "Good morning" and scurried to work. Had that one small choice—his choice to abandon his children—shaped everyone and everything in Gretel's life?

When Hansel came down from his bedroom, though, she doubted it. "Hello, dear sister," he'd say jubilantly, planting a quick peck on her cheek. "I think I shall go out today to try to bag a stag." Or maybe, "I'm off to spear a deer." When he'd laugh at his own rhyme, Gretel couldn't help but laugh with him. Hansel was what he had always been—funny and likable and full of plans. He spent his days hunting and making friends in the nearest town and doing who knew what else. The terror of those days in the gingerbread house in the forest hadn't cast their shadow on him.

Maybe if his had been the hands that pushed. Maybe then he would still hear the witch's screams in his nightmares.

Gretel would stir whatever she was preparing on the stove that day, whisking the sounds out of her brain. Hansel would grab some frybreads from the table and head out the door into the forest. She wondered how he could do that, walk into the woods so nonchalantly. But she noticed he never headed the direction they'd taken that day so long ago, and he always followed the signs he had cut into the trees. Notches in wood don't disappear like breadcrumbs.

With the men gone, Gretel would be mercifully alone again. She did not go into town often, as they did. The townsfolk all knew her family—they had even known her stepmother—but no one knew what had happened those months when Gretel and Hansel had disappeared. Since no one knew the truth of her family's story, they could not know the truth of her. And because they did not know her truth, everything felt like a lie.

Her housework, on the other hand, was dependable, understood. She swept, sewed, gathered vegetables from their little garden plot. Quiet, peaceful work she could relax into. Each activity was automatic, her hands and fingers going through the motions she'd set for them and repeated daily through the years. That way she could set her mind adrift, floating on a sea of soothing nothingness until the men came home at night and she was wrenched back into the world.

It had been five years. Surely life should have gotten better by now. And some days it was. Some days the supper conversation was gentle, or laughing, or loving, full of the events of the day and thoughts of the future—but then she would remember.

She remembered the blankness in their father's eyes when he and their stepmother took them into the woods to die. She remembered how he wouldn't lift a hand to save his own children. She remembered the fear when she and Hansel knew they were lost, how their breadcrumb path had been eaten away by birds they hadn't thought to plan for. The hope when they saw the gingerbread cottage in the forest. How that hope turned to horror, days and nights and weeks and months of it, ending in the final horror of the witch's burning flesh.

Remembering, she would rise from the table, politely excuse herself to her room, and scream her rage and despair into her pillow.

Such was every day for Gretel, an endless round of remembering and forgetting and restlessness and stillness.

She couldn't say exactly when she decided to leave. It was like baking—there was no single moment when a loaf went from dough to bread, it was simply a process of time and heat. Maybe it was watching her father slink off to work every day, never meeting her eyes, yet never seeking forgiveness. Maybe it was the way Hansel laughed when she shuddered suddenly as the oven door caught her gaze. Maybe it was the slow-burning realization that they could all easily spend the next ten years together as they had spent the last five, nothing changing. She was nearly seventeen now; most of the girls in town were betrothed or married, heading out to new lives and worlds. They were not her friends, and she did not envy them, but maybe a seed of change had come free, floated away on the breeze, and settled in her soul.

Whatever the reason, Gretel lay awake in bed late one night, staring at the rafters, realizing she could not stay in this place another day. She'd been waiting for something to magically change, as it always did in the fairy tales from her childhood. She could barely remember those tales from when her real mother was still alive, filling her head with stories of wonder and filling her heart with love. Planting dreams of happy endings.

But real life wasn't that way. Yes, there were the villains—she'd met them, after all—but no fairy godmother was ever going to appear just because Gretel was good and kind and hardworking. No djinn would emerge from a bottle and offer her heart's desire. And maybe that was because she too was a villain, because she had blood and ashes on her hands, but she didn't care anymore. If change wouldn't come by itself, she would bring the change.

She woke the next morning to a scream in her mind. She curled in on herself, for a moment sucked into the darkness of reliving that sound. It's over now, she remembered, and she opened her eyes to look around her bedroom and smooth her hands across her worn coverlet, reminding herself where she was. And where she would never be again. She brushed away hot tears. She would not let those memories conquer her any longer. She rose from bed and went through the usual morning routines, but her heart pounded with a new sensation, a precarious sort of excitement.

After the men had left for the day, she picked up the knapsack she'd already packed, placed a dagger in its sheath around her waist, left a note of farewell for Hansel and her father, and headed for the door.

She pushed it open and gazed out into the woods.

Don't think, just go.

But where? She rarely traveled and never alone. She didn't know where to go, though a tiny, insistent voice inside told her that no matter where she went, there was one place she must return to before she could start anew.

If she followed the path from her home, she would arrive in town and eventually at the carpenter's shop where her father worked. She could tell him goodbye. She doubted he would stop her, but if she went that way, she feared she might stop herself. If instead she turned left, stepping off the path, she would head in the direction of the gingerbread house. If she turned right, every step would take her farther away from it.

Fear told her to take any path but toward that little house, but the voice inside spoke louder. What good was it to leave behind one nightmare only to take another with you? She took a deep breath and turned left. She did not look back. She would not be dropping breadcrumbs this time.

Gretel walked a steady pace now across the soft sponge of the mossy forest floor. She breathed in the crisp air of the forest. The sun was high overhead, but the ground was still cool in the dappled shadows of the leaves. The woods did not frighten in reality as they had in her memory; the trees were still large, but they didn't loom.

Even knowing where she was headed did not fill her with the terror she'd expected. It was as if, with every step away from her old life, something new rose within her, something green and growing and fragile, easily crushed but straining into life.

An hour passed, then two and three, and Gretel began to finally feel an uneasy sense of familiarity. It came with the breeze, and at first she didn't recognize its scent. But then it wafted past again, and she knew it: the tang of molasses and ginger. Her steps slowed as the tension she'd been releasing returned in full, filling her stomach with nausea. For the first time she looked back, *away*. It wasn't too late to turn another direction.

She stopped and took a deeper breath, letting the scent fill her nose and her lungs, clinging to a nearby tree trunk to keep herself from running. She closed her eyes, waiting for the terror to lull, then pushed forward. Only another minute passed before she saw her living nightmare at a distance through the trees.

In a small clearing stood the little brown house. White icing in cheerful scallops ran around the windows, under the eaves, across every shingle of the pitched roof. Around the foot of the walls brightly colored gumdrops, red, yellow, green, blue, sat in neat rows like a sweet, sticky garden. The windows were delicately tinted poured sugar, sheets so thin she knew they let light into the house yet still strong enough to keep out the wind. The walls, of course, were gingerbread. The whole cottage seemed perfectly preserved, exactly as she had last seen it those years ago.

Gretel's stomach clenched, and the blood pounded strangely through her veins. Her head was light, but her feet felt glued to the ground. Surely time should have decayed such a confection. Surely it should have been a ruin by now.

Surely, Gretel tried to tell herself, the witch was not still alive and tending to her home.

Gretel's stomach squeezed again, and this time she dropped to her knees to retch up the remains of her breakfast into the leaves and dirt. When she was through, she wiped her mouth and forced herself to look again. She noticed other details this time. The striped candy shutters, the poofs of divinity lining the walkway, everything exactly as she had tried to forget.

In the middle of the cottage stood the only element that could not be consumed: a tall stone chimney, rising up like a monument. Though it was indoors, Gretel could see its base clearly in memory—an oven door, wide enough to admit the entire body of a child. Or a witch.

She watched that chimney, holding her breath, waiting to see the telltale smoke of a burning fire, but the air was still. Nothing stirred in or around the house, but Gretel didn't trust its appearance. Truth be told, she hadn't trusted that house the first time she saw it either, but hunger and fear had driven her to ignore her instincts.

She would not make the same mistake this time.

So she stood longer, watching the house from a distance, waiting for signs of activity. Minutes passed, then hours. In the stillness of watching, every sound became amplified. A leaf falling to the ground crackled as it landed. The rustle of the breeze through the tree branches thundered. She noticed, however, that no animals chittered nearby, no birds called in this area. She shivered with more than the chill of the wind.

Maybe the cottage truly had been abandoned, and only its lingering magic preserved it. Nothing had changed in hours. Nothing had changed in five years. Maybe nothing would ever change here. Maybe it was time to move on. She tried to convince herself that she was being practical, not cowardly, as she turned her back to the house, studiously ignoring it as she picked up her knapsack and fetched a snack to settle her uneasy stomach.

In the stillness, she heard a distinct *snap*.

She twisted back to face the house and saw, with horror, that a man had walked out of the forest and was standing there. The snapping sound came from a hand-sized chunk of gingerbread that he'd broken from the eaves.

"Don't eat that!" she shouted, rushing from her hiding place toward him. She reached the man and swatted his gingerbread to the ground, stomping it to pieces.

He stared at her, eyes wide, then glanced at the crumbled remains at his feet. "Why not?" he asked.

Gretel panted from the exertion of the dash and the sudden terror that had flooded her. "Believe me . . . you don't want it. You shouldn't come here!" She grabbed his hand and tried to pull him back into the safety of the trees.

The man resisted. Gretel hesitated, torn between saving herself from the witch and trying to save the foolish man as well.

"I've come here before," he said, and his voice had gone soft, the way you talk to a wild creature. "It's safe. It's . . . peaceful, even. Not even the animals come near."

Peaceful. Gretel's stare darted to the house. She could not think of this place as peaceful. She looked at the man again. He was younger than she'd first thought, perhaps only a few years her elder. Handsome, in a gentle way, with dark hair and the muscles of a woodsman. But the expression in his brown eyes suggested sorrow and pain that was fresh. "You find *peace* here?"

"I know the house is a little strange. It's in perfect condition, and the gingerbread grows back." He shrugged and gazed out into the distance, seeing things she couldn't. "But there are worse things than strange."

Gretel's hands were still shaking with the remains of terror, but she realized how foolish she seemed. Of course the witch was gone. Of course nothing bad would happen from eating the gingerbread now, but she hadn't been able to think logically when she saw that piece of gingerbread in his hand. "You're right, I'm sorry. I just . . . "

"What did you *think* would happen?" he asked, returning his gaze to her.

She shook her head. "Nothing, nothing. I apologize. I overreacted." Now that the moment had passed, she felt a new fear. She wasn't sure about trusting a stranger in the woods. She carefully reached for her dagger and drew it from its sheath.

"I've never seen anyone else here before," he said, watching her cautiously. "I didn't think anyone else even knew it existed."

"I haven't been here for five years."

"And why are you here now?" He kept his eyes on her, hardly blinking.

Gretel's inner voice, the one she could sometimes hear when the pain was quiet, suggested that at this moment he was not the dangerous one. She lowered her dagger but did not put it away. "That is my business."

"Fair enough." He gestured toward the knife. "I'm not going to harm you. I only came here to think." Then he pointed to a long log bench near the edge of the clearing. "Do you mind if I sit?"

Gretel shook her head and gestured an invitation.

"I made that bench. Decided if I was going to keep coming here, I needed a spot to sit." Sorrow appeared in his eyes again, but he said nothing more.

In spite of herself, Gretel was curious. She followed him and sat on the bench too, but as far from him as she could. She leaned back. "It's comfortable."

"Yes. A must for thinking." He stared out into the woods while his hand moved to touch a bag at his side. Gretel tightened her grip on her dagger, but he didn't seem to notice. He drew a wooden box from the bag, about the size of a round of bread. His finger traced a pattern painted on it, a strange shape like a red waterskin with several drinking spouts. It looked familiar, but she couldn't place it. "She wanted me to be a murderer," he said, almost to himself.

"I am already a murderer," she responded, surprised into honesty as she stared at the chimney that held both an oven and a grave.

He looked at her, snapped briefly out of his thoughts. He didn't seem afraid. "Really?"

She nodded once. "Here, in this place. I killed to save my life and the life of my brother."

A moment of silence, then, "Tell me," he said.

Only once had she ever told even part of this tale, to her father, the night that she and Hansel had returned from the forest. Since then she'd held it close and guarded it in her heart, afraid of what the telling would do to her, of how the hearer would react. Yet here, in the shadow of the gingerbread house, with a stranger her heart told her she could trust—here it flowed from her lips.

The young man listened as the words poured from her, revealing each little morsel of the world she had lived in every day of her life since they'd come home—the pain at her father's betrayal and cowardice, the fierce but terrifying relief of the witch's death, and the news of her stepmother's death as well. The unbearable guilt of killing, no matter how justified.

She cast out the words, the feelings, with an energy that at first made her burn with their power. She had never said these words this way before, with the freedom to tell the truth. Who cared what this stranger thought, this stranger whose story held darkness too? If once she could say it all, without care to soften the words, to hide the scars, who knew what might happen?

She told him of the unchanging years of forcing herself into numbness, of hiding from everyone—her family, the townspeople, and especially herself. The more she told, the more the rage quieted, the more she found relief in the words. They slowed, they soothed her. They reformed themselves almost with a will of their own. They began to feel like a different story altogether. A story where she wasn't the villain any longer. She wasn't the victim. She was just Gretel, someone new, someone transformed, someone—maybe—free.

She knew, instinctively, that it was a story she would have to tell herself again and again. But for the first time it existed, and *that* felt like the budding of hope.

Finally she fell silent, and the two of them stared ahead into the beginnings of dusk falling over the house.

"You are not a murderer," he said firmly. When she didn't respond, he continued. "You did it to save yourself and your brother. No one can call that murder." He pointed to the house. "Think of all the other children you may have saved too. Who knows how many she would have killed."

She bit her lip in thought. "I hadn't thought of them. Maybe I did save them." She smiled, and the idea of those children, safe now, took root in her soul. She breathed deeply—her first unfettered breath in five years—and though the scent of spices on the air called to her fears, she didn't let them overwhelm her.

"I had never told anyone all of this." She tilted her head to the side. "I owe you much. I think maybe more than I can repay."

He opened his mouth to reply, but she waved her hand to stop him.

"No, I know you weren't looking for payment, but I owe you nonetheless. I can't do much, but I *can* do one thing, the same thing you did for me." She turned to face him fully. "Tell me your story."

He still held the box in his hands, and now he opened it. Within it lay a darkened, bloody object that matched the picture on the box—a heart; that was why she recognized it. She looked into his eyes, hers widening again. Had she been wrong, after all, to trust him? "I thought you said you were only *meant* to be a murderer."

Quickly he shook his head. "No, no, it's not human. It's a pig's heart. But I must take it to my queen and pretend it is human, or she will hunt the owner of the heart she really wants."

The young man's tale was nearly as mad as her own. He told of a coldhearted queen in the neighboring kingdom who wanted to be the most beautiful woman in the land. He told of a girl who threatened that beauty and of the queen's command to take the young woman into the forest and kill her. Gretel shuddered. She wondered, would it be better to be killed outright in the forest or, as Gretel had been, merely left to die?

Either way, the man couldn't do it. He'd let the girl go, showing her a way to safety. He'd slaughtered a pig and taken its heart. He was on his way back to deceive the queen.

"I loved her," he said softly, closing the lid on the heart.

"The girl?" she asked.

He shook his head. "No. The queen."

The words rang for a moment in silence.

"I loved her from afar of course. For too long I loved her. I tried to pretend she wasn't as she seemed. I came out here to pretend, to forget, so I could go back and be her servant again." He laughed without mirth. "But I can't pretend anymore."

She knew too well that pain.

He shrugged, trying to lighten the mood. "My mother was right when she told me I should acquire better taste in women."

Gretel smiled. "Next time pick someone who doesn't like to kill." She blushed and looked away.

"I'll do that." He chuckled ruefully.

"You saved a child without having to kill anyone. I envy you that."

He reached his hand out to comfort her but pulled back.

"If your queen finds out you tricked her, she'll kill you."

He nodded. "Yes."

"Run away."

He hesitated a moment, staring into the distance. "Maybe."

"Leave. Start somewhere else," Gretel urged, uncertain why her throat tightened at the thought of his danger. "You owe her nothing."

"No, but I owe the girl. I have to at least deliver the heart. Then? Then we'll see."

The noisy rustle of a sudden gust of wind through the trees broke the spell woven by the mutual telling of tales. They both looked around for what seemed like the first time in hours. Darkness was falling quickly now.

"I must be on my way back," the man said, reluctantly.

She rose. "I'll be going too."

He looked straight into her eyes. "Maybe we'll meet in the woods again someday."

"Maybe. On a better day for us both."

"This day has turned out far better than I expected when it began." He stretched out his hand to take hers in a gentle grip. "Thank you, Gretel."

What could she say to this man to whom she had broken her silence? She had said so much already. In the end she could only nod, her throat clogged with emotion. He turned away, and she watched him go, following his shape through the forest until he was beyond her sight.

A moment later, she looked toward the house. She had lied; she wasn't going anywhere yet. There was one thing left to do here.

She steeled herself and walked to the door.

Her fingers trembled as she reached toward the door latch. She sucked in a breath, and the scent of sugar and cinnamon and nutmeg overpowered her senses and dragged her away again, back to that time in the gingerbread house, when she wondered every day if she would once again be able to convince the witch that Hansel was too thin to eat for supper.

She shuddered, then shook her head to dislodge the memory. That's all it was, a memory. The house held no power any longer, no witch to harm her. Still she hesitated, her fingers a breath away from the latch. She swallowed and tried to breathe through her mouth, but even then the scent, so strong this close to the house, threatened to pull her under again.

She drew back. She could see the inside of the house in her memory. The last light of dusk filtering through the sugared window panes tinged the room blue and green and red. The witch's chair stood in the corner with a bag of knitting. The stove, the shelves, the door to the witch's bedroom, she saw them all in her mind. And there, in the center of the room, the oven that had filled her nightmares for so many nights.

The recollection made her dizzy. She pressed her hands against the smooth gingerbread doorpost to keep herself from falling. She couldn't go in. Not tonight. This day had swept away so much of the nightmare, and yet so much remained.

It didn't matter. This house was just a house. Going inside it was not some magic spell that would solve all her problems. She could do that herself. She could leave here and move on.

One day, someday soon maybe, she'd wake to the sounds of birds chirping a morning greeting instead of vivid, echoing nightmare screams. One day she wouldn't fill every moment with tasks deliberately chosen to make her forget. Maybe then she'd come back and step into the gingerbread rooms without fear. Maybe she'd come back and sit on the log bench to wait for a thoughtful stranger to appear. Maybe she'd offer him a loaf of bread and they'd sit in the sunshine and talk and laugh and when the meal was done she'd break off a piece of gingerbread for dessert.

Or maybe she wouldn't.

Gretel turned away from the house, facing the darkening woods. What would she do next? She'd focused so long on forgetting that she almost didn't know there was anything else.

But now a memory rose up from her childhood, like a tiny curl of leaf unfurling from a seed long lost in the ground. She'd wanted to travel the world, back then, when she didn't know how much danger the world could hold. She'd wanted to see lakes and mountains and caves, meet dwarves and fairies, find out if unicorns were real.

She'd buried that dream under gingerbread nightmares, but now bits of the nightmares crumbled and fell away as the dream rose again within her, struggling out into the light. Gretel touched her dream gently, brushing gingerbread crumbs from its leaves. So delicate, but with strength in its roots.

She settled her knapsack firmly on her shoulder, picked up the sprout of a new dream, and headed down an unknown path into the woods. The gingerbread house faded into the distance behind her.

SPRING'S REVENGE

Anika Arrington

CHAPTER 1

*O*nce upon another time, not so distant from the first, Snow was queen. She had married her prince in the bitterness of winter, uniting neighboring provinces, and then given birth to a fine son, whom she named Bertram, in spring of the year following. Bertram grew in the same love of his parents that the kingdom did. He learned under their justice and grew in their mercy, by turns, as all children do. Their kingdom was prosperous and peaceful and lacked nothing until the day the king died.

King Ross Redmond had loved Snow and their son for more than a decade before succumbing to a fever just before the boy's eleventh birthday. Snow was grief-stricken for some time, but soon turned her energies to the *care of her son. And though the boy expressed sorrow at the loss, to the shock of all, he never cried.*

Bertram pined for the father he'd lost, and strove to be like him. He often doubted that his skills would be sufficient to shoulder the mantle of kingship when it came. He hired tutors in every subject to improve his learning. Snow assured her son again and again that she would be there to guide him and that he would be an excellent king so long as he continued to walk in his father's footsteps. And so in the days leading up to the prince's coronation his people saw him less and less as his tutors endeavored to instill the wisdom he craved.

No one likes the cold, but all of Thuringia loved my mother, Snow.

The people dropped flowers as she passed by or rushed to bow before the steps of the palace when she stood on the terrace. She had ruled with a gentle grace since my father died, and we flourished for it.

But soon she would stand aside for me. Soon I would be the one waving before the crowds on the festival days, making trade decisions, leading the way. I wasn't sure they loved me so well.

My history tutor certainly didn't. He came so highly recommended, I had to engage him. I wanted to be a wise king, someone the people could admire as they had my father. As one of the best, Master Matthaus had little patience for lack of scholarly interest. I had little patience for history. I only tolerated the hour I spent in his company each day because I rewarded myself with a hunt or a fencing lesson afterward.

Master Matthaus's switch came down with a crack on the table. He never struck me, but the desk took a fair bit of punishment.

"Who brought the end of Queen Marwyn's reign?"

"My father did," I said, not looking at the massive tome before me. Everyone knew the story of how Prince Ross had gone searching for the lost princess in the forests that marked the border between Altenburg and Eisenach, how he had restored her to both life and her place among the nobility through the power of his love, and how they had joined the two provinces to create Thuringia.

"How?" My tutor narrowed his eyes. I was trying his patience, as I so often did.

"By bringing my mother back from the forest alive." I stifled a yawn.

"Yes, but what happened to Marwyn?" His gnarled fingers stabbed at the page in front of me.

I let my eyes skim the page, not reading the words.

"For all you go on about wanting to be wise, you seem perfectly willing to be a historical dunce. Ignorance of one's own history would be a tremendous failing for any ruler. You must learn from the mistakes of your forebears if you do not wish to repeat them." He waved an irritated hand. "Read the passage aloud."

I shifted in my chair. My parents' mistakes? The people certainly didn't think they made any. I had never seen my mother slip a stitch, let alone a blunder that warranted noting in the history books. I turned my attention to the page, curious what it might have to accuse them of.

"Upon returning to his palace, Snow White and Ross Redmond announced their marriage, but kept her identity a secret. They did this knowing that her mother would seek Snow's death if she discovered her alive, but also knowing that she would attend the wedding of a neighboring prince. When Queen Marwyn arrived at the palace, they had her arrested for her repeated attempts on Snow's life."

I knew all of this.

"Go on," Matthaus prompted.

"At the wedding Marwyn was brought before the guests and amidst cries for her torture and execution Prince Ross called forth his blacksmith."

I looked up at my tutor. "What did he need his blacksmith for?"

"Keep reading."

"The blacksmith came bearing a pair of iron shoes which he placed in the bonfire until they glowed red. The queen was forced into the shoes and told to dance before the guests." My own feet grew hot and my stomach lurched.

Matthaus must have seen some hint of queasiness in my face because he took the tome from me and continued the paragraph in his voice like rasping paper.

"The guests chased Marwyn from the wedding feast and into the forest. She was left to die of her injuries amidst the bitterness of the winter elements and given no burial. No one in either province contested the justice of this."

"Is that true?" I did not want to trust the words in front of me any more than I would trust a dwarf with a diamond.

"Yes," he insisted. "I was there." He stared at me with a fierceness he reserved only for those with soiled fingers near his books.

"And my mother did nothing while her mother was tortured like that?"

"The histories do not say it, but your mother could not even watch. She said nothing, neither asking Ross to spare her nor interfering as Marwyn was driven into the night."

I could picture her serene face, eyes lowered to a perfectly placed napkin in her lap while the screams and jeers landed around her. For a moment I could even smell the burning of Marwyn's flesh.

"She said nothing," I repeated. The truth settled on my shoulders with the weight of those iron shoes. "But how can the people support her? How did they support my father if they knew?"

"It was the people who called for Queen Marwyn's torment. They were enthralled with their princess, as was your father. He simply gave them what they wanted. The question you must ask yourself as his heir is: 'Will I?'"

"I think that's enough history for today," I said.

"I think that's enough for today," my tutor echoed, as though he hadn't heard me. "We will meet—"

But I was already halfway out the door; desperate to drench myself in sunlight, away from the dusty tomes that detailed my family's legacy.

CHAPTER 2

*B*ertram had been told since the day of his birth that he possessed all the handsome features of his mother, but behind their hands the servants and the people whispered that perhaps a young man should not be quite so soft and fair. So he strove every day to learn the manly arts: battle strategy, swordplay, the hunt. As his skills grew, so did his enjoyment of these pursuits, especially the ride out to a hunt.

Snow watched her son's progress with beaming pride, but she could never quite hide her concern when he went into the forest. He assumed that it still held the memories of her own fears and the time she lay near death. Whenever he rode forth she reminded him of three things: never ride the deer trails, keep your men-at-arms with you, and carry your own water.

"Prince Bertram, you must slow down. We can't keep you in sight."

"Turn back then," I called over my shoulder. Not that I expected them to, but I wouldn't lose this chase for their lethargy. I would outrace the storm clouds within, each roll of thunder one of Master Matthaus's revelations.

My captain said something else, but I couldn't be detained or I'd lose the magnificent hart that had darted out of a thicket, and driven away the internal gloom.

The day reveled in the glory of the season: warm sun, the whipping air of the ride, the scent of green things growing and dying in a biting bouquet. I refused to lose my quarry in the dappled light that hid it so well. The pace of the chase drove all other concerns away. My mind narrowed to the blood coursing to each limb, my breath coming in snatches.

Nothing but the present moment.

Watch the foliage.

Follow the tracks.

My horse's breathing grew labored. Just as I thought I'd lost the hart, and in the same moment I was certain I'd left my companions far behind, it dashed across my path once more. My horse reared, but I leaned in and spurred him on after the beast.

The stag was beautiful, a creature of powerful muscle and rippling coat. And when the light filtering through the trees reflected off it, I was blinded for just a moment. Perhaps more than a moment, because I followed the beast up an embankment on a narrow deer track I would never have taken on any other day.

I crested the hill. The soft, carpeted undergrowth gave way to a treacherous incline of jagged rocks. I couldn't slow us fast enough. My horse lost his footing.

As I was thrown I thought I saw the hart prancing away down the stream at the bottom of the ravine. I landed against a massive flat stone that drove the breath from my lungs. I gasped for air as the momentum carried me onward down the slope. My head made contact this time. Sparks of white light blazed before me, and then a view of darkness.

When I could open my eyes, my head protested, and my stomach heaved. I lay still, hoping the nausea would pass. I raised a hand to the worst of the throbbing and found crystalized blood, red as rubies, had matted my hair and now winked in the sunlight. I needed water.

A strangled, despairing noise drew my attention. My horse. I had no idea how long I had lain there, but that whole time the poor beast suffered near death. Two of its legs had broken in the fall. One bone, a jarring whiteness, tore through his dark coat. I tried to stand and found my right foot wouldn't hold my weight. He made the most horrific keening as I limped over the rocks to him. His eyes rolled with madness and pain.

My pack, and with it my waterskin, lay trapped beneath him. With an injured foot and a battered head, I'd never be able to move him.

I drew my sword and, with one merciful stroke, ended his anguish. A torrent of red flowed down the rocks to a stream that ran along the bottom of the steep bank. Everything downhill would be tainted now. I stumbled and slid my way down to the water's edge and limped along upstream until I judged myself far enough away from the carnage.

I knelt and dunked my bleeding head in the frigid water. It was torment and relief in the same instant. I pulled up gasping, the icy cascade soaking into my shirt. I shivered and blinked my eyes clear. The crimson evidence of my meager triage pooled in the stream. I cursed myself for not drinking first. But the cold had cleared my head somewhat, and when I stood to move farther upstream I didn't waver.

I hobbled just a few feet before I decided the water was clean enough again. This time I paused and looked at the reflected face that shifted with the current: wan with wide, frightened eyes and blood streaking the pale skin. I was a mangled mockery of my mother's perfection. I swallowed two great handfuls, and the icy snowmelt stung all the way to my stomach, but my thirst insisted. The cold seeped into my flesh until the tips of fingers and toes sparked with numbness. I had to hold myself back, panting. Drinking excessively in the throes of dehydration would make me sick, and I didn't have the strength for that.

Sheer rocks rose on either side of the stream, with the occasional sharp, jutting ridge. I couldn't climb, not in my condition. It would be easier and likely safer to go downstream to wherever the water let out. There would surely be a homestead, if not a village, where I could seek help. But the thought of passing by my horse again choked me. I felt the water in my stomach sour.

I let my head drop to my knees, cursing my weakness. None of my men-at-arms would have thought twice about putting a suffering beast out of its misery or even walking past a dead animal. I knew what they would all say back at court. How foolish I was to ride off alone, how soft to get thrown and bashed up so badly, how pathetic to balk at walking past a beast I had dispatched with my own hand.

"Bertram."

I lifted my head. There was no one. And the voice calling my name had been no more than a whisper. The trees that stood sentinel at the top of the ridge rustled with a passing breeze that didn't penetrate down into the ravine. It must have been a trick of the wind and my head wound. Except, I realized, my head had stopped hurting.

I reached up to the gash to find it healed. No tenderness, no stinging, just smooth skin beneath my hair. Cautiously I stretched, testing the extent of the miraculous healing. I found no bruises or aches. I balanced on my right foot, now perfectly sound. A place of such perfect healing would be a great blessing to my people, and might well bring even greater prosperity. I looked about for some landmark.

"Bertram."

I whirled.

No one. I was just as alone as I had assumed. My mother's warnings to drink only from my own water supply echoed in my mind. Perhaps she meant to keep this place hidden. Perhaps, like so many magical things, it was not without its price. I turned to leave.

"Bertram."

There was no mistaking it now. The voice beckoned from upstream, away from certain safety and yet—

"Come, good prince."

The voice was neither menacing nor cold. It filled me with a certain familiarity. This was a place I could be safe. Never laughed at or looked down upon. Within the sound of this beckoning voice, I was home.

CHAPTER 3

ertram returned from one such outing covered in blood, but with no injuries; his clothes in tatters, but not a scratch on his skin. His men-at-arms had returned to the woods after a rebuke and the promise of demerits from Queen Snow. They searched in vain for the prince in the woods, and not until many hours past nightfall did he come walking up the palace steps. His mother raced to his side, but he waved her away. She insisted that he sit by the fire to warm his skin, which carried a clammy chill. But Bertram insisted he was more than warm enough and wanted only solitude and rest.

He locked himself in his room and didn't emerge for three days. He refused all company, all food, all drink. When he finally came forth among the court, everyone stared at the transformation. His once ivory skin was now a sickly grey. His soft, buoyant curls hung lank in his eyes. And the red flush of his lips looked stained with purple wine. He went about shirtless, sweating, complaining of the oppressive heat and demanding that all fires be extinguished. Queen Snow did her best to raise her son's spirits and convince him to seek help, but he only replied, "I need no help. I'm home."

The sweat trickled down along my hairline. This incessant wave of heat would surely bring drought. It drove me to distraction.

"Another pitcher of cold water," I said, pouring the last drops into my cup. I drank it down, but nothing could slake my thirst since I strode from the woods. I did not wish to go back, but I began to think that finding the stream once more might be my only hope of relief. I paced the floor, wearing out my restlessness on the rich carpet.

At last I heard footsteps in the corridor, but when the door opened my mother stepped into the private parlor we shared. I found myself retreating to its seclusion more often than usual. She shut the door behind her and stood watching me. Her eyes held the same love and concern I had always known, but also fear.

"Bertram," she began, but the knocking of the servant returning with my water interrupted her.

She took the pitcher from the servant at the door and dismissed him with a wave. She set it on the sideboard, and I moved to refill my perpetually empty cup. She laid a hand on my shoulder, and an oppressive warmth radiated down my arm. I brushed her away, certain she would leave burn marks with her fingertips. The irrationality of it all only fueled my frustrations.

"Bertram, this can't go on," she said.

Every syllable seared itself onto my ears.

"You must let me summon a physician, or at least the apothecary," she insisted for the thousandth time.

"I'm not ill."

"You cannot think you are well."

"What would you know of it? You can't even gaze on the suffering of others."

She recoiled as though struck.

"I'm sorry," I said. "It's just this infernal heat."

She didn't reply. She turned with a haughty air, strode to the window, and pulled back the draperies. The low clouds of a spring storm hung in the air. She opened the window, and the wind whipped at the open pages of a book. But I felt no cool relief.

"It is freezing outside, Bertram. We haven't had a full day of sun since we thought you lost."

"What is this witchcraft?" Indeed, I could see the clouds and the stirrings of the winds, but they could not penetrate the fire of the air around me. "No, this is some kind of illusion."

"It is you who are under an illusion," she said, taking a step closer. "No one feels the fire you speak of. No one here is athirst like you."

"No one spoke up at your wedding either," I snapped. I hadn't been thinking of it, but the words came from somewhere deep within.

"Bertram, you aren't making sense."

"You let her die, my grandmother—" I had never even thought of Queen Marwyn as anything other than a villainous wretch, but she was family I had never known.

"She tried to kill me—"

"And you tortured her!" Snow drew back a step, as though I'd laid hands on her. "You sat by while the people tormented her to her death. How can you say I am the one who does not see when you could not even raise your eyes to the spectacle of your own mother's demise?"

Steam came with each panting breath as I struggled to master myself. I could see the damage each barbed word did as I spoke them.

Tears rolled down her cheeks. She went to the cabinet, the one that held the royal jewels and a few of her favorite keepsakes. She removed the key she kept on a chain round her neck, and unlocked it. When she returned she held a mirror.

"That was Grandmother's." I heard the condemnation in my voice and lowered the accusatory finger I hadn't meant to raise.

"And if you ask it, it will show you the truth of what happened that night."

"I know the truth," I spat. "Everyone knows it. Ross—"

"Your father," she said.

"No. I won't be that kind of tyrant." I took the mirror and flung it away. Though it hit the ground with a solid clang, it did not shatter. I fled to the safety of the only place I knew that would soothe my soul.

"Why do you return?"

I did not answer. Rather I dove into the depths of the pool that fed the stream of miracles. Passing the days-old carcass of my horse meant nothing to me as I sought the final resting place of my grandmother. The sweet, crisp water and her loving smile were my only thoughts. When I surfaced, she stood before me, just as she had before. Not like the paintings I had seen, austere and distant, but comforting and inviting. Her form, the picture of what she must have been as a young woman, stood with bare feet atop the pool's surface.

"Bertram, why are you here? Your coronation is so near, you must prepare," she said with all the tender feeling of a doting grandparent.

I heaved myself up to the edge and sat with my feet in the blessed waters.

"This place is good for me. I cannot think when I am away. This heat—"

"The heat will pass after you become king," she assured me. "Until then you must bear it the best you can."

She came and sat, her feet, hidden in a cloud of mist, never moving beyond the water's surface.

A question still lingered. One I had not dared ask the first time she had beckoned to me, one that I could not ask my mother, one I was not sure even my tutors would have an answer for.

"Why did you try to kill her?"

Her eyes became frosty.

"Some have said I was jealous of her beauty or the doting favor my husband showed her, but those are the lies of the blind. I would be a monster if such were true." My grandmother extended a leg as though to tap the water. The pool rippled until it showed her sitting by my grandfather, another family member I knew only from portraits and tales. A little girl came bounding up to him and alighted on his lap. He smiled. So did my grandmother's image. She seemed genuinely pleased to see her daughter so happy. With another flick of her foot the image was gone. "I knew that she was dangerous."

"How?" I splashed a handful of water over my neck, the relief running down my back.

"She had power over people. She could always make any servant obey her, even to do terrible things like killing a favorite laying hen of mine for dinner or hiding others' belongings. She often laughed at the pain and surprise of others. The guests at her wedding who drove me out did it because they were under her sway. Perhaps she has learned not to be so flagrant, but no one should have that kind of control. She is a danger to you and your people."

"Then why would she let me take the throne?"

"Because all good must end. Just as she could never ensnare me, so she can never quite enchant you. The people are prosperous now, but the wheel of all fortunes is ever turning, and soon they will face hardships of war and famine and disease. She wants to place the burdens of kingship on you so that you will turn to her of your own will. She can rule through you, and if anything besets the kingdom she can blame your lack of judgment and experience."

A ray of sun glittered on the pool's surface, playing tricks with the water, making a mire of its crystal purity. Marwyn stood and the light blinked out, shuttered by the canopy of green around us.

"She cannot stand to think that anyone might not adore her." A bitterness touched the edges of her voice. It suffused the taste of the water dripping from my hair and down my face.

I thought of how my mother had begun to cry when I laid the accusation of her indifference before her. It made sense that the people would be only too happy to blame the soft, young king when times grew hard. If I said it was her guidance that brought us there, they would turn on me.

"How do I stop it?" I wondered aloud.

"Take this with you." My grandmother waved a hand, and water rose before her. The exterior shone, and when it rested in her hand it was contained in a crystalline flask. "It will keep your vision clear and the torment at bay. When the time comes, you will know what to do."

The day reveled in the glory of the season: warm sun, the whipping air of the ride, the scent of green things growing and dying in a biting bouquet. I refused to lose my quarry in the dappled light that hid it so well. The pace of the chase drove all other concerns away. My mind narrowed to the blood coursing to each limb, my breath coming in snatches.

CHAPTER 4

*T*he reality of the grim scene at Ross and Snow's wedding is recorded well, by many hands. But what is known by few is that while the revels continued, Snow slipped away, into the woods. She followed the trail of melted snow, the dragged footfalls, and eventually the muddy gouges of a figure crawling up a narrow deer track, until she came to where Queen Marwyn, now a disheveled wreck, lay moaning.

Snow fell to her knees, trying to remove the shoes and begging her mother's forgiveness, but the flesh had melted to the metal. Marwyn kicked her away, screaming her vengeance anew. She drew all her power around her and with her last living breaths pronounced this curse:

Fair as Snow your children may be
But poison bitter shall yet flow free.
As keys the binding locks unhinge
So winter's death brings spring's revenge.

Marwyn then transformed herself into a pillar of ice with a darkness at its heart. Snow knew, staring at her reflection in the ice, that not only would there be no forgiveness for holding her silence, but she was still not safe. As each new year passed, she dreaded the coming of the spring, never certain if this time she would face the fulfillment of her mother's curse upon her children.

I washed and dressed on my return to the palace. A sip from the flask every now and again kept the worst of the burning at bay. A day passed, then two. My supply dwindled.

I knew I could not return to the pool before the coronation, but I could not wait any longer to be king.

Grandmother Marwyn was right. I could see so clearly now. Soon the rest would, too.

I decanted the wine and added a few drops from my flask.

"They will support me." I knew anyone that drank of my grandmother's pool would, and yet—

I summoned a page. "Send word that I wish to meet with the councilors."

The lad looked confused. "They are with your mother even now, my lord."

Anger ground my teeth against one another, but I could not let them see it. Not until they were free of her influence.

"Bring the wine and follow me then," I instructed.

I made my way to the council hall where the learned of my kingdom were gathered. My mother stood before them, placid and dour.

"You all look as though someone has died," I said.

No one laughed. One man stood. I couldn't remember his name.

"My prince, your mother is concerned, as many of us are, about your well-being."

The page placed the tray on the table with just enough force to rattle the glasses against each other.

"I am perfectly fit, as you can see."

"What we see is not a defect of form, but of mind—" another chimed in.

"Nonsense," I replied, struggling to smile. I poured a glass for each of the dozen or so men and women seated at the table. I handed the tray back to the page, indicating he should distribute them. "I was shaken by a revelation, and it was quickly followed by my own blundering in the woods. It took me longer to sort out the truth from my own little tumble."

I laughed. None laughed with me.

"Please, join me in a salute, to my father's memory." I raised my glass. They followed suit, though with hesitancy. The page placed a glass before my mother, but she made no move to take it. As was her wont, my mother said nothing and stood motionless, cold, waiting.

"To the mercy of Prince Ross." I took a gulping draft that quenched only the tiniest sparks of the heat within.

They echoed and drank. A few spit it out upon tasting it. One or two others did not even touch it.

"What is this?"

"How dare you try to—"

"Poison! Treason!"

But despite the cries from those who could not abide the taste of truth, those who had swallowed the draft became aware. They blinked and looked about them as though they had never been cognizant of their surroundings before.

They looked to me and then to my mother. One by one they came and stood at my side.

"Your power here is broken," I said.

"You drank," she began, then choked back a sob. "After all my warnings."

"I am free of your lies."

Those who had not swallowed also rose, but went to stand beside my mother.

"You will not be crowned while you ramble in madness," one of my mother's champions spoke up. "It has already been decided."

"You tricked us, persuaded us to deny Prince Bertram his right while we were under her spell," called one of those with me.

Soon everyone was speaking back and forth. A few approached each other and I was certain it would come to blows. I drew my sword and the room went silent.

"You cannot deny my ascension without making war. Arrest Snow White," I commanded my loyalists. No one moved. "I said arrest her. She is a danger to this council and to our people. She must be held until we can decide a fitting punishment."

At once two guards strode forward, not to take hold of my mother, but to disarm me.

I raged. "You dare approach your king? You think me feeble and tender because I have the complexion of the woman that bore me? Come then, I'll show you the strength of your king."

CHAPTER 5

*B*ertram engaged his own soldiers in single combat, and though his court cried out for him to stop, he would not hear even those who stood loyal to him. His years of practice showed in his skill as he wounded one man and pressed the other.

Seeing her son slip deeper into the darkness of Marwyn's curse, Snow fled, hoping he would pursue. She used the mirror, which she had kept with her since he had tried to smash it, to lead her to the one place that perhaps this wickedness could be undone.

Bertram proclaimed, "See how she flees justice," and bounded after her. The servants tried to stand in his way, but one glance at his flashing sword and they scrambled aside.

He chased her beyond the palace walls, determined to capture her at first, but as his quarry eluded him, his intentions became less and less his own. Bertram became more enraged with every step, shouting his vitriol and her betrayal to the skies. The forest came to Snow's defense as it had before, hindering his progress. Roots of good trees rose to trip him, and stinging nettles tore at his ankles. Birds brought beak and talon to bear on his face and arms. Blinded by these obstacles and his consuming fury, the prince did not see where she led him.

How had we come here? I stood by the pool's edge, my sword in my hand.

My mother stood on the opposite side. The mirror, the one my grandmother had used to find her, was clutched in her hand.

I heard myself screaming. "I won't let you hurt anyone else, you selfish brat."

I sounded deranged. Spittle, in white flecks, collected on my lips. The maddening heat flared again, radiating up through the soles of my feet. I took one step into the water, then another, not sinking below the surface, but striding across it like my grandmother had. I was wrapped in the certainty that only the death of Snow White would bring the relief I sought. It was the only justice for the things she had done.

Justice. I blinked and tried to stop, but my feet, still burning, were not my own. I strode across the water with a dark purpose I did not feel. I balked.

Could I truly kill my own mother? *Hadn't she tortured hers?*

Would that make me no better than my father? *She is the one who deserves it.*

Snow waited across the water. So still.

I gripped my sword before me, poised to strike. She was only steps away from me now. But I couldn't take them.

A wave of self-loathing washed over me. *Disgusting. Weak.*

Her composure made my frayed consciousness all the more tangled. It wasn't fair. I felt a seething rage at her perfectly statuesque indifference.

"Say something!"

She held up the mirror to her face.

"Mirror, mirror, in my hand, show the truth as I command." She turned the mirror around so that I saw my own face reflected in it. I was withered with fever and fatigue. I wondered when I had last eaten and couldn't remember. More shocking still, I did not stand on the surface of a clear spring, but rather atop a pool of blood. Bile rose in the back of my throat, but the true taste of what I had swallowed lingered on my tongue. My sword fell from my trembling hands as I gagged on my own revulsion.

I stumbled to my mother's side, and skidded away from the pool's edge until my back came against a tree trunk.

The spirit of my grandmother rose from the pool as she had before, but now her eyes burned. The cloud of mist that once obscured her feet had vanished. She wore the slippers of iron that had been her death, and they still glowed red.

Marwyn did not smile. She did not look at me with the concern of days before. Only disdain.

"You mewling little fool. She must be destroyed."

"I won't do that," I said. The very idea horrified me, and I remembered my horse. Even that act of mercy, needful as it was, had left me shaking and pained.

"You're pathetic." Marwyn's voice seethed. "More worthless than your soft-headed mother."

My mother knelt next to me and laid a hand on my shoulder as she so often did. It did not burn. I looked into her eyes. Compassion and fear mingled in her face.

"I can't do this," I said again.

"I know," she replied.

"No, I can't be king. I'm not strong like Father, and the people will hate me." My fears poured out of me, down my cheeks, and into the tainted pool.

The queen's tirade never ceased. "Stop your whimpering, you little worm!"

But I couldn't. The illusion that all I had to do was be like my father had been shattered the day I read the truth, and now the realization crashed over me that no matter how I tried, I could never be a king like him.

My mother pulled me to her, and I wept as I had not done since before he died. Waves of loss washed over and through me.

Marwyn's screams became merely a swirl of unintelligible noise, drowned out by my sobs.

At last I was left with nothing but a hiccup or two, and I looked up.

Where there had once been a pool, full of the bitter essence that was Queen Marwyn, now there was a dry pit, crusted in salt, with a pair of iron shoes sitting at the bottom.

My mother's arms stayed wrapped around me. "She told you I was dangerous?"

I nodded.

"And she believed it."

I looked at her, astonished.

"Like me, like you, she could bring anyone she wished under her sway. She was beloved by her people, but when she realized that I, too, could lead with just a gentle command, she felt her hold on those around her slip. She grew more and more desperate. More deranged."

My mother told me every detail of how she barely escaped death again and again after her father passed away from a fever, very like the one that took my own. She told me of how my father had insisted on arresting Marwyn for her crimes, and how she had no idea what the people or my father had in store. She told me of the curse and the pillar of ice that had stood as a quiet reminder that her own happiness would be short-lived.

"But now this place is dry. Its cursing is wrung out, and you are restored to me, my sweet boy." She kissed my head.

"What if Grandmother is right? Do we hold too much power over our people?"

"People want to be led. The people loved your father because he made them feel as though they were righteous and just, even when their actions were vicious. The people loved my mother because she made them see her as lovely. You have asked the right question. What have we done to deserve their praise? If I can answer honestly that I have done my best to respect their will and lead without coercion, then I can sleep at night with an undisturbed heart."

A glow lit her from within. Demanding though ruling by example could be, I saw in her the peace of knowing she led by her own daily walk of unselfish kindness.

"How could you love Father after what he did?" I asked.

"It took time for me to forgive him, but he did what he thought he must to protect me. Sometimes I even wonder if Marwyn influenced his decision herself, to justify her own cruelty." She sighed and took my hand in hers, just like when I was a boy. "And you can choose to be better than he was, learn from the mistakes he made."

"I miss him," I confessed.

"So do I," she whispered. "The ones we love don't have to be perfect. They just have to be loved."

"I think"—I wiped my nose on the sleeve of my shirt—"I think I'm ready to go home."

The jubilation of the week-long coronation festival drove all memory of the strange days before it out of the people's memory. Prince Bertram's ensorcelled madness was branded as a strange manifestation of nervousness preceding the assumption of his new place as king. He made amends to those he had harmed, even promoting the guards who had stood against him in defense of Snow White.

Queen Marwyn's words of troubled times that would surely come his people's way did not leave him, however, and as soon as the kingdom settled back into the rhythms of daily life he began to lay up stores, to educate those within his influence, to build alliances with his neighbors. Snow watched her careful, thoughtful son grow into a wise and prudent king with beaming pride. And though turbulent times did come, as they always must, Bertram and Snow faced them with grace and fortitude, leading by example, and even at times finding happiness thereafter.

THE ORIGINAL TALES

Jack and the Beanstalk
Country of origin: England

"Jack and the Beanstalk" is a classic story in which Jack trades a cow for magic beans, climbs the beanstalk, and steals treasures from a giant. The tale has roots in the oral tradition and has been recorded numerous times; a common version was penned in 1890 by Joseph Jacobs in *English Fairy Tales*.

Rumpelstiltskin
Country of origin: Germany (related stories can be found from Slovakia to Japan)

In "Rumpelstiltskin," a miller's daughter must spin straw into gold in order to save her life and marry the king. The most well-known version of the story is included in the 1812 edition of *Children's and Household Tales* by the Brothers Grimm.

Tsarevitch Ivan, the Firebird, and the Gray Wolf
Country of origin: Russia

A wolf helps young Ivan on his quest for the firebird, the horse with a golden mane, and a beautiful princess. This story was collected by Alexander Afanasyev. Both Ivan and the firebird are common characters in Slavic folklore, appearing in multiple fairy tales.

Tatterhood
Country of origin: Norway

An ugly princess with a goat and a spoon fights trolls (or in some versions, witches) to rescue her sister's head; her heroic efforts results in her marriage to a foreign prince. This story was collected by the Norwegian folklorists Peter Christen Asbjørnsen and Jørgen Moe.

The Little Mermaid
Country of Origin: Denmark

A mermaid makes a trade with a sea witch so she can become human; when her prince marries someone else, she turns into sea foam. This story was written and published by Hans Christian Andersen in 1837.

The Yule Cat
Country of Origin: Iceland

The Yule Cat is a traditional monster from Icelandic folklore that would eat children who did not receive new clothes on

Christmas Eve; today, Icelandic children still receive clothing at Christmastime. Other Icelandic Christmas traditions focus on the tricksters known as the Yule Lads.

The Princess and the Pea
Country of Origin: possibly Sweden; first published in Denmark

A prince tries to find a "real princess" without success; when a soaking princess arrives at their door, the queen tests her by placing a pea underneath twenty mattresses. Hans Christian Andersen retold this story in 1835.

The Pied Piper
Country of Origin: Germany

When a town refuses to pay the rat catcher, he leads away their children with a magical pipe. This legend originated in the Middle Ages and has been retold by many, including Goethe and the Brothers Grimm.

The Nutcracker
Country of Origin: Germany

A girl's Christmas toy comes to life, battles a mouse king, and then brings the girl to a magical land. "The Nutcracker and the Mouse King" was written in 1816 by E. T. A. Hoffman, retold by Alexandre Dumas, and then adapted into the ballet *The Nutcracker* by Pyotr Ilyich Tchaikovsky.

Hansel and Gretel

Country of Origin: Germany

Two children are abandoned in the forest by their father and stepmother. When they are captured by a witch living in a gingerbread house, they must trick and ultimately kill her to avoid being eaten. This story was collected by the Brothers Grimm and published in their 1812 edition of *Children's and Household Tales*.

Snow White

Country of Origin: Germany

Snow White hides from her wicked stepmother (the queen) with the help of seven dwarves; the queen poisons Snow White. Snow White is saved by a prince and at their wedding the queen is killed. This story was collected by the Brothers Grimm and published in their 1812 edition of *Children's and Household Tales*.

ABOUT THE AUTHORS

Anika Arrington

Anika Arrington is a devoted wife and mother of six. As a Hufflepuff and a pluviophile, curling up with a good book and a mug of cocoa on a rainy day constitutes her personal heaven.

She's written fantasy fiction since her early teens, and her first novel, *The Accidental Apprentice*, was a Whitney Award finalist. You can find her quipping/griping on Twitter @AnikaArrington and talking movies on her website www.anikasantics.com.

Sarah Chow

Sarah Chow is an editor who lives in the desert outskirts of greater Los Angeles with her husband and two quirky kids. Every morning the kids ask her to check for coyotes in the wash behind their house. Sarah is the communications editor for Cesium, an open source library for creating 3D maps. But she's also worked on everything from children's magazines to computer graphics research books. She loves stories and books of all types, but any time she walks into a library, she winds up in the folklore section (call number 398, if you're looking) because fairy tales are her favorite—especially problematic ones.

Katherine Cowley

Katherine Cowley loves European chocolate, steampunk fashion, and videos of goats doing parkour. She has worked as a radio producer, a documentary film producer, and a college writing professor. She is an award-winning author of short stories and essays, which have appeared in publications including *Steel and Bone*, *365 Tomorrows*, *Mad Scientist Journal*, *Defenestration*, and *Segullah*.

Katherine lives with her husband and three daughters in Kalamazoo, Michigan. You can read many of her published stories on katherinecowley.com or follow her on Twitter @kathycowley.

Scott Cowley

Dr. Scott Cowley is an award-winning digital marketing professor at Western Michigan University. Prior to completing his Ph.D. at Arizona State University and beginning an academic career, he was a marketing strategist and consultant in Salt Lake City. You can learn more at scottcowley.com and on Twitter @scottcowley.

Chris Cutler

Chris Cutler is an immunologist. His experiments in world-renowned labs at Emory University and Harvard aim to unravel the mysterious role that sugars play in immune cells. When not growing cells or staring through microscopes, he can often be found writing poetry. He collects words of all kinds, from the scientific (e.g., *glycoproteomic*, *lemniscate*, and *bleb*) to the poetic (e.g., *vituperative*, *anodyne*, and *elide*). He loves lyrical language and good stories, and he regularly stays up all night to read "just one more chapter." Despite living a mere thirty minutes from Walden Pond, he has yet to embrace a solitary life in the woods, though he does like to take his kids there for walks.

Sarah Blake Johnson

Sarah Blake Johnson is the author of the fantasy novel *Crossings*. She has an MFA in Writing for Children and Young Adults from Vermont College of Fine Arts.

She has stepped in quicksand in Brazil, walked on the frozen Baltic Ocean in Finland, cooked dinner in a geyser in Iceland, learned to play an ancient instrument in China, explored abandoned castle ruins in Germany, worked as an economist in Nigeria, and scuba dived in the Red Sea in Egypt, all countries where she has lived.

Learn more about Sarah at sarahblakejohnson.com and www.sarahblakejohnson.blogspot.com.

Ruth Nickle

"Take this weapon forged in darkness; some see a pen, I see a harpoon."
—Tyler Joseph

Barely tethered to earth, Ruth Nickle spends her days weaving reality into colorful tapestries of art with her computer. She began writing at age eleven after her wildly popular fan fiction of *The Hobbit* received rave reviews from her mother. However, with a family full of math teachers, she was woefully unaware that she could, in fact, sculpt her daydreams into a career. Now, after a twenty-year hiatus, she is plunging head first into the beautiful torture that is writing.

Ruth is a wife, mother, writer, graphic designer, photographer, and artist. You can read her diary at https://elsanickle.wordpress.com.

Kaki Olsen

Kaki Olsen is always in search of a place to visit and a story to tell. Though her mild-mannered alter ego has a desk job, Kaki can tell you what it's like to hike a pilgrim's trail in Austria or eat the world's best gazpacho in Barcelona. Closer to home, she loves following the Red Sox and contributing to a local speculative fiction symposium. Not all of her stories are inspired by ballet, but her debut novel, *Swan and Shadow*, is based on another Tchaikovsky classic. She blames the Boston Ballet and the teacher who once gave her *The Nutcracker* for Chanukah. She has also published personal essays, writing articles, and a science-fiction fantasy with a dragon-smuggling android. Links to her published works, her blog, and news can all be found at www.kakiolsenbooks.com.

Robin Prehn

Robin Prehn has always loved fairy tales and spent her early school years reading (and re-reading) her way through Andrew Lang's "color" books. After wishing she could grow up and become Laura Ingalls Wilder, she found a way to start and run her own one-room school for seven years—and discovered for herself how fairy tales really end (some good, some not as good).

Like the princess with her pea, Robin has also had sleeping issues. One of her tricks involves telling herself stories about what comes after "the end" in her favorite books, and that's how she learned she loved to create tales and build worlds.

Currently, she lives on the edge of the Rocky Mountains with her husband and their two teenagers, and life is mostly happily ever after (with a fair amount of work, of course).

Jeanna Mason Stay

Jeanna Mason Stay has always been a sucker for a good fairy tale. The romantic kind, the gruesome, the utterly bizarre—she'll take them all. And then she'll rewrite them. Her favorite fairy tale of all, though, is the one she lives daily with her dreamy husband and their four charming children. They are currently happily-ever-aftering in Maryland.

When she's not getting lost in a book or keeping the baby from eating one, she's probably debating one with friends or listening to the older children reenact literary scenes. Along with books, Jeanna also loves fireflies, serial commas, and birds of paradise. She dreams of one day owning a herd of Chia sheep. You can find her blogging when fancy strikes at calloohcallaycallay.blogspot.com and fortnightly-ish at mormonmommywriters.blogspot.com.

PJ Switzer

PJ Switzer is a child of dreams. As a girl she dreamed of being Princess Leia but that job was already taken. So was lead singer of the Eurythmics and first woman in space. As a grownup she dreamed of being an Olympic rhythmic gymnast but middle-aged, goddess-sized ladies don't usually make the team. Today she's a writer because the world always needs more stories and there's no age restriction. PJ is encouraged in these and all her endeavors by her husband and three sons, as well as the wonder pooch, Rosie. You can follow her on Instagram at @pjswitzer and on Twitter @switzerpj.

Made in the USA
Columbia, SC
07 April 2018